Disorder and Ch

Simon Lovat is 36 and liv
literature critic and journali

Disorder and Chaos

Simon Lovat

Millivres Books
Brighton

First published in 1996 by Millivres Books (Publishers)
33 Bristol Gardens, Brighton BN2 5JR, East Sussex, England

Disorder and Chaos
Copyright (C) Simon Lovat, 1996
The moral rights of the author has been asserted

A CIP catalogue record for this book is available from the British Library

ISBN 1 873741 26 X

Typeset by Hailsham Typesetting Services, 4-5 Wentworth House, George Street, Hailsham, East Sussex BN27 1AD

Printed and bound by Biddles Ltd., Walnut Tree House, Woodbridge Park, Guildford, Surrey GU1 1DA

Distributed in the United Kingdom and Western Europe by Turnaround Distribution Co-Op Ltd., 27 Horsell Road, London N5 1XL

Distributed in the United States of America by InBook, 140 Commerce Street, East Haven, Connecticut 06512, USA

Distributed in Australia by Stilone Pty Ltd, PO Box 155, Broadway, NSW 2007, Australia.

ACKNOWLEDGEMENTS

Grateful thanks go to my editor, Peter Burton, and Sebastian Beaumont for their comments on various drafts of the novel. Thanks are also due to David Pollard and John McLean for their help with the preparation of the manuscript, and to Dr A. Phillips BDS (Lon.) LDS, RCS (Eng.) for his specialist knowledge. Very special thanks also to Dr Joan Draper, for her long-term support and her faith in my writing.

For Sebastian

DISORDER AND CHAOS

PART ONE

CHAPTER ONE

Today, Monica is searching for the final photograph – the one that will make her famous. She may find it lying on the pavement, like some of the others, or abandoned on the windowsill outside Woolworths, or it may have been relegated to a street bin, but she's certain she'll find it. And with that her fate will be sealed. That's what she wants more than anything, and she knows that if somebody wants something badly enough, then it must happen. Some things are inexorable.

Monica walks the High Street with languid steps, her eyes locked to the dusty pavement. She is haunted by a dragging lethargy which seems new, but as she stares, passive, through the window of a bakery at the anaemic cakes and pies within, she realises it has always been with her. She wonders why. Now that school is over and everyone has trickled off to revise for the exams, the answer stares her full in the face, like an exposed corpse: she is exhausted from the effort of years of waiting. She has been waiting, always, for the saviour who will find her and rescue her from this suburban nightmare; who will place her in the full glare of public scrutiny.

And come he will, this saviour, but he will not appear at her side, as if out of a dream, to sweep her to her destiny. Rather, she will discover him – an incongruous man with the collar of his overcoat turned up against the December cold. He will be aiming futile punches at a postbox, and she will talk to him, as suggested by a Tarot spread. She will be twenty-two years old.

But today, Monica is only sixteen – seventeen next month – wandering through the White Lion Centre, looking for that final photograph as she inhales the artificial precinct air and stares at herself in shop windows.

The first thing she notices is that she's turned into a Lipo-Freak. Wearing black is supposed to make people look thinner – according to the glossy mags she consumes nightly in her airless little eyrie of a bedroom, stuck at the top of the house – but it doesn't seem to work for her. She's gross. Probably forty-five kilos. She pinches the excess fat at her waistline with white fingers crowned with blood red nails, and frowns. *Oh, Em, please don't let me turn into a Lipo,* she mutters under her breath, a supplication to her Strong Goddess. *I'll get three A's, I swear. Just don't let me be a Lipo.*

There's one standing next to her right now, squeezed into an olive green gabardine mac and wheezing through her puggy nose, trying to suck up enough air to feed her sweating hulk. Monica studies the Lipo's reflection in the shop window, her outline punctuated by the shoes ranged in tasteful displays within.

"Expensive, aren't they?" says the jelly-woman, turning her tight face to Monica's hollow jawline.

"Hideous. Seriously gross," says Monica.

The Freak's lips flutter like obese butterflies, unable to formulate any reply, and Monica stares her down. Another victory for angular youth. As she saunters away, she imagines the Lipo with no clothes on, and retches. The bitter sting of yellow bile rises at the back of her throat, and her stomach suddenly hurts. How long is it since she last ate anything?

Monica walks slowly through the hushed precinct, bathed in fake daylight, and remembers her stash of Mars bars. They have been wedged behind her books of W.H. Auden poetry for some time, forgotten until now. Nine of them, waiting to be gorged; waiting to coat her tongue with thick, sweet-toffee-fondant goo. With a smile, she pushes through the glass precinct doors and steps out into an early-summer street thronged with wealthy Surrey ladies, and meanders towards the railway station, her spirits lifted by an abstract sugar high.

Oh Em, Strong Goddess, may I find one more today, she intones as she waits at a zebra crossing, fingering her single silver earring. It is startlingly bright amongst her raven hair as, for an instant, the sun catches it.

Once on the station concourse she begins her search in earnest. First she checks the ticket booths, but they are all closed, and empty; then the buffet, purveyor of brick-orange tea and pukey scones, but still nothing; there is nothing on the floor, nothing in any of the bins, and nothing in the rest room. So it will have to be the machine itself.

Monica hates to do it this way, it's like reading a thriller after someone has told you the end, but she has no option this morning. People have been more careful than usual. In truth, casually found strays are somewhat rare, and therefore precious, and Monica has had to cut the hunt and go straight to the kill in this way for most of her Icons. She's practised at it, skilful, has learnt how to exercise her art without being seen. Success lies in knowing when to grab, and when to walk away empty-handed. To date she has never been caught stealing from any of the three Guildford Photo-Me machines. Monica hums a snatch of an old song as she ensconces herself near the booth, and sits on an uncomfortable metal seat as red as her fingernails. Hardly anyone comes: an old man with glasses; a zeccy middle-aged woman with a briefcase.

After three quarters of an hour a train comes in from London, disgorging more zecs in suits, and some Inter-rail foreigners. Cautiously watching the booth, Monica gets up and inserts fifty pence into a drinks machine which spits out a can of diet Tango, and prays to the Goddess for luck. Instantly a tiny white feather, dislodged from some young pigeon's downy front, rocks earthward into Monica's waiting palm.

Monica smiles. *Thank you Em*, she whispers. There are many signs – rabbits, special mushrooms, magpies, cats, pennies – but a white feather is one of the best signs of all. The only sign more potent than that is an aircraft at the point of take-off, at that moment when the wheels first detach themselves from the runway. Monica dreams of seeing that magical refracted hot air between earth and sky, shimmering beneath the belly of a jumbo in the moment of its leap of faith. But this feather, with which she now caresses her cheek, is sufficient to her current purpose. She knows she will be successful now.

Sitting by the booth once again, Monica watches the foreigners laugh with large mouths as they jostle each other. Two disentangle themselves from the crowd, shaking their heads at the others, and point towards the Photo-Me. Then one of them disappears behind the orange pleated booth curtain and begins to fiddle with the plastic stool, adjusting it's height. The stool complains with a rusty farting sound. Monica watches with rising excitement as the first foreigner emerges from the booth, running a tanned hand through his thick hair, and grinning. He pushes his friend into the booth and Monica soon hears four dull thuds as the flash fires. Then the second foreigner emerges, somewhat dazzled, shoves his friend playfully, and they both stand beside the booth, waiting for the photos to develop. Suddenly, there is an abrasive call from the group, a cranky teenage male voice, and the two foreigners join their friends.

Monica clutches her white feather in a sweaty palm as her eyes fix on the chrome slot mouth of the Photo-Me, where the strip of Frankenstein poses will soon emerge. She is near enough to the machine to hear the gentle hum of chemicals and rollers doing their work, then the tick of the first four photos as they fall gently into the wire cage. The first foreigner scoots over to the machine, grabbing at the photos with careless hands, and Monica knows he will have smudged the still-wet emulsion, super-imposing fingerprint whorls over his face. He returns to his friends, brandishing the photos like a hard-won scalp, and the group descend on them in a squawking huddle, like seagulls swooping behind a fishing boat. So captivated are they, that they do not notice Monica as she steps up to the machine and removes the second strip of photos, which have just slid out.

The power of the feather, says Monica to herself as she walks away from the machine, nonchalantly flapping her arm to and fro in order to dry the pictures, which she holds by the edges, between thumb and forefinger of her right hand.

Back home, in her room, she studies them. The subject is in his mid-twenties, with several days of beard growth. He has lank, longish hair which is parted in the middle, a cold sore nestling at the left hand corner of his mouth, and ghostly skin. All excellent characteristics. But it is the eyes she likes best. They look wild and confused. The subject is doing something weird with them, rolling them back up into his head, eyelids half shut, so in the pictures they appear entirely white. The pose is identical in all four pictures: Foreign Student Experiencing Seizure.

Delightedly, Monica rips the top picture off the strip and affixes it to her photo-wall, between an Indian woman with spots and a bald man with a fat moustache. She steps back from her xeno-collage for a moment, and sighs with deep satisfaction at the fruit of three years' diligent work. Her face glows, expectant. Something is bound to happen now. She has the exact number: one hundred and eleven. The number of the Cosmic Gateway. One Eleven. One One One. All she has to do is focus on her desires and they will materialise.

To this end, Monica draws the curtains against the bright summer sun, then lights a white candle – white for purity of thought – and sets it down at the foot of her altar, beneath the picture of The Strong Goddess which forms the centrepiece of her Shrine. Monica wishes she had blonde hair like the Goddess's, but hers is black and cannot be lightened. Then she lights a stick of cinnamon incense and sits before her Icon, watched by one hundred and eleven pairs of Photo-Me eyes.

As she mumbles her ritual devotions, Monica takes a few minutes to reflect on her life, wondering if any area is deserving of special prayer. She is not concerned about her impending exams. She'll get three A's for certain. And besides, it doesn't matter if she doesn't. Cambridge have offered her two E's, and she wants to go to drama school anyway. But not the one here in Guildford, it's too close to home. She fancies Bristol Old Vic, or Central. Somewhere where she can start *living*, instead of this somnambulant existence.

With bowed head, she pushes a stray wisp of hair from her brow, and her thoughts turn to her parents – that strange, mismatched pair who almost never speak, neither one happy. They have always seemed beyond her help, creating for themselves a house of quiet demons, but Monica is sure that home life will improve now, because she doesn't hate her mother any more. She stopped hating her last night, after a campaign lasting more than six years, due to a sign from the Strong Goddess. (It was so unexpected to receive such a message. After her evening Communion and ritual reading of the Testing Trial, she had visited the toilet, and when she had evacuated, examined her stool as usual. It had been dark, knobbly, and submerged. This was significant. After a brief consultation with the Book of Truth she had understood it's meaning: something long-standing and difficult was to be expunged from her life. It could only mean her war against her mother, as she had been thinking of this whilst she sat on the toilet.) Thinking about it now, as she mutters her prayers before the Holy Shrine, it all begins to make sense. Hating Zoe hadn't stopped Zoe from hating her father, her original intention, and so it had served no purpose. But now she is uncertain of the way forward. She needs another sign. At once, Monica switches from the Litany of Power and begins to recite the Mantra of Coincidence in a low voice. She calls on the Strong Goddess for guidance, reaches for her stack of old 45s which lie beside the Shrine and selects one at random, then puts it on the turntable and awaits the message it will surely reveal. It crackles horribly, resolving at last into an old Beatles tune which was famous before she was even born: *All You Need Is Love.*

"Of course. Love. That's the answer."

The Goddess is instructing her. Rather than hate her mother, she must love her father unconditionally. Lenny needs her love, she realises. He has had so little from anyone else, and none of the right kind. There will be a bond between them now, a love-bond. He will tell her his secrets, and she will be able to use them against Zoe. This notion pleases her, and a small smile perches on her magenta lips as she happily intones the remainder of her prayers and mantras.

Her devotions completed, she opens her eyes and regards her newly-completed xeno-collage ranged across the wall, her face still shining with the magic of the One Eleven, the Cosmic Gateway. "What do I want? What do I really want?" she asks aloud, her eyes bright, knowing that her wish today will be granted. The Holy Bird, which lies mummified on top of the Book of Truth, to the left of the Goddess, glows warmly in the candlelight. And suddenly she knows the answer. Making the sign of the Triangle with her index fingers and thumbs, she begins a final, most heart-felt, prayer to the Strong Goddess. *Oh great Em, living Goddess, grant me this my perfect wish. Let me rise like you above the ordinary into the realm of the extraordinary. Show me the way to be strong. Let me know the path of strength so that one day I may walk the shitty Guildford streets and people will blanch in recognition. In the power of the One Eleven, and the xeno-collage representing all people, grant me fame and glory. Fame and glory. Oh Em, I want to be famous.*

Exhausted by the intensity of her feelings, Monica is abruptly seized by a nauseous pang of hunger, her stomach clenched shut after two days with no food. Slowly, she rises and makes for the bookshelf above her computer. She sticks her hand down behind Auden and retrieves three Mars bars, unwraps them hurriedly, and consumes them one by one. As soon as she has finished eating, a wave of disappointment crashes over her, leaving behind flotsam of disgust, regret and self-loathing. But this will pass, as it always does, after she has stuck her ruby-tipped fingers down her throat and vomited discreetly into the toilet. It's all under control.

CHAPTER TWO

It's seven-thirty a.m. and Keith, after another sleepless night, stands in his small white-tiled bathroom, staring down at the milky detergent which fills his hand basin. The hot water prickles his hands as he presses his sweater into the suds, and the wool darkens as it absorbs the water, becoming slick with soap, almost slimy. He massages it for some time with his strong fingers as hot, clean-smelling vapour rises up to his face.

This sweater is one of his favourites. He wore it last night when he went to the theatre, and then to the pub afterwards, so naturally it needs washing this morning. Now, he wishes he had done it last night, as soon as he arrived home. Then, perhaps, his somersaulting brain might have got some rest.

Keith tells himself it's the smoke from the pub, smoke which has inveigled itself into every fibre of his sweater, which has forced him to wash it this morning. But this is a deflection of the truth, a mirror thrown up in self-protection. In fact, Keith washes *everything* after a single wearing: underclothes, socks, shirts, trousers, sweaters. Even handkerchiefs. He washes it all by hand, every day, except jackets, coats, and ties, which he has dry cleaned in a shop across the road. So frequently does he wash that his hands have become sensitive to the chemicals, and he has to switch brands regularly to avoid serious allergy problems.

If he doesn't wash all his clothes before work, he knows he will not be able to leave the house. It is impossible to leave when there are dirty garments lying unwashed in the laundry basket. They will burn into his brain all day, like a fire-brand, if he does that – he won't be able to concentrate, will find it hard to catch his breath. And so, every morning, he makes sure that all his clothes are washed, spun, and hung out, and that any items for dry cleaning are dropped across the road to be collected on his return from work. It's a harmless enough obsession, he reasons, and is actually useful in some ways. Most people he knows detest washing, even with the advantage of a washing machine – an appliance Keith refuses to use because they're too rough with clothes and make them wear out more quickly.

Recently, however, the washing thing has been getting worse. He finds himself on occasion unable to sleep, instead lying awake thinking about his soiled clothes. And sometimes he gets out of bed at two or three in the morning to wash them, the clothes he has been wearing that day, knowing this is the only way to ease his mind, the only way he will be able to sleep. Last night had been a monumental struggle. He had lain in bed, rigid and alert, determined not to give in to his compulsion, determined to sleep. He had done neither and now, standing blearily at the hand basin in the bathroom, he feels quite unready for work. If it continues like this for much longer he will have to talk to someone about it.

As he rinses his sweater, he reflects that perhaps he should, at least, confide in his old friends Bob and Derek – The Bookends. Keith doesn't know how they came by this nickname, but he thinks it suits them perfectly: they look and dress alike (although Bob wears his wavy hair slightly longer than Derek), they have been together for twenty years, and he has never seen either one of them independent of the other. They are the permanent fixture in his life, his best friends, having taken him under their wing more than ten years ago, when he was taking his first halting steps on the road towards a homosexual lifestyle. They had exhibited parental concern for his welfare in those days, and even now maintain a proprietorial interest in him, like some kind of benign vigilante. He loves them very much, they are the people to whom he turns in times of need. Yet the idea of talking even to them about his obsession fills him with cold fear and horror. They might think he is unbalanced, needs help, when in fact it is nothing.

❈❈❈❈❈

Keith is standing in his bedroom, staring through the open doorway. He can see the upstairs landing beyond the threshold, with elongated golden rectangles of sunlight falling across the carpet. He is eleven years old, and today is the first big exam of his life. He likes tests and exams, he always does very well at them, but lately his parents have been telling him that this particular one is important. They've begun to say that it will affect his future, building it up into something huge and frightening. Keith is worried that his parents think he's cleverer than he really is, that he will fail. He doesn't feel very clever, in fact he feels a bit stupid. Especially today, because he can't figure out how to get out of his bedroom.

It started a while ago, as a kind of game, after he was told about his forthcoming Eleven Plus exam. The next morning, on his return from the bathroom, he had folded up his towel in a special way, for luck, before going down for breakfast. And from then on, he found he had to do it every day. The towel had to be precisely folded, with the corners touching exactly, and it had to form a perfect square, otherwise he'd have to start all over again. Only then, when he'd folded his towel correctly, could he put on his clothes and go downstairs for breakfast.

Sometime after that, the towel folding exercise extended to his bedclothes as well, and then to his pyjamas and dressing gown. Soon after that, he found he could not leave the room unless the curtains hung in a particular way, the regular pattern of the material matching up on both sides. It often took him fifteen minutes to straighten out his room, before he could leave it.

But today is different. He's folded his towel with enviable precision, along with his pyjamas and dressing gown; his bed is perfect, with the sheet turned down exactly one foot; and the curtains are straight and proper, their geometric patterns in absolute alignment. But still he can't leave the room.

He can hear his parents downstairs, and birds calling in the thin morning light outside, and he is dismayed. Somehow, it has become impossible to walk through the doorway. Something stops him (he doesn't know what), every time he tries. It's like a force field which repels him, will not let him through. Keith reasons that if he can find the formula, the right ritual, the door will let him pass. Obviously, it has nothing to do with the precision of his bedroom, so it must be to do with the door itself. Pleased with his logic, he touches the wooden door frame, first the left side with his right hand, then the right side with his left. Finally, he touches the door frame with both hands at once, pressing his knuckles against the frame on either side of him, at the same time counting backwards from ten. It's the right sequence, and he steps through.

He finds that all doors are the same from this moment onwards, although some are trickier to pass through than others. Sometimes the numbers have to be recited before the touching sequence, sometimes during, and sometimes after it. As the weeks pass, he tells no one about this strange phenomenon, instead adopting surreptitious gestures, honing his technique to a rapid-fire drumming of the lintel and a blur of counting – a two second impediment to his passing through a door – so as not to draw attention to himself. But the strategy fails. His merciless classmates dub him 'Loopy Lewis', and ritual humiliation becomes a part of his school day. His parents, thankfully, never mention his strange behaviour when passing through doorways – they have never taken a great deal of notice of him. For five years every door, everywhere, demands the entry ritual, in spite of the heavy price of ridicule.

Until he meets the man in the toilet:

Keith is on his way home from school one day, shortly after his sixteenth birthday, and, in dire need of a piss, scoots into a nearby toilet to relieve himself against the yellow-stained ceramic wall. He is about to leave when he notices a man at the other end of the toilet, standing by the door of the furthest cubicle. Keith thinks he looks old – about thirty – but he has a nice face and smiles in a friendly way. Keith smiles back. He glances down at the man and notices that he must have an erection, as there is a large swelling in his trousers. The man, seeing Keith looking at him, beckons Keith over, and without knowing why or how, Keith approaches the man.

When Keith reaches him, the man tells Keith to go into a cubicle, indicating the one he means with a nod of his head. In the doorway Keith executes his entry ritual, touching the left side of the frame with his right hand, and the right side with his left hand. Then he uncrosses his arms, as always, and touches the frame on either side of him with his knuckles. The man looks at him oddly, and Keith flushes with shame, feeling foolish.

Once the door is closed, the man undoes Keith's trousers, and Keith stands rigid as a statue. He is paralysed, but not with fear. He just doesn't know what to do. The man tries to kiss him, but Keith turns his face away. Instead, he lets the man masturbate him, although he derives little or no pleasure from it. This is his first time with anybody. He did not expect it to be like this, in a smelly cubicle, with an old man.

When Keith comes, the man takes his hand away and undoes his own trousers. With his free hand, the man gently pushes Keith down onto his knees, and presents himself for Keith to suck. Keith finds it difficult to breath, as the man is large and he has never done this before. His jaw tires quickly, his neck begins to ache, and he pulls back his head. At that moment, as Keith pulls his mouth from the stranger's cock, the man ejaculates copiously onto Keith's jacket and trousers. Then, wiping himself, but not Keith, with some toilet paper, he zips up his trousers, turns, and leaves without another word.

Keith, still on his knees, stares in horror at the thick albumen drying on his clothes. At last, sweating, he gets to his feet and notices a large wet urine stain on either knee of his trousers, dark and spreading. Unsteady now, he turns and vomits into the toilet, quickly flushing it away, then leans his head against the cool wall, breathing deeply. Suddenly, he has to get away. He turns and runs – out of the cubicle, out of the toilet, and all the way home. When he arrives, he does not pause at the front door, or at the door to the bathroom, so urgent is his need of sanctuary. Once inside, he strips off all his tainted clothing – every last garment, blazer and all – and dumps them in the bath. Then he turns on the taps as hard as they will go and watches the water seep slowly over them. He feels filthy. Unspeakably filthy. It is only now, as the water rises over his clothes, that he realises he has crossed four thresholds without using his entry ritual, and somehow he knows he is cured of that childish obsession.

14

As Keith hangs out today's laundry and surveys his small square of garden, he is suddenly aware of its silence. Somehow this moves him profoundly. It seems an absolute statement of his existence as a solitary being, a single unit, when what he wants more than anything is a partner. Not just a lover – how transient that sounds to him – but a life partner to live with for always.

Over the years there have been many men in Keith's life, and it has been then, in these periods of companionship, and even love on two occasions, that he has felt most real, most whole. But none of them have been substantial mates. Running through his list of attributes, as he affixes wooden pegs to the waistband of his Levi's and fastens them on to the revolving washing line, he believes he has a great deal to offer another person. He's sure he has. So why do his lovers always float off like fragile ghosts at the first hint of commitment? Why do his relationships always dissolve into nothing just when he is beginning to rely on them?

The Bookends, of course, have their own theory.

"You've got to find someone your own age," Bob told him when Pete, the most recent departure from Keith's life, exited without warning, leaving an enormous phone bill as a memento. "You're thirty-eight now – almost twice Pete's age. These age gaps are a disaster area."

"But he didn't leave because he was younger than me."

"No. He left because he was young, full stop," said Derek with an avuncular smile. "He's still learning. What you need is someone who has finished growing up. Someone who threw away their L plates years ago."

"The trouble with you is you're a soft touch," added Bob.

But Keith can't help it. He is attracted by youth. For him there is nothing more exciting than the angular thrust of a petulant jaw; the insolence of a gum-chewing face; the studied, super-cool nonchalance of a boy too trendy to dance. Youthful indifference to anybody over thirty drives him wild with desire. He has always harboured this proclivity.

"Guess I'm just a sucker for a pretty face," he smiles as he returns to the bathroom, wipes condensation off the mirror and checks his appearance.

And once again he feels lonely. It is months since he last held Pete in his arms, months since he last made love to that greyhound body. Keith still misses him, even though he knows it was never love. He knows he was simply a stepping-stone for those youthful, indifferent, Peter Pan feet.

Later, having showered and shaved, Keith sits down to a high-protein, low-fat breakfast in his black-and-chrome kitchen. It's an attempt to gain muscle bulk, as he has a bet on with his training partner, Ian. Keith maintains he'll be able to bench press seventy kilos by Christmas and Ian asserts that he won't. At the moment he's pressing about fifty-five, but six months should be enough time to make the gain. At the very least it will give his training more purpose, in the absence of a man to keep fit for.

Draining the bitter dregs of coffee from his mug, Keith checks the time with a reflex gesture of his wrist, quickly dumps the dirty breakfast crockery in the dish-washer, and leaves for work. It is a journey he enjoys: a short trip from his modest little semi-detached house, through quiet lanes the colour of oatmeal, flanked by verdant hedges, to the statistical nerve centre of the civil service, on the outskirts of an inconspicuous town in the Hampshire countryside. Most often he cycles, in an effort to keep fit, only resorting to the car in bad weather.

Keith works for the government, at the Office of Population Censuses and Surveys – a job even duller than it sounds. But it is secure at least, and he has been promoted to a level where there is no immediate boss leaning over his shoulder, which makes for relaxed working conditions. He has a pleasant workforce under him, including Maggie, who is a lesbian, and Tom, another gay man, so they manage to have some good times in the office. He is well liked and respected, especially by Tom and Maggie who find his open attitudes refreshing in this usually faceless regime, and he has tried to sweep away the stilted, oppressive atmosphere which was so all-pervasive when he arrived here ten years ago as a graduate entrant.

As he walks from the security desk, through cool, dim corridors, towards the shiny lift which will take him to the fourth floor, he remembers his first day in the office as an Executive Officer. Especially, he remembers the six resentful faces staring at him as he, young and nervous, was introduced as the new boss. All six faces were considerably older and more experienced than his own. He remembers the panic of realising that he was supposed to be in control of this office, that he was supposed to know what to do.

Now, having climbed another three rungs up the ladder, he has learnt how to run a team, and enjoys the responsibilities demanded by the post of Principle. But best of all, he has been promoted out of the open-plan area – a mêlée of grey filing cabinets, looming shelves crammed with statistical data, and spider plants – into a private office with a pleasant rural view.

Keith emerges from the lift and swipes his yellow plastic I-D card through the time-clock on the wall opposite, which flashes up his hours worked this period. He notices that he's down on hours, owing the office almost a whole day due to his recent trend of early exits to catch up on the sleep his has been missing. He admonishes himself, and suddenly flushes with panic at the thought that his obsessive behaviour is, for the first time, affecting his work. He knows it has to stop. He hadn't realised it had got so bad. Perhaps he really should get help. This idea, sharp and sudden, unnerves him.

He takes three deep breaths to calm himself, then walks the last few yards of corridor to his office. Halfway there, he encounters an unhappy looking Doug Grimmond, the SEO immediately beneath him.

"Keith. I'm glad you're in. Something's just come through on the fax," he huffs.

"Oh yes?" says Keith, focusing on Doug's immobile glass eye, a rude habit which he seems unable to break. "What is it?"

"I'm afraid it's a PQ."

Keith clicks his tongue in exasperation. Parliamentary Questions are a nightmare, being massively labour intensive, time consuming, and very boring for those unfortunate enough to have to collate the data. Everybody hates them.

"Who's it from?" he asks heavily.

"The Department of Health. From the Minister, no less."

Keith raises his tawny eyebrows, surprised by this news, and hurries into Doug's office. Usually, PQs are from batty MPs who want to know how many cars are owned in their particular constituency, in order to campaign for more parking spaces, or something equally trivial. This is obviously quite different.

"See for yourself," says Doug, handing Keith the fax.

He reads the message from the Minister's office, and is surprised again.

Without having to check, Keith knows this is a part of the census data which has not yet been keyed into the computer system. It will have to be collated the old fashioned way, by poring over the printed volumes of tables from previous censuses, all thick as telephone directories, which are housed in racks which extend the length of the open-plan office area. Extracting the data will be a laborious task.

"I don't think this sort of stuff is running yet, is it?" says Doug in a wooden voice.

"Absolutely not," says Keith, "it's a manual job. I'm afraid the whole section is in for a riveting day." He pauses to look at Doug's leathery face. "Under the circumstances, I think I should tell them the good news myself," he adds, and Doug's countenance brightens considerably.

Keith is almost amused by the obvious frisson as he enters the open-plan EO/CO area. He regards most of them as friends – especially Maggie and Tom, his fellow homosexuals – but nevertheless, he is several grades superior to them, and a certain formality goes with it.

"I've got an exciting project for you all this morning," he says with mock brightness, leaning on a squat filing cabinet in an attempt to seem less formal. His movements are solid and confident, the movements of a sportsman. "We've got a P.Q. from the Minister of Health." Several groans go up, and Tom buries his face in his hands, theatrically, amidst some ironic applause. Keith clears his throat, catching Tom's eye as he raises his head again. "What she wants to know," he continues, raising a hand to quieten them, "is how many never-married women," and he looks at Maggie as he says this, "have children. And she wants it broken down into Social Class and Socio-Economic Grouping, both regionally and nationally, as well as total numbers."

Everyone goes completely quiet.

"Bloody hell, that's a manual job," comes a distressed voice at the end of the room.

"She also wants to — "

"You mean there's *more*?" wails Tom.

"I'm afraid so. And it's a killing blow, I warn you. She also wants to know what qualifications were achieved by children of never-married women, as extrapolated from the 1971 *and* 1981 censuses."

Everyone is staring at Keith in horror. The atmosphere is loaded.

"And she wants it by four p.m. this afternoon, to take into the House," Keith tells them. Then, into the gloomy silence: "If it's any consolation, Doug and I are going to join you for this one."

"She's really got it in for single parents, hasn't she?" says Maggie wearily.

CHAPTER THREE

Lenny sits down, presses a button on the pad beside him, and closes his eyes as the chair tilts backwards. Comforted by the shiny black leather beneath him, which he caresses with a chubby forefinger, he stares up at the brilliant white ceiling and wonders how long it can go on like this.

How many more silent breakfasts can he endure, faced by the catty, porcelain features of his estranged wife? How much longer can he endure the daily, ritual soul-slaughter wrought by those terrible, reproachful eyes, so full of unarticulated accusation? And why does she stay? Surely she is as unhappy as he is? These daily questions have become Lenny's litany as he lies in his dental chair, waiting for the working day to begin. It is eight-thirty, and his first patient is due in half an hour. His nurse, Diane, won't be in for another twenty minutes.

These days he likes to come to the surgery early, to sit in the ordered quiet, surrounded by things he understands, and think. This is an environment he can control: X-ray machines, drills, high-tech lamps and mirrors, state-of-the-art measuring devices for recording the merest gaps between disordered teeth; shiny, clean surfaces and sensible drawers sectioned off in trays, where everything has a practical purpose. This is where he feels safe. At home, in his comfortable house on the hill, nothing makes sense; the mess that is his life crowds in on him like a malevolent ghost. Given the chance, he'd prefer to live on a desert island surrounded by nothing and nobody.

Lenny is shaken from his brooding thoughts by soft banging sounds from next door, where his colleague, Michael Whiting, is preparing for the day's work. He doesn't like Michael very much, and the feeling is mutual. Michael makes Lenny nervous, always so self-absorbed and cock-sure. Always asking after Zoe with that sly smile of his. But Lenny has to be polite, always. This is Michael's practice and chairs are hard to come by these days, with government cuts and all.

Lenny sighs a jagged, uneven breath, an unconscious reaction to the memory of his lost life. A year ago he had his own, very successful, practice with plenty of clients. He ran a large car, was the master of all he surveyed, and answered to no one but himself. But Zoe put an end to that, destroying fifteen years' carefully nurtured work at a stroke, and now he finds himself here, renting a chair from a second-rate colleague. It feels all wrong, and he doubts that he will ever get used to it. In fact, he actively resists it, fostering instead the vague hope that one day he will be able to start again.

It's an embarrassing situation as it stands. Whilst Michael's client list has shrunk since Lenny joined him, Lenny's has already expanded dramatically. People always ask for him, not Michael. Some of these are loyal patients from his old practice, but by no means all. Lenny puts it down to his good hands. Whilst Michael sees him as nervous and bumbling, in the surgery he possesses the confident hands of a sculptor. This cannot be taught, it's a gift.

For a moment he feels intensely proud of this fact, until the shame which is the rest of his life floods around him again with the force of a tidal wave. There is no escape from it. It comes to haunt him every day, even here, and the pain never lessens, the hurt goes on and on. Tears of anger at the injustice of it spring to his eyes. That he should be . . . he can't even bring himself to say the word.

Angrily, Lenny switches on his disposal unit and listens to its vapid gurgle, thinking of the pints of baby-pink water which will be spat into it throughout the day, washing away pieces of amalgam, scale, and blood. Flushed, he wipes newly formed pearls of sweat from his forehead with the back of his hand. Once again he feels thoroughly cheated. Nothing in his life to date has compensated for the self-disgusted celibate hell he has been inhabiting for the last seventeen years.

Except, perhaps, for Monica.

Monica, his beautiful, hugely gifted daughter. Lenny smiles as he assembles his dental tools – pick, probe and mirror – and takes comfort from the knowledge that he created her, that she came out of him. But, he thinks, her sharp smile, striking cheekbones and unhurried aristocratic air have all come from Zoe. And as for her immense brilliance – where did that come from? Idly fingering his mirror, Lenny catches the small, round reflection of his own brown eye and is touched with sadness. He can see nothing of himself in her, nothing at all. And he knows that in time he will become a mere spectator watching from the sidelines as his extraordinary prodigy marches on to success, leaving him far behind. He does not understand his fate at all, and curses it. His whole life feels like a party that he has inadvertently gatecrashed, and although none of the other guests have intimated it, he knows they would all rather he left because, frankly, he doesn't fit in.

There was a time when he really thought marriage was the answer, but it has turned out that Zoe is the biggest mistake of his life. Rivers do not run uphill, however much one might want them to. He tries not to blame Zoe for her coldness and disdain. Perhaps, were the situation reversed, he would feel same the creeping hatred for Zoe that she feels whenever he is near her. All he knows is that he has never lied to her. She has known since before they were married. It's a scene he often replays to himself in his mind's eye, as much to remind himself of the facts as to assuage his feelings of monstrousness. He really did tell her; there was never any duplicity on his part. He is not guilty of that charge.

❋ ❋ ❋ ❋ ❋

Zoe, thin and beautiful, is standing at the bar in Lampton's, a club that neither of them can really afford to be in, as they are both still students. He is nervous and diffident, smiling too much in the presence of this goddess, whose perfect beauty is constantly remarked on by his fellows. She leans forward a little, and he knows she is about to say something important, something she's been working up to all evening. He runs a dumpy hand through his hair and awaits the killing blow. He knows it will happen now, because his best friend Anthony, with girlfriend in tow, has just drifted off to another part of the room, to observe from afar. Perhaps they are even in on it. Zoe's eyes flame, but not with passion, and her expression is unreadable.

Unexpectedly she asks him straight out if he is a . . . and she fails to articulate the word, blushing crimson. She's only asking because there have been rumours, she says. Lenny, taken completely off guard, answers candidly that yes he is, but it disgusts him and he will never, ever, do anything about it. He says his dearest wish is to get married and have children.

He does not realise that as of this moment Zoe intends to make him her lifelong crusade, that her failure to cure him will lead to disappointment, then resentment, and ultimately a hatred as cold and solid as the heart of a mountain.

❋ ❋ ❋ ❋ ❋

Lenny hears the voices of Diane, his nurse, and Wendy, the receptionist, through the wall as they hang up their coats and make ready for the day. They are discussing the lead singer of Right Said Fred, saying how good looking he is, and whether or not he is one of *those*. Lenny does not like their sneering tone of voice, but neither can he bring himself to condemn it, even though they are unwittingly sneering at him also. He is one who believes that his condition, his desire of men, is morally wrong and unacceptable, but this is not through religious conviction. It is something he feels instinctively. Sometimes he wishes there was a cure, a pill which would render him heterosexual – a pill he would willingly swallow without hesitation – but most of the time he simply wishes he were dead. Or at least alone.

And this is the essence of his problem. Zoe will not leave him of her own accord because her life is comfortable, albeit less so now. Moreover, her pride is at stake. For eighteen years, she has been telling friends and family that Lenny is wonderful. To leave now, to admit that it was nothing more than a charade, bolstered by the profligate use of a cheque book, would be an unendurable humiliation.

And neither can he ask her to leave. Last year, when he finally discovered that Zoe had run up debt after debt, totalling more than £50,000, he at first suggested the obvious solution. They would sell their too-big house and move somewhere more modest, paying off the debts with the capital generated by the transaction. But Zoe refused, was adamant about keeping the house. Instead she told him to sell his practice, and for her part, she would curb her spending. There was no question of her getting a job. The equation was unreasonably balanced, but the lever Zoe used on Lenny's conscience was hard as diamond. She had told him, with the glittering eyes of an Egyptian goddess, that she would expose him as a ho-mo-sex-u-al if it ever came to it, and he believed her.

Zoe's anger is complete. If he destroys her by asking her to leave, she will make sure that he is ruined. It would be easy. Dentistry is a sensitive area for a man of his sort to be working in.

As he stares up at the ceiling, Lenny knows that he is absolutely trapped. And all because of some freaky gene.

CHAPTER FOUR

Keith, The Bookends, and Tom are on the train from Portsmouth to London, sitting in a compartment that can seat eight, but nobody will ask to join them on this journey however crowded the train becomes. They are too obviously homosexual. They have all had a few drinks at Keith's house, although it is barely eleven-o-clock in the morning, and are feeling buoyant and excited because today is Gay Pride.

The Bookends are dressed in identical denim outfits, perfect clones of one another except for Bob's longer hair. The waves at his temples are mid way between black and white. "We don't take the clone thing seriously," says Bob, with a wave of his hand, when Tom enquires about it.

Everyone smiles, especially Tom, who has not met The Bookends before today. "How long have you two been together?" he asks.

"Since before you were born, I shouldn't wonder," comes the reply.

"Awesome," says Tom, in a voice which could mean anything.

Keith has said little so far, but he has been watching it all. He hopes it isn't a mistake to invite Tom, his work colleague, along today, and at the same time he hopes very much that Tom will come home with him tonight. It's not impossible, he thinks, Tom seems interested enough. But Keith worries that it might make things difficult at work.

Once they arrive in London, the four of them make their way to the South Bank, where the march is due to start. They have to fight their way through the crowds at the tube station, which is virtually at a standstill, and this thrills Tom beyond words. It is his first experience of Gay Pride, and the sheer number of outrageous people all around him is electric. He has been changed forever by this, he can feel it. So many homosexuals in one place. "Awesome. Just totally awesome," he says to Keith as he stares about him.

"Isn't it?" Keith smiles, and he takes Tom's hand, which happens to be available. "I told you it would be like this."

"I know, but . . . " Tom shakes his head, unable to form the words.

The Bookends have meandered off in the direction of a contingent from Southampton, and Keith wonders when he will next see them. Perhaps he will bump into them again at Brockwell Park, which is the destination of the march this year. His hand soon becomes sweaty in the heat, holding Tom's, and he lets it go, casually, as they weave through the excited crowd, making towards the back of the assembled gathering.

Once there, they stand about for some twenty minutes, taking in the scene around them as more and more people flood out of the tube to join the throng. Up ahead is a formation aerobic display team, clad only in sparkly jockstraps, all oiled pectorals and defined abdominals. Keith finds this rather too exhibitionist to fully accept and instead ruminates over the slogan emblazoned on a nearby chest. Why is it gay *pride?* he wonders. He is not proud of being homosexual, just as he is not proud of having blue eyes, or of being five feet eleven inches tall. These are things which merely define him, he had no say in any of them. So where does pride fit in? One has pride in achievements, but surely not in physical facts? He is certain that he would not be 'proud' to have no legs, for example.

Perhaps, he tells himself, what it really means is gay self-respect. Or indeed pride that one has *achieved* self-respect against some considerable odds.

Satisfied with this, he lets the carnival atmosphere wash over him as the procession at last slides its way forward, to shrieks of delight from the assembled mass. All around him is the booming of at least five different sound systems all competing with one another, and a cacophony of whistles.

Keith and Tom shuffle through the hot black London streets together, the crowd thrillingly loud as it passes under cavernous bridges, but after half a mile, Tom disappears from his side. Keith watches him up ahead, talking with a young man he doesn't recognise, and wonders if he is an old friend, or whether Tom is making a conquest. With a sigh, he decides to drop out of the procession and watch it stream by for a while, camera at the ready. Perhaps he'll get a good shot of The Bookends as they go past, and then join them.

Several minutes later, he sees them walking arm in arm beneath a banner advocating heavy sex. The incongruity amuses Keith, and he snaps a shot as they wave in his direction, then he plunges once again into the human river to join his friends, who now walk either side of him. Tom's name is not mentioned.

Later, they take an absurdly packed tube to Brockwell Park. At each station the train doors open and close, but nobody gets on or off. It is impossible. Then a booming voice from somewhere in the crush makes an announcement.

"This train is overcrowded. Will all heterosexuals please alight at the next stop."

This delights the ninety-five percent homosexual throng, and a deafening chorus of whistles and whoops breaks out right along the train.

"Quite right!" cries Bob with a smile.

Several hours pass as they wander through the park, buying junk food, dropping in on the cabaret tent, and looking at the hundreds of stalls and specialist shops, all laid out on trestles beneath canvas canopies. The Bookends spend some considerable time debating whether or not they should join Stonewall, whilst Keith kills some time in the writhing, one-hundred-and-ten-degree disco tent. Later they buy beers, and lounge about on the grass listening to mediocre bands, simply enjoying the spectacle of human diversity. This year, they notice, as their eyes scan the crowds, there is an added attraction in the park. A funfair.

Keith has never before seen a funfair entirely full of homosexuals, and is astonished at the difference in the atmosphere here as compared to a regular one. No flushed, almost-drunk youths with their loud mouths, no frightened children, no impatient fathers reluctantly doling out money for rides. Just a crowd of fizzy, enthusiastic adults who are not ashamed of showing fear or delight. It enchants him, although he doesn't ride on anything himself because he knows it will make him sick.

At the end of the night, after dazzling fireworks have exploded over the swollen London sky, the three friends make their way home, their return journey more silent than the outward one. On the train, Keith dozes fitfully, more from the heat of the sun and the alcohol he has consumed than through actual tiredness. Once, when he opens his eyes briefly, he sees that Bob and Derek have cuddled up together, and Bob has lightly draped an arm around his partner. And for an instant Keith is inexpressibly happy. He knows it can be done. But not, he reflects, with Tom, who is even now, Keith imagines, at a club with that young stranger, high on alcohol and the promise of sex. Or perhaps they are already in bed.

When he finally enters his dark house, pleasantly cool after the pressing heat of London, he runs himself a glass of water, then goes to the bathroom and peels off his clothes, for washing. The night air licks his body like a refreshing tongue.

As he checks through the pockets of his jeans, a habitual precaution, he discovers a sheaf of folded fliers, some of the bounty he has collected during the afternoon. He has thrown most of the fliers away over the course of the day, but he received these ones early on, and was at that stage keeping them – thrusting them, unread, deep into his pockets. Flicking through them now as he sips his water, he finds that most advertise clubs or organisations, none of which are of interest or of use. But one intrigues him. It is called the Self-Insemination Group.

He remembers the woman who handed it to him, a flame haired, handsome woman in her thirties, with the bones of a horse. He had liked her, she reminded him of Maggie. "We want your sperm," she'd cried as he passed.

He reads the flier with interest. It explains the planned changes in the law excluding lesbians from artificial insemination either privately or on the National Health, and asks gay men to come forward who are willing to donate sperm to the group.

Keith thinks again of Maggie – what a fine person she is, what a splendid pair of parents she and Linda must make – and is in no doubt as to his moral stance. Without hesitation he goes in search of a pen, then fills in the form at the bottom of the flier and seals it in an envelope, to be posted in the morning. He does it for Maggie, and he does it to spite the Minister of Health, who had him poring over all those figures earlier in the week. He does not do it for himself. Personally, Keith loathes children.

Then, without another glance at the envelope lying on the dining table, he returns to the bathroom to wash his clothes.

CHAPTER FIVE

Michael Whiting, whose major talent has always been to see through people immediately, to pierce through their emotional defences and examine the person beneath them, is disconcerted by his new colleague, Lenny. He has drawn something of a blank with him. Lenny is remote and unreachable. But Michael is certain – and has been from the day Lenny interviewed for the associate chair – that there is something just a little off-kilter about him. That was why he decided to take him on. Michael, who must always be in the ascendant position, assumed at the time that this flaw, this something, would make Lenny easy to manipulate, but it has not proven to be the case. Now, Michael knows that he will have to discover the nature of this 'something' if he wants to gain mastery of his associate, and he has begun to search for clues. All that is apparent at present is mutual dislike.

As he casts a keen eye around his associate's surgery he takes in Lenny's photo of Zoe, which is ostentatiously displayed on a side cabinet, where no patient can fail to see it. There is something about this, too, which Michael finds irritating, disconcerting. Yet why should Lenny not display it? An exquisite photograph of a woman as striking as Zoe surely deserves to be admired by all. As he stares at her chiselled, flawless features, he can feel the stirring of desire for this woman once again; a woman wasted on a man as clownish as Lenny. He thinks of her often, trapped beneath her sweaty, bumbling husband in the dark night. In his dreams it is he, Michael, who penetrates her, who licks her salty skin and makes her gasp and murmur. How can it be that he is divorced, and single, whilst Lenny the Lumpen takes the prize?

Feeling resentful and envious, he looks up from the photograph and meets the meek eyes of his associate, who stands behind his chair as if for protection – sweating as usual, nervous as usual. Dumpy little Lenny, trying to hide his belly inside a flashy suit, awaiting the pronouncement from The Boss. Michael holds the silence a little longer than necessary, then allows himself a practised, insincere smile.

Michael loves this feeling of superiority. He has had to crawl a long way to get it, from the backstreets of a small, unheard-of Yorkshire town, out of the cloying mediocrity of both his family and his bitchy, ungrateful wife, to arrive at this surgery. A respectable profession, with plenty of opportunity for making a stack. The perfect combination. Until now.

"So, how's it going Lenny?" he asks in a confident, actor's voice. The vowels are lengthened and smoothed to hide any trace of the background he longs to expunge from his memory. He wishes it could be neatly excised, scraped from his psyche like an unwanted foetus.

"Busy," Lenny replies with polite deference.

"That's good," says Michael, his eyes drifting once again to the picture of Zoe. "It's just," and here he becomes serious, shifting his gaze to Lenny's dental chair, poking it with a finger, "that costs are going up again next month. I'm sure you saw it in the *Journal*. And I'm a little concerned about our overheads, especially with the NHS patients you've taken on. You must know that it can actually cost us to treat them?" Once again he looks at the photograph of Zoe, imagining his lips on hers. "I don't want to see us getting into difficulties," Michael adds, and there is an edge to his voice.

Lenny, wondering where this is leading, says nothing. True, the government pays him less than the actual cost of materials per NHS patient, but it is Lenny who shoulders that cost, not Michael. But then again Lenny, as an associate, pays fifty percent of his earnings to Michael. Fifty percent of a little less really does represent a shortfall for Michael. Anxious, Lenny waits for his boss to speak, then, realising that Michael has nothing more to say, answers: "Yes, of course." It occurs to him for the first time that Michael's chair might not be paying for itself, but Lenny is in no position to take it on, and Michael knows it. Perhaps Michael is about to raise the premium for Lenny's chair?

"I thought you should be in the picture, that's all," says Michael.

"Thanks," says Lenny in a wooden voice. A part of him is relieved, but he is unaccountably certain that Michael knows something, something bad about him. Why else would he be here? Why else would he be staring so pointedly at the picture of his wife? The sweat, which always flows freely from his body, is now a river on his back. His shirt sticks to him, between his shoulderblades.

Michael regards Lenny for a long time, searching his expression for clues, then leaves the room without expanding on his theme.

Back in his own quiet surgery, Michael hopes that he has sounded threatening. Frankly, he is at a loss as to what to do next. If he doesn't get hold of some money soon, he's going to fold. Depressed, he looks down at his thin hands, which lie on his desk top like dead leaves, and thinks he can discern a slight tremor in them. Horrified, he counts the days. It's three days since he had any gear. There's no way he can be suffering withdrawal . . . He tries not to think of the money he must have spent on his habit in the last two years.

Michael puffs out his cheeks and looks up towards the ceiling, as if he may find inspiration there, emblazoned on the plaster. There is something in the air between himself and Lenny, he can almost smell it. Michael hopes it's something he can use against Lenny for financial advantage. Everybody has a lever, it's simply a question of discovering what it is, and how it can be manipulated. Lenny is obviously a frightened man, but frightened of what? His face had drained of colour quite perceptibly as Michael cast a weary eye over his surgery. Particularly, Michael now recalls, when he allowed his eyes to linger on Lenny's photo of the beautiful Zoe. Instinctively, he knows this is significant, a way in, and he prepares a plan of action. He will monitor Lenny in infinitesimal detail. Goody Two Shoes may yet provide a useful escape route from the financial quagmire in which he, Michael, is currently sinking.

CHAPTER SIX

In the second week of July, Keith receives a letter from the Self-Insemination Group. He had all but forgotten about them, and is surprised. Somehow, he had imagined he would never hear from them again.

Inside the letter, which as far as he can tell is an exact copy of the flier he was given, there is a long questionnaire which asks many personal details, both physical and mental, concerning hereditary illnesses and diseases, general state of health, and willingness to submit to an HIV test, as well as a straight physical description. The reverse side of the form explains that all these details will be kept in the strictest confidence, for the exclusive use of the women of the SIG, and that if any woman feels his details are suitable, they will get in touch by letter.

On reflex, Keith completes the form, saying that he has had no operations or diseases, except the regular childhood ones; that he is HIV negative and willing to take another test; that he is five feet eleven inches tall, with swarthy skin tone, black hair, blue eyes, of medium build, and fit. For profession, he writes, 'Government employee'.

Keith smiles as he checks over the details of his application. He feels like a high class stud, or a prize bull, waiting to be called on to service some anonymous woman – a strange, but not unpleasant, notion. At the same time he fully expects never to be called on at all. He wonders how many men are in this gene pool, and how the women come to select this man or that man to be the father of their children. It all seems extremely arbitrary, he thinks, as he posts his completed form to the box number in London.

And so he is astonished when, some nine weeks later, he receives a letter from a woman, asking to meet him. The letter has been typed on a word processor with a very old dot matrix printer. The individual dots are visible, and the print itself is faint as cobweb.

Dear Mr Lewis,
I am a member of the SIG, my name is Rebecca Kilbride, and I have seen your details on our files. I am interested in you as a father. Even writing this feels weird. Perhaps we could meet to discuss?
Yours,
Rebecca K. (01483 175654)

The shortness of the letter, its lack of information, surprises Keith and fills him with a vague sense of doubt. The tone is cagey. He knows nothing about this woman, whilst she knows a fair amount about him, including his address. The imbalance disturbs him.

As he sits back, surveying his kitchen, he realises that he has regarded the entire affair in the abstract until now. But this letter has made the whole thing real. If he goes ahead, and it works, it will not simply be the exercising of a political act but the creation of a real baby, a new human being. It's a strange idea, and suddenly he has misgivings about it. It's a much bigger issue than he had at first thought. He decides he needs advice.

That evening, having invited himself round for dinner with The Bookends, he asks their opinion.

"Ethically, I think it's highly laudable of you," says Derek, "but as you say, theory and practice are rather different." He is sipping dry white wine from a long-stemmed glass, twirling it between index finger and thumb as he speaks. "What do you know of this woman?" Derek continues, "is she in a relationship? And how do you know she won't sting you for maintenance as soon as she spies the chance?"

"I don't know anything about her at all," Keith explains, "but I think it's worth meeting her, at least. She's vulnerable too, don't forget. She has to trust *me*."

"In what way?"

"In the largest possible way," Keith answers, his words slurring, shunted together by alcohol. "She has to trust me with her life. She has to believe that I haven't got it." There is a tight silence. He has broken their rule never to mention the disease – they have all lost too many friends to it – but it seems entirely legitimate in this case. "So you think I shouldn't do it?" Keith presses, unaware of any shift in the atmosphere.

"I think you should get some legal advice first," says Bob. Then: "You know Simon?"

Keith nods, remembering an attractive man in his forties whom he has met several times, here, over dinner. He's a lawyer.

"Why don't you give him a ring?" Bob suggests. "I'll get you the number."

Next morning, Keith phones Simon, but he doesn't know how to begin the conversation. His brain seems not to be working very well. He feels heavy and hung-over, as if someone has injected lead into his limbs and head. The Bookends have been liberal with their measures again.

"Hello, Simon?" Keith begins in a dry voice, "I expect you don't remember me, but I'm a friend of The Bookends. My name's Keith Lewis. We met at dinner . . . "

"Of course I remember you," Simon replies pleasantly, "you were with some miraculous youth as I recall. Pete, wasn't it?"

"Yes," says Keith, not bothering to tell him that they parted more than a year ago. "That's me."

"And what's yours?"

"What?" Keith has no idea what Simon is talking about.

"Problem. What's your problem? I assume you've got one, or you wouldn't be ringing."

Keith tells him about Rebecca Kilbride, and awaits Simon's professional opinion.

"I'm afraid the whole thing comes down to trust," Simon tells him. "Legally, she can sue you for maintenance, so long as she can identify you as the father, which is quite straight forward – blood tests and whatnot. But what with this new Maintenance Act, the state can also insist on the same. They're rather sharp on the absent father front at the moment, I have to say."

Keith is silent, disturbed by Simon's words. He stares at the Matisse print which hangs in his hallway and notices that the glass needs dusting.

"But if you *are* going to go ahead with this – by which I mean if you believe her intention is guileless; that she doesn't intend to involve you in anything but the purest biological sense – then you must insist on absolute anonymity from the beginning. Demand that she declares 'father unknown' on any birth certificate.

"You might even suggest that you draw up a contract, stating that she intends not to name you, and that she will not sue you for maintenance at any time. It wouldn't hold up in court, but it would at least establish innocent intention on your part, and a retraction of that intention on hers. They'd be on your side. But with regard to the state, it's a gamble. If they find you, they will make you pay. As I say, it's all a question of how much you trust this woman to say nowt."

After his conversation with Simon, Keith is more frightened than ever by the legal and financial implications of getting involved with Rebecca Kilbride. Everyone he's spoken to seems to feel the same. They all warn him to be wary, imagining the worst of her, whilst he instinctively feels the situation is more innocent than they describe. He has sought advice for ethical reasons only. It has not occurred to him, until now, that the woman would be anything but entirely honest. Yet now he is consumed by a creeping unease.

Keith lies in the bath whilst his head clears and reads the letter again and again. He thinks he can detect a certain trepidation in it, and this encourages him. He believes that the woman has not come to this decision lightly – that it is a massive, terrifying step for her to have taken. His friends are wrong. He decides, in the end, that he will talk to her.

Wrapped in a towel, he picks up the phone for what seems like the umpteenth time this weekend, and dials the number at the bottom of Rebecca's letter. He doesn't know where in the country he's phoning, the code is unfamiliar. It's answered on the fourth ring.

"Hello?" It's the soft voice of a young woman, slightly accented. Keith imagines it to be West Country.

"Hello . . . uh . . . sorry to ring you on a Sunday, but my name's Keith and I'm phoning about your letter. From the

SIG."

There is a tense pause and Keith realises he is actually very nervous. The sensation is unpleasant, and his throat feels strange.

"Oh, I see," comes the surprised answer. "Then it's Rebecca you want."

"Yes, Rebecca. I'm sorry, I assumed you were her."

"No, I'm Nin. Rebecca's in the garden. Hang on, I'll fetch her for you."

There is no doubt about it, the woman's voice is bubbling with undisguised excitement. This, more than anything, calms the beating of Keith's heart. These are ordinary women, a couple, who simply want a baby. It's absolutely safe.

After a few moments someone picks up the phone, and a voice full of light says: "Hello, you really are speaking to Rebecca now. Sorry about that."

"That's okay," says Keith. His throat has closed up again.

There is a difficult pause. Then Rebecca says: "Listen, seeing as it's all my idea it'll probably be easier if I do all the talking, and you tell me if you agree or disagree. Yes? I know these things can be embarrassing. And thanks ever so much for phoning."

"No problem," Keith manages.

"Okay, now this is the system," says Rebecca, her tone growing more serious, her words slower and somehow larger. "Actually, it's very simple. We'd come down to see you, you'd give us some sperm, and that would be that. No strings, no nothing. And we'd keep doing that every month until it worked. Nin and I haven't discussed how long we'd keep trying for . . . You'd be free to say you're fed up with it at any time, of course. Even after the first go." She pauses. "Still interested?"

"Yes."

"Brilliant." Rebecca can't believe she's having this conversation. The stories from other women in the SIG have not been encouraging. The men they contact almost never respond, they say, but her man – the first she has written to – has phoned her. And she has only been a member for two months. She wants to scream in excitement; she wants to jump up and down with Nin in her arms, and kiss her all over. "Then I think the next step," she continues, trying to sound businesslike and in control, "is to set up a meeting, and then see if we still think it's a good idea after that. How does that sound?"

"Okay."

"Good. As for a venue . . . " she makes a clicking sound with her tongue, like a dolphin, as she thinks. "We'd be happy to come to you, of course."

"I suppose," says Keith, uncertain, after a pause.

"But perhaps it would be better if we met on neutral ground," Rebecca adds quickly. "A bit more impersonal, which I think is a good thing. We'll pay your petrol, of course. It won't cost you a thing. Now let's see . . . You live in Stubbington, we live in Guildford . . . "

"Why not meet up in Brighton?" Keith suggests. He has warmed to Rebecca already, and is responding to the atmosphere of adventure. "It has the right sort of feel, don't you think?"

"Yes," Rebecca agrees. "But it's a lot further for you to come than for us."

"That's okay," he replies. "I have friends there, I can make a day of it." He's thinking of Gary – an old friend from university – and his lover, Paul. He hasn't seen them in ages and owes them a visit.

"Alright then, if you're sure. Where shall we meet?"

"I know a café on the sea front,' says Keith. "You can't miss it. It's on the border between Brighton and Hove, and there's a bloody great statue beside it. An angel, I think. How about there?"

"That's fine, I'm sure we'll find it," she says. "The only question now is, when? Any time to suit you."

Keith considers this for a moment, knowing that he should strike whilst the iron is hot, or else run the risk of loosing his nerve completely. "Why not this Saturday, two-o-clock?" he offers. It seems very soon and very sudden, but he supposes it is better like this.

"That's fine," says Rebecca. Then, as an after-thought:

"How will we know you?"

"I'll be easy to spot," Keith says in a jokey manner, "I look fairly gay."

"So does everyone in Brighton!" counters Rebecca.

Keith laughs briefly. "You should recognise me from my description on my form," he adds.

"Of course! Stupid of me," says Rebecca. "See you on Saturday, then."

As the week progresses, Keith grows steadily more nervous until, on Saturday morning, he is at such a pitch that he is unable to eat his breakfast. He forces himself to drink a pint of milk, but even this sits uneasily in his stomach, awaiting the slightest provocation to re-emerge.

As he drives along the busy coast road towards Brighton, he wonders what Rebecca and Nin will be like, and how they are going to decide if he will make a suitable father. Once again he is filled with panic at the thought of deception, and arms himself with the strategies that Simon has suggested to him. The nightmares of maintenance payments – or worse, actual parenting – whirl around in his head like frantic moths, and he reminds himself that he must demand certain rights from the outset. Could the state force him to look after his child? he wonders. He must talk to Rebecca about this. But how to broach these subjects without appearing unpleasantly suspicious? Perhaps it's a bad idea after all.

He arrives at the café early, and sits at a table where he is easily visible, sipping coffee and darting nervous glances at the other patrons. He spots two women who might be a couple sitting three tables away, but they are in their mid-thirties. Nin and Rebecca must be younger than that. By ten minutes past two, nobody has approached him. He wonders how long he should wait, and on reflex glances at his watch for the fifth time. But as he looks up, two silhouetted figures meander through the surrounding tables towards him, and he smiles to see it's the pair of women he had ruled out as too old. One of them has a blue cardboard file under her arm.

"You must be Keith," says the woman with the file. "I'm

Rebecca. And this is Nin."

They all smile and shake hands, then Nin excuses herself, moving up to the counter to order more tea for them all. Once left alone, Keith and Rebecca appraise one another. Rebecca is very fair, with almost invisible blonde eyebrows and pink, sensitive-looking skin. Her eyes are watery.

"So," she begins, once Nin has returned with the tea, "here we are!"

There follows a brief, trivial conversation about their journeys to Brighton, and the weather, characterised by an air of sublimated embarrassment. After all, it is, essentially, an interview of which Keith is the subject: Rebecca is trying to find out if she wants Keith's genes, and if he is psychologically suitable for her needs. To qualify, Keith must fulfil certain criteria.

"Do you mind if we ask you some questions now?" Rebecca says, once their uneasy conversation has stalled. She fiddles with her cardboard file, and smiles a thin smile.

"No. Go ahead," says Keith.

"Okay, first question," says Rebecca, reading from a piece of paper in her file without looking up at Keith, "what do you think of children?" She is worried that he might desperately want children, and is only doing this in order to get one. As soon as it is born, he may demand visiting rights, expect actual input into the upbringing of the child, or even worse, sue for custody. He may demand to be named as the father. She has heard examples of all of these things, and of women who have lost their children through it. What she wants is a man who will inseminate her, then forget about it.

"In what way do you mean 'what do I think of children?'" asks Keith, flustered. He's playing for time. He's certain it's a trick question.

"I mean, do you like them?" smiles Rebecca.

Keith frowns. He's sure he is supposed to say he loves them, and isn't it a shame that he'll never have any? Everyone is supposed to love children. If he says he doesn't, they'll think there's something wrong with him. But if he says he likes them, then they'll ask him for money as soon as the child is born, and make him visit it and be a 'father'. He'd rather die than that. "Well, actually, it may sound rather shocking but I loathe them," says Keith, looking apologetic.

"I see. So you wouldn't be interested in any practical parenting, if I were to have a baby?"

Keith feels the colour drain from his face. It's his nightmare come to get him. "No. Absolutely not," he answers, more forcefully this time.

"Wouldn't you even want to see it? Surely you'd be curious?"

To Keith, the question seems loaded with emotion. "Not at all. I'd be pleased for you, but not at all curious. As I said, I really don't like children. I don't want anything to do with them," says Keith, wondering if he sounds as terrified as he feels.

"Okay. Then why are you interested in doing this? What made you put your name down?"

This question is asked flatly, with no clue as to the expected answer, and Keith decides to be quite honest. "It was a political action," he says. "I'm fed up with other people telling you what you can and can't do with your own body, so I wanted to help a lesbian couple have a child if they wanted one. I know the system is stacked against you, and it's not right. I've a lesbian friend who is a wonderful mother, and . . . " Keith stops talking because Rebecca and Nin are no longer listening to him. They are smiling at one another across the table.

Rebecca turns to look at Keith. "That's a good answer!" she whispers. And her voice is the voice of fragile leaves. Then her face clouds, troubled by a question she doesn't want to utter. "I'm afraid there's no delicate way of asking this," she says, biting her lower lip as she laughs with embarrassment and tosses back her hair, "but it's important that I know you're a safe donor. I know it says so on the form you filled in for the SIG, but . . . " Her voice trails away to nothing.

"It's okay," says Keith. "I've had a test before. I'd be happy to have another."

"Is that alright?" Rebecca asks, concerned.

"Quite alright." Keith is not remotely worried. He knows he is negative.

Later, as they walk along the sea front, Rebecca tells him that she is a freelance graphic designer, and Nin announces that she is a teacher. They almost skip along the esplanade, filled with teenaged excitement, as they tell him these things.

Keith looks at the two women and smiles. He can tell how much they love one another by the light in their eyes, and is pleased that he is helping them. "So why did you choose me?" he says.

"Because you're so dark and I'm so fair," says Rebecca. "I've always had trouble in the sun with my skin, so I thought I'd take advantage of the choice of genes, to rectify that problem for IT."

"And why you, or are you both going to have one?"

"I work from home, but Nin would need time off school, so it's just more practical that it should be me."

Keith looks out at the shimmering sea to make his next remark. He wants it to sound casual. "A friend of mine suggested writing out a contract about all this," he says, "about anonymity on the birth certificate and so on."

"Oh god yes," says Rebecca emphatically. "I don't want you barging in and claiming to be the father! But there's no point in doing all that unless I get pregnant."

It's the first time the word has been uttered and it makes Keith feel like a stud again. It reminds him that he has been selected for his physical appearance, his dark-skinned genes; that she merely wants his seed. It's an uncomfortable thought. But at least he is now certain that they are as keen for him to have nothing to do with the child as he is.

"So when do we begin?" he asks.

"I'm due to ovulate again on the 14th and 15th of next month," Rebecca explains. "That's almost three weeks away. I suggest that we all go away and think about this, and decide how we feel. Then I'll phone you nearer the time, to arrange when we can come and get the sperm. Providing we all still want to go ahead, that is."

Later, in the pub, Keith tells his friends Gary and Paul his exciting news. They listen, eyes wide, thrilled at the subversion. But he can tell they're glad it is he who is doing it, and not themselves.

CHAPTER SEVEN

Monica is lying on her bed reading some French literature, a novel included on the reading list for her first term at university. She has decided to begin her studies early – good discipline if she wants to achieve a First. The house is silent, profoundly still, and Monica is content. She likes the ambience of the house at this time of the night; she feels she owns these thick early hours.

Sometimes she wanders the house whilst her parents are asleep, alone in their separate beds. Naked, she stands in the centre of every room with arms outstretched, and claims the space as her own. She touches everything – especially the photographs, with their powerful energies – as she bathes in the purple darkness, and then returns to her room replete, as if after a heavy meal.

But not tonight. Tonight, she is re-reading *La Porte Etroit*, in French, relishing the religious strength and conviction of the heroine, Alissa. Monica identifies with her struggle to achieve her saintly goal, whilst having little sympathy for the ingrate Jerome, who never speaks his mind. He reminds her of her father in his meek acceptance of anything that Alissa demands, in his belief that he is powerless to effect change. But Jerome has got it all wrong. What he needs is the Litany of Power.

"Lesson One: Set Your Goals. Lesson Two: Devise A Plan To Achieve Your Goals. Lesson Three: Never Be Deflected From Your Plan," Monica chants in a low voice. Strength is the key to the city of success. Monica is learning to be strong, learning not to be deflected from her plan.

Half an hour later Monica finishes the book, then makes a list of useful quotations and memorises them. She hopes there will be discussion of religious conviction in her seminars. *Oh yes, Em, then we can talk about us,* she murmurs with feeling, but the words seem to make no sound. When she's talking to Em, she's never quite sure if she's talking aloud or in her head.

Now, her studying over for the day, Monica decides it's

time to weigh herself – her nightly ritual before sleep. Rising from the bed, Monica moves over to the weighing scales which sit at the foot of her chest of drawers, and, stepping onto them with bare feet, she peers down at the dial which swings back and forth between her toes. When it settles, it reads forty-five dead. She's gained half a kilo – disastrous. She's becoming obese. She'll never be famous if she turns into a Lipo. There are no famous Lipo-Freaks.

Panicked, she runs into the bathroom and stares at herself in the mirror there. Her skin looks yellow in the artificial light, her eyes staring and lifeless. Her usually obedient fringe is flopping over her forehead, a strange kink in her hair making it fall the wrong way. And her teeth look like the teeth of an old woman, or a heroin addict, with receded gums and stained, ruined enamel. Somehow they seem worse than usual tonight, and she vows never to smile again, especially not in front of Lenny. He has already mentioned her teeth a million times, pressing her to let him fix them – advances that she has thus far repelled. But the current state of her mouth might be all the ammunition he needs to make her submit finally to the drills and needles. This is a hideous prospect, she doesn't want one of his freaky Stepford Wife smiles. Unfortunately, it will prove hard to avoid, without special help from the Living Goddess, as her Campaign of Love demands that she smile at Lenny constantly. He will be certain to notice.

To date, her Campaign does not seem to have worked particularly well. Lenny has remained a silent, creeping thing despite her new gift of affection for him. In ten weeks, her giant love has not been able to prise open his heart to reveal whatever lies within it. She imagines it now, dark and wet like a deep cave, only without the coldness. She knows he is not cold. But she acknowledges that such things as the healing of her father will take time. She will be patient, because patience is a sign of strength, and eventually her love will reach him and heal him.

Most of all, she wants the hunted look to disappear from his eyes. Every evening, when he comes in from the surgery, his face wears the expression of a man who all day has had to carry an enormous, invisible weight on his back. Lenny thinks he is the only one who sees it, but Monica sees it too. Or perhaps her father cannot see it. Perhaps he merely feels its oppression, without understanding its source. Could it be that she is the sole witness of his burden? And should she tell him that really it is as inconsequential as dust?

She walks away from the grotesque reflection of herself in the mirror, and buries herself in the darkness of the house. Let it swallow her disgusting body, hide her corroded teeth. The mezzanine landing sighs at her passage down the stairs, and as she walks through the dining room she feels aimless, with no clear idea of where she is going.

She lets herself out through the back door and stands shivering in the garden, pinned to the ground by the hard light of stars. The cedar tree at the foot of the garden, which she has climbed so many times, casts a giant silhouette against the crest of the hill behind it. As she looks up at the dark planes of this tree – which, more than anything else in her life represents her childhood, laced with a thousand memories of games played, friendships forged, and minor injuries sustained – she crosses her arms over her flat chest, the palm of a hand on each shoulder, and sways from side to side to still the pain. A pain she feels welling up from an unknown spring, to drown her.

What will she do now, with her three A's? She's supposed to start at Cambridge in three weeks, but she'd rather live on Mars. Everything's happening much too quickly. She's only just seventeen, after all. Where did her childhood go? She never asked to be so clever, in fact she'd rather she wasn't – expectation after expectation heaped on her head until she can hardly stand it. When will it end? And the One Eleven, the Photo-Me collage, seems not to have worked. She had expected something spectacular to have happened by now, to rescue her from it all. Suddenly afraid, she throws back her head, exposing her white neck to the stars, and begs the unseen moons and planets to save her.

❋❋❋❋❋

Monica is nine years old, hunched over the dinner table, crying into her soup. Timmy died today, and she loved him so much. Big, cuddly Timmy, with that fresh, pink tongue; always licking her a slobbery welcome home from school. And now he's been smashed to jelly and jam by a fat man in a lorry. Just thinking about it renews her anguish, redoubles her choking sobs.

Her mother glowers at her across the table as snot and tears mingle on her chin. Monica makes no attempt to wipe them away and glares back at her mother, who never loved Timmy the way she did. Never even liked him. She rowed with Lenny about him for weeks, when he said Monica could keep him. She's probably glad Timmy's dead.

Who will be her friend now? At school they call her Brain-Box and Witch, and no one will come near her, after what happened to Darren. Timmy had been her only companion, and now he's gone too. So now she has no one, no one at all to play with.

Monica bows her head towards her untouched bowl of Heinz 57 Tomato and thinks of Darren, and his strange squashed face at the bottom of the cedar tree, staring up at her. They'd been playing House in the crook of the tree, a safe dark nest where the trunk split into three parts, and she'd been telling him about Magic. Telling him about thistle down, and how you got a wish that really came true if you could catch it as it drifted past. Like the opposite of stepping on cracks in the pavement, which was bad, very bad. Darren nodded gravely at this. Then, as if summoned by her words, a smoky, fairy bubble of thistle down had floated past them, up through the dark fronds of cedar.

A wish, a wish that will really come true, Monica said, and Darren jumped up, snatching at it with impatient fingers. The motion of his hand disturbed the air and it floated away. But Darren clambered after it as it moved off, tantalisingly slow; climbed out on to a flimsy branch, and stretched out his arm . . . Then there was a crack, his face changed, turning white, and he fell. Something happened in his head when he hit the ground, and he couldn't move.

Monica didn't cry when Darren fell, or when the ambulance came to take him away, or even when their teacher told them, weeks later, that he was dead. But she's crying now, for Timmy, and she doesn't know if she'll be able to stop, doesn't know if she wants to. And for the hundredth time she wonders what Darren was wishing for as he fell.

Since Darren, Monica has been careful to observe the rules of Magic to the letter. She never walks under ladders, she spits if she sees a single magpie, says her name backwards three times if she sees a black cat. She has a hoard of lucky pebbles in her bedroom, and she touches wood (it has to be living wood) at least once a day. And she's been lucky, until now. Always top of the class, always her teachers' favourite. But today, someone put a curse on her, someone put a shiny black jackdaw's feather in her school locker and she just knew something bad was going to happen. All the way home from school she searched for lucky signs to counteract the bad omen, but found none. And when she arrived home, she saw her mother's brittle face, heard her blurt out that Timmy was dead, without warning, in a voice stripped of any possible comfort, and Monica blamed it on the bad black feather.

Now, as she pushes her soup bowl away from her, with a stomach clenched tight shut with grief, she realises that she needs more powerful forms of protection from the world, but exactly what she doesn't know.

Years go by, and Monica surrounds herself with talismans, slowly building a wall. Her silent parents hardly talk to her, Zoe encased in her hard, impermeable shell; Lenny loving her, perhaps, but it feels as if it's coming from far away. It touches her like the light of stars, almost imperceptible, almost cold. She is bored, lonely, ignored; she has just become a teenager. And this is when she decides not to eat. But it's not a decision that is made in her head, it comes from somewhere else. Even she doesn't understand it. Her parents, of course, seem not to notice.

She wonders, with dark fury, just what she has to do to get their attention. Being clever hasn't done the trick – eleven GCSEs at fourteen seems barely to arouse the vaguest approbation. And so she begins to read about famous women, women who were noticed: Ruth Ellis, the last woman to be hanged in England; Lizzie Borden, whose parents maybe noticed her too late, as the glinting axe swooped down on their unsuspecting heads; and that other, perhaps more terrible, heroine whose friend was killed *in a childhood accident, like her. Whose dog was run over, like her. Whose birthday is less than a week from hers, and who shares her initial. They are linked. Monica has found the ultimate talisman, the ultimate goal. Em will protect her forever, and one day, she will be noticed.*

❋❋❋❋❋

Monica feels silent tears on her cheeks, then turns and runs back into the dark house, where she stands motionless in the kitchen, holding her breath and chanting the Silent Mantra in her head. Somewhere there is the ticking of a clock, and fainter, behind this sound, she can hear a car up on the hill, but she is not calmed. The curse is on her.

She crosses the kitchen and pulls open the door of the refrigerator, stocked to the roof as ever by her efficient Barbie Doll mother, and peers inside. Buttery light spills onto the tiled floor immediately in front of the refrigerator, defining a space, like a stage, and rendering the surrounding darkness more profound. Monica is suddenly hungry, and yet she knows she must not eat. She already weighs forty-five kilos.

Monica continues to stare into the refrigerator, at all the food ranged on white wire shelves: A half-consumed chicken carcass; some slices of ham; the floppy remains of some trendy ethnic salad wallowing in pale pink vinaigrette; some cheese, wrapped in cling film; some eggs; four packs of butter; a tub of margarine; a cup full of some undisclosed liquid, blood-dark and thick; a jar of mayonnaise; some milk; a plastic bottle of cooking oil. As she looks at the food, something inside her dissolves, her will to abstain crushed by the weightier demands of a baser, more powerful force deep within her, and she knows she does not have the strength to resist it.

Kneeling, Monica reaches into the refrigerator, grabs the cold plate on which the half-eaten chicken rests, and pulls it to her. She cradles the plate in her left arm as she picks at the flesh with her right. It rips away easily, flaky and white, becoming pinker near the plastic-looking bones. Her head is bent down low to the carcass and her fingers barely move as they push the flesh between her greasy, craving lips. Soon she is taking bites directly from the bird, her fringe trailing in the fat which has gathered at the edge of the plate. When she has finished the chicken she wipes her lips on the back of her hand and without pausing, reaches into the refrigerator again to snatch up the slivers of ham in her fist, cramming them into her mouth all at once. She breathes heavily through her nose, making a wheezing sound as she chews and swallows. After the ham, Monica eats the limp salad, drinking down the bitter-sweet vinaigrette from the edge of the bowl. Then she unwraps and eats the cheese, a mature cheddar which makes her mouth tingle.

Now Monica is lying on the floor, propped up on her left elbow. She reaches for the row of eggs which sit in holders in the refrigerator door and cracks them open on the edge of the bottom shelf, then tips them into her waiting mouth one by one. They slip down the back of her throat like snot. Then she reaches for the jar of mayonnaise, and slowly unscrews the lid.

Upstairs, the mezzanine landing sighs again at the tread of another foot, but Monica does not hear it. She is unreachable in her world, past caring, and feeling nothing at this point. She is quite unaware that she has an audience until she looks up towards the kitchen doorway and sees Lenny, her father, staring at her out of the shadows. Suddenly she sees herself as he must see her: lying on her back in front of the refrigerator, stomach taut, scooping gobs of mayonnaise into her mouth with her hand and making guzzling sounds.

She struggles to her feet with a body weighing tons and pushes past him, wiping dribbles of raw egg and mayonnaise from her chin as she runs upstairs to shut herself in the bathroom. She does not dare to look in the mirror. She was gross before, so what must she look like now? Terror and disgust course through her as she sees Lenny's confused face once again in her mind's eye. "Now he knows," she moans, her voice a whisper. Leaning back against the door she tries to breathe deeply, but her ribs feel constricted. And then, as her stomach begins to protest at its abuse, she begins the second phase of her solitary, inexorable ritual.

Slowly, she kneels before the toilet, raises the lid, and stares down at the calm rectangle of water beneath her. Then she holds her throat, with thumb and index finger at the point where her tonsils might be, pressing inward and upward, and regurgitates the contents of her swollen stomach. And again. And then again, this time bringing up blood. Weak and sweating, she sits herself down on the toilet, puts her head in her hands and cries like a little girl. Like the little girl who wouldn't come down from the cedar tree, who shouted down to her father that she'd never come down because she didn't want to go to school – because after that, she'd have to go to another school and eventually she'd have to get a job and that would mean that she was a grown-up. That was what she didn't want. To be a grown-up.

Monica rises from the toilet and splashes cold water on her face, still not looking at herself in the mirror, then returns to her room. Ashamed, humiliated, and feeling worthless, she flings her wardrobe doors wide open to reveal the Holy Shrine and prostrates herself before the Strong Goddess, her face pressed into the carpet.

Oh Em, living Goddess, I'm weak, so weak. I have no strength, no will, no control over myself. I am base and abased, I am unworthy even to worship you. You achieved your goal, withstood the Testing Trial, yet my will is broken like a stick in the wind. Give me your strength. Forgive me, Em, your humble acolyte, for this weakness. It will not happen again. It will not.

Monica lights a lemon scented candle, to aid her concentration, and reads herself the salient passages of the Testing Trial from the Book of Truth. Then she snips a strand of hair from her fringe, cuts off a sliver of bright red finger nail, and places them at the alter, making the Sign of True Repentance. Feeling better now, she settles down to recite the Litany of Power until morning.

CHAPTER EIGHT

Since his meeting with Rebecca and Nin, Keith has been feeling much more relaxed about helping them to have a child. They seem eminently sensible, stable, and responsible people – qualities he believes to be important for good parenting. But as the week goes on, he begins to curse himself for not asking them more questions. In fact, he doesn't remember asking any.

As he sits in his quiet office, staring out over countryside rendered inexplicably charming by a wash of early autumnal sun, he realises that there are things he badly wants to know about the process. For example, how exactly is Rebecca hoping to become pregnant? On both occasions to date euphemisms have been bandied about, and Rebecca has spoken of *coming to get the sperm*. What does that involve, precisely? It could mean anything! Suddenly, the appalling thought occurs to him that he is going to have to have sex with her. He is going to have to go into a room with this woman, a complete stranger, and copulate with her.

Panicked, he rises from his chair and takes a short walk around the fourth floor, past offices containing earnest workers speaking in hushed tones, and arrives at the drinks machine. Selecting hot chocolate, the least unpleasant drink that the machine has to offer, he watches steaming water jet into his brown plastic cup, then carries it back to his office, cautiously sipping at the hot froth.

Back behind his desk, Keith stares at the wall distractedly, taking tiny mouthfuls of his drink and worrying about how he is going to impregnate Rebecca. He simply can't do it. He will be unable to have sex with this woman, or any other woman. It will be a nightmare. Fretting at the end of a pencil with his teeth, he decides he will have to tell her that he's changed his mind. He will explain why; she will understand. It's easier for a woman. She doesn't have to do anything – she can just lie there – but a man has to become physically engaged. The very thought of it terrifies him and he breaks out in a cold sweat. Nervously, he bites right though his pencil.

That night, just as he returns home from his evening session at the gym, Rebecca phones. Keith, his gym bag still slung over his shoulder, is caught off guard.

"Hello again, I'm just ringing to see if you still want to go ahead?" Rebecca asks, her voice level and controlled.

"Uh, yes." Keith responds on reflex, without knowing why.

There is a bright pause. Then: "Oh, I'm so glad. Okay. Right. Let's sort out the practicalities, shall we?"

Keith summons all the courage he has. "Uh . . . there's something I wanted to ask you, actually," he says in a thin voice, leaning against the wall for support.

"Yes?"

Keith has no idea how to say this. He burns with embarrassment and discomfort, his only salve the fact that Rebecca cannot see him at this moment. Then he steels himself, and talks quickly: "It's just that I'm a little uncertain about . . . That is, it's no offence to you personally of course, but do I . . . uh . . . I don't think I would be able to actually . . . uh . . . make love . . . " The phone feels as slippery as a fish in his sweaty hand.

At the other end of the line there is silence, then a thud followed by a rasping sound. The sound goes on for some time before erupting into snorts of recognisable laughter. Rebecca at last regains control of herself. "Oh you poor man," she begins, "I should have explained better. Have you been worrying all this time that you'd have to — " and once again she shrieks to the heavens.

When she is finally calmed, she tells Keith how it will work. "We'll come down to see you on the 15th – that's next Thursday – and we'll arrange a specific time to meet. Say six-o-clock. So, we come to your house at six, you hand us a jar with some sperm in it, and then we go away again. End of story."

"Will that work?"

"Apparently, yes. Sperm can live outside the body for about two hours, provided they're kept at the right temperature. But the fresher it is, the better. That's why we need to arrange a specific collection time."

"I didn't know that."

"No. Anyway, once you've handed it over we'll run off to a guest house and do what we have to do with it. And then we'll do a repeat performance the following evening, if that's okay."

Keith, relieved beyond belief, will now agree to anything. Now that it's been explained to him, he can't imagine what he had been thinking of, and feels extremely foolish. "Six-o-clock is fine for both days," he says.

"Brilliant. And if anything crops up I'll call you, but otherwise, expect us next Thursday, at six."

"Okay, see you."

Keith smiles at himself as he puts down the phone, then dumps his sweaty gym kit in the hand basin, for washing, together with his work clothes. He experiences a pleasant sense of adventure; he feels useful and valued, a productive person. Happily agitating his clothes in the suds, he wonders who he might tell. He knows his family are out of the question – his sexuality is cross enough for them. This added idiosyncrasy would simply be too much. After some thought, he decides to tell The Bookends, Gary and Paul (who know part of the story already), and of course Maggie at work, but nobody else. Other people's moral codes are unpredictable, and best left untested, in his experience.

Throughout the following week Keith is decisive and purposeful, striding round the office and tackling small, niggling jobs which have lain unfinished on his desk for weeks. He demands the same vitality and enthusiasm from those working beneath him, which makes them suspect that he is in love.

On Thursday morning, the big day, Keith relaxes his regime, turning his gaze to the window, but mid-afternoon some urgent paperwork comes in, something from Computer Division which needs his attention. It seems some multiple-occupancy housing tables have been scrambled by George, the computer, and nobody knows where the original data has gone. After lengthy phone conversations with Wallace in Computers and Davison in Census, it becomes clear that the information is, in fact, permanently lost. This is a pity, as multiple-occupancy housing – and here Keith imagines opulent Regency houses converted into flats – is the most interesting and largest growing statistical area. As he puts the phone down for the last time, he knows that it will be up to him to do what is always done in such situations. He will have to extrapolate the figures from other data. In short, he will have to invent them.

With a wry smile Keith sighs, then he glances at his watch and snaps upright. It's five-thirty-five! With a lurching stomach, he realises he has only twenty-five minutes in which to get home and manage an ejaculation. The figures will have to wait until tomorrow. As he flees his office, grabbing his coat on the way out, he hopes he is not going to be late. He drives home as fast as he can, through the dark winding lanes which he knows so well, and arrives home at twelve minutes to six.

He hurries directly into the bathroom, where he runs a shallow basin of hot water and stands a small Marmite jar in it, to warm. He has saved it especially, having cleaned it with great care. He feels it's the perfect vessel due to its associations with yeast and growing things, and because it has the advantage of being opaque. After a minute, he takes it into the bedroom with him and lies down on the bed. He looks at his alarm clock: five-fifty-one.

In vain, Keith tries to conjure sexual thoughts, but the stress of his day together with the panic of getting home in time, not to mention the added pressure of having to produce his semen to order in the next nine minutes, makes things difficult. He strokes himself hopefully, but his penis does not respond, and true panic sets in. What if he can't perform? What if they ring the doorbell whilst he is still masturbating?

The minutes tick on, but his member becomes increasingly uncooperative. In a final effort to arouse himself, Keith reaches for an old edition of *Vulcan* and gazes at his favourite picture whilst masturbating at crazy speed, trying to bully his still only half-interested penis into action. Finally, by some tremendous effort which seems to involve every muscle in his body, Keith manages to produce some sperm and guide it into the jar, a harder task than he had anticipated. He is still lying back staring at the ceiling, panting and relieved, when the doorbell rings.

Hurriedly, he screws the lid on the jar and proceeds to the door, carrying it in his right hand. Rebecca and Nin are standing on the doorstep, flushed with excitement. Nobody says anything. In a slow, self-conscious movement, Keith extends his arm and hands the jar to Rebecca, his eyes averted.

"Thanks," Rebecca breathes. Then: "Same time tomorrow?"

Keith says nothing, just nods. He watches them turn and walk away, grinning at each other.

The next evening he is more organised. He arrives home early, prepares another jar, this time courtesy of Robertson's, and allows himself time to create the right bedroom atmosphere. For some reason he is certain that Rebecca is more likely to become pregnant if he feels relaxed and happy whilst producing the necessary sperm. To this end, he puts on some music and lowers the lights; he removes all his clothes and lies on the bed, thinking of Pete. Then he masturbates slowly, depositing his semen once again in the jar.

Whilst he is waiting for Rebecca and Nin, he puts the jar in his pocket, to keep it warm. Six-o-clock comes and goes, but they do not arrive. At six-twenty, Keith peers anxiously into his jar to inspect his sperm, as if he might be able to tell whether or not they are still alive. He notices that the fluid has separated. It is no longer opaque and thick, but clear and runny. Does this mean it is no good? There also seems to be very little of it. As he stares at this peculiar soup, he is freshly amazed that this is the stuff of life, that it contains real living things that can make a human being, and for a moment he is awed.

Ten minutes later, Keith is handing over his sperm to an apologetic Rebecca.

"Traffic," she says. "Mega-traffic."

Keith smiles at them. "Good luck," he says, indicating the jar, "I hope it works."

"Thanks," says Rebecca, "and if it doesn't, we'll see you next month?"

"I don't think that's going to be necessary," says Keith, looking up through ragged clouds at the full moon. "I think you're going to have a boy."

"If we do, we're going to call him Martin," says Nin. She digs Rebecca in the ribs with her forefinger and they scurry away, giggling.

"Martin," Keith muses as he closes the door, shutting out the night.

CHAPTER NINE

Lenny is standing in his surgery, peering into the mouth of a fifteen-year-old girl. The girl, Rachel, is very pretty, except for her teeth, which somehow manage to dominate the rest of her face. She has already undergone a good deal of orthodontic procedure (Lenny has previously straightened and spaced her two front incisors, and extracted two molars), and today he is correcting the last fault, applying a facing to her right canine, which is set back somewhat and appears as a black space in photographs, as if it were missing. He prefers this kind of work to the routine of treating cavities and leaking fillings. Although he finds it rewarding to put people out of pain, nothing can compare to the thrill he feels at mending a person's looks. He loves to watch their faces as they peer into the mirror and see their new smile for the first time.

Today's procedure is a lengthy one and his back has begun to ache, but he tries to keep his expression benevolent. He is not wearing his mask because Rachel is terrified of dentists and Lenny especially wants her to see his friendly smile. He wants her to relax. She has remained rigid, with large wild eyes, for almost an hour.

When Lenny encounters a frightened patient, he usually talks about something which will interest them, connected with their job perhaps, or a favourite hobby (he makes a note of such things in his patient's details, having found over the years that it builds a bond of trust). But Lenny doesn't know anything about ballet, Rachel's sole interest, and can think of nothing to say which might take her mind off his probe, the sharp tooth clamps, and the aspirator, which periodically attaches itself to her tongue and the side of her cheek as Diane moves it about her mouth. Bravely, with small hands clasping the sides of the dental chair, Rachel has allowed him to do whatever he wishes with her mouth.

When he has finished, Lenny hands Rachel a mirror and she takes a cautious look at herself. Tentatively, she smiles

– a radiant, perfect smile – and then bursts into tears.

"I'm beautiful!" she exclaims with genuine surprise.

Lenny, pretending there is something in his eye, wipes away a tear with the back of his rubber-gloved hand. "I told you so," he smiles.

Rachel is his last patient. He ushers the delighted child to the door and then prepares to leave himself, tired but pleased with his work. As he passes through the reception area on his way out, Wendy points towards her desk.

"Letter for you, from Canada," she says.

Lenny catches his breath. "From Canada?" His voice comes out strangely and she gives him a quizzical look.

Lenny runs to the desk, snatches up the envelope in his small, dumpy hand, and stares down at it. It is! It really is from Anthony! How could he not recognise those loops and curls as they stretch three-quarters of the way across the face of the envelope? And how long is it since he last saw this writing? Sixteen years.

*****

Lenny and Anthony are in their final year, the terrible, inseparable duo of Guy's Hospital. They sit next to one another during classes; they eat together at the refectory; they share digs; they go out together on double dates. They are the original Siamese twins.

Their tutors continually try to separate them, deliberately putting them in different groups, but somehow they always find their way back together again. Rumours spring up about the two of them like eager weeds, but Anthony dismisses them as palpable nonsense. He tells everyone that Lenny is as straight as they come.

Lenny, for his part, wishes to pursue his friendship with Anthony far beyond the constraints of Plato. He is desperately in love with him, yet hopes that his friend will never discover it. If Anthony ever guesses his true feelings for him, he will break off their friendship, Lenny is certain. This is the reason for the double dates. It is a means by which to throw everybody off the scent, yet also spend time with his friend.

Sometimes, the two of them go out alone, two young men on the town together. On one such drunken night, after a particularly unpleasant exam, they treat themselves to an evening at Lampton's, an upmarket casino. Anthony, certain that he has failed his exam, gambles away the last of his grant money on the roulette table in a morose, almost hypnotic fugue, and for the next two weeks, Lenny finds himself paying all the rent and buying Anthony meals. This pleases Lenny. It is a way of showing his love. Eventually, they decide to return to Lampton's, where Lenny stakes all his savings on a single hand of black jack. Miraculously, he wins the lost money back. In fact, he wins a great deal more than that, and they go away on holiday with the proceeds.

The holiday is not a success. A whole group of them have taken a house on a Greek island, but Lenny feels excluded because Anthony, the handsome ladies-man, has invited his new girlfriend, Helen. She and Anthony spend the whole time in bed together, leaving Lenny to contend with the rest of the group, most of whom are strangers. This is not what Lenny had imagined. Really, he wants to be alone with Anthony, and he spends most of his time kicking along deserted beaches on his own, baked by the Mediterranean sun. He does not enjoy his unrequited passion, because he knows it is wrong. In fact, he hates feeling this way about his friend, forever worrying that it must show.

And then Zoe appears on his horizon, shortly after their return from Greece. She is a friend of Helen's and follows them everywhere. Anthony encourages Lenny to date Zoe – she is regarded by all to be the most beautiful woman ever sighted at Guy's, with the added cachet of being a civilian, not a dentist – and Lenny adopts her as a means to continue their friendship. Zoe, however, misreads these signals and finds herself falling for the self-conscious man in the unfashionable clothes, who always blushes when she looks at him. She sees in Lenny a malleable man, someone whom she can easily mould into a future husband.

One night they find themselves in Lampton's once again, and Zoe asks him if he is homosexual. Ten minutes later, she proposes. Lenny, desperate to escape the torment of his shameful love for his best friend, agrees to marriage at once. It is the only way forward. He wants to please his parents, and he knows that being homosexual will not please them. Homosexuals are weak and unhappy. He believes that he must get married and have children, for their sake. His desire to be conventional is great. And why not marry Zoe, the only person in the world who knows his monstrous secret? If he cannot live with Anthony, the person he actually loves, then it is immaterial who he lives with.

His parents are delighted by the news and make elaborate plans for the wedding, which takes place shortly after Lenny qualifies. The entire event is gruelling. Throughout the service Lenny secretly wishes that Anthony, his best man, were beneath the veil instead of Zoe. A word from him now, and Lenny would gladly turn on his heel and walk back down the aisle in front of all those watching eyes, regardless of the consequences. But instead, rings are duly exchanged and he is invited to kiss the bride, his new wife. He lifts the veil and kisses her on the lips, feeling nothing. He might as well be kissing a balloon.

To his surprise, the marriage works well at first and Lenny is pleased. He finds, contrary to expectation, that he is able to couple with Zoe, and within two months he has managed to make her pregnant. Feeling vindicated, he convinces himself that perhaps he is normal after all. They stop having sex during the pregnancy, and when Monica is born he is delighted, but now that the fervour of role playing has evaporated, he finds himself unable to touch Zoe sexually. Now, their nights are spent staring silently at the ceiling – Zoe furious, Lenny terrified. After an excruciating month of sighs and apologies Zoe admits defeat and moves into the spare bedroom. They never share a bed again.

Soon after the onset of Lenny's impotence, and a year after the wedding, Anthony comes over for dinner one night. He arrives alone, which is a surprise. These days Anthony and Helen are an item, and everyone expects them to marry soon. Anthony says Lenny and Zoe look happy, that marriage obviously suits them, and congratulates them on the baby. Zoe tells him that yes, they're very happy, whilst Lenny stares into the fireplace, unable to take part in the charade. During the meal, Anthony tells them that he and Helen are emigrating to Canada, to set up a practice there. He mentions it casually, as if it were a trip to Cornwall rather than a new life on the other side of the world. Lenny is mortified. He cannot contemplate a life without Anthony, it will be unbearable. He had expected them to go into practice together at some stage, but now his imagined future crumbles around him.

Shortly before Anthony leaves the house, Zoe takes him aside and talks to him in a low voice. Lenny can't hear what they are saying, but he is convinced that Zoe is talking about him. Sickened, he's sure she's telling Anthony about his homosexuality, a spiteful gesture to pay him back for his inability in bed. Embarrassed, he can't look at them. Then Anthony picks up his thick overcoat, smiling and thanking them for a wonderful evening, and walks out into the night. Lenny feels deserted.

He hears no news for sixteen years; there is nothing – just a staggering silence the size of the Atlantic ocean.

At first, Lenny forgives Anthony's silence, imagining that he is busy setting up his new life abroad. But as the weeks resolve into months, and one, then two Christmases pass without a card, the silence extending into years, his heart hardens. He writes two letters to the Dental Association of Canada, but both are returned unopened, unread, and this tears Lenny apart. Really, it would be cleaner to discover that Anthony was dead. At least then he could begin to deal with the pain.

Slowly, he builds a wall around his hope, a wall that Anthony's silence cannot penetrate, and as the years pass, the bright pain resolves into a dull ache. Finally, it softens into an almost undetectable niggle which, like an old injury, is mostly forgotten but flares up without warning every now and again.

✻ ✻ ✻ ✻ ✻

So Lenny trembles as he clutches his letter to his breast, the unacknowledged pain of the last sixteen years re-kindled in his heart. He wonders how long he has been standing here, motionless in the reception area, under the steady, curious gaze of the receptionist? Smiling a hesitant, apologetic smile to her, he retreats into his surgery to open his letter in private. After so long without a word, he is daunted by the prospect of news, and cannot guess at his reaction. He pulls at the envelope with nervous fingers, his eyes misting with tears as he sits down on the edge of his dental chair. His throat is dry.

Dearest L,
I expect it comes as something of a shock, to hear from

me again. I imagine you're angry, very angry, with me for my long silence. I can understand that completely, but there were reasons, which I can't go into here. Actually, it's taken quite a while to track your practice down – it seems you don't own it, which surprised me! In the end I wrote to the Dental Council. You know how omniscient they are.

As you can see, I'm still in Canada, but I'm coming over to Britain for a while soon, mainly on account of my father's health. I'd very much like to see you. Is this possible? If so ring me on 001-403-862298. Don't feel obliged.
Yours,
A
PS. Sorry to keep this letter so brief.

Lenny lies down on his chair and covers his face with his hands. Anthony is right. His overwhelming emotion now is one of anger, anger at Anthony's assumption that he can sail back into Lenny's life as if he had just walked to the corner shop for a newspaper, rather than spending the last sixteen years in self-imposed exile on another continent. His letter – and how short it is! – appears featureless to Lenny, without any of the characteristics that he has come to associate with his friend. The wording is almost formal, and this frightens him a little, although he doesn't know why.

What to do? All these years he has imagined such a letter arriving on his doorstep, and in each fantasy scenario he has been delighted, rushing off to meet his friend with open arms, his smile wide and genuine. But here he is, trembling, reticent to make that contact. He finds it excruciating to unwrap this parcel of his past, which he has assumed will never be disturbed again, and regard it without flinching.

Anthony, for him, encapsulates his deviance. He married Zoe in order to rid himself of that deviance, but despite his every effort, his desire is still for the male body rather than the female. He denied himself the company of Anthony in order to become heterosexual, and when that failed, he denied himself any other sexual outlet. To deny himself Anthony had been difficult; to deny himself a host of other, lesser men, easier. Is he strong enough now to inflict on himself the only person he has ever loved?; to stick hot needles into his soul and taunt himself with the long-evaded truth: *I am a homosexual?*

Lenny's thoughts turn to Zoe, queen of the house, who silently judges his every move. How she peers constantly at him with silent accusation, over the top of books; and prepares ostentatious meals which Monica will not eat. He thinks of his last sleepless night, that solitary vigil of the dark hours, and recalls the sight of Monica lurching through the shadows towards him, her bloated, ghostly face floating past only inches away from his, her breath like the breath of a corpse. He does not wish to confront what she might have been doing in the kitchen that night, but he knows it was something strange, and it scares him.

It strikes him, as if for the first time, just how empty his life at home has become, how he has been trapped in this creeping, insidious charade. And now that Monica has gone to Cambridge, there will be nobody at all to round the edges of his solitude. Left to themselves, what will Lenny and Zoe do? Tear the house down? Destroy themselves? Or each other?

Even here at the surgery, usually an island of escape from his strange, oppressive home life, there is no respite. He cannot explain it, but even here he feels watched, regarded from all angles by some unseen scientist conducting an experiment of which he, Lenny, is the subject. Instinctively Lenny knows that Michael is behind it, playing a bizarre game of cat and mouse, and he worries about his motives. Now, Lenny is constantly wary when he is at work, monitoring his every word, every gesture, eradicating all possible traces of homosexuality from his behaviour, speech and mannerisms. He has become completely assimilated; no one would ever suspect. And yet he's half-convinced that Michael knows already. Whenever Michael leaves the room he always gives Lenny a look, a greasy smirk, as if he is party to some secret information. And what will he do when he is certain of it?

For the first time, Lenny has a sense of real panic. Too many things are happening in his life and they're all running out of control. He can't talk to anybody at work about his problems at home, and he has no one at home with whom to discuss his problems at work. He has no friends. Suddenly Lenny feels like the last person on Earth, and in his misery he decides that he will call Anthony – the only person he has ever truly regarded as a friend – to arrange to see him.

He uses the phone in reception and dials the number, wondering what time it is in Anthony's part of Canada. He can't remember if they are ahead or behind, but hopes it's behind as it is six-thirty here, which will make it late morning for Anthony. If they're ahead, it will be the middle of the night, scarcely the perfect moment to receive an unexpected phone call from a long-lost friend. Nervous, Lenny swallows, waiting for someone to pick up the phone. After four rings, an answering machine cuts in and Lenny hears the familiar voice of his friend, rendered strange by a Mid-Atlantic accent. He is caught by a wave of emotion, and sits down on the edge of the desk.

"You've just got through to Tony Merrills," says the message, "but I'm not in right now. If your message is urgent you can call me on the following number: That's the international code for the U.K., plus 171-875-2739. Catch ya later!"

Without giving himself time to back down, Lenny dials the London number, his heart pounding. It is answered abruptly.

"Hello?"

Lenny would not have recognised the voice had he not just heard Anthony's message. It is deeper than he remembers, the accent disconcerting. "Anthony? Is that you?" says Lenny with some trepidation. He is nervous beyond measure, and feels awkward.

There is an agonizing pause. Then: "Oh my god! Lenny!"

"Yes. I just got your letter, so . . . "

"My letter? I can't believe this," says Anthony, stunned.

"Yes. I've just read it."

"Listen . . . uh . . . God, it's been so *long* . . ." Anthony drawls. "I mean, I guess I expected you to ignore the letter, after all these years. I wrote it in a fit of nostalgia at the thought of coming back to England. I never imagined it would bring the two of us together again. I'm a bit freaked out."

"Me too," says Lenny.

"So, listen. Let's meet, yes? I'm no good on the phone." Anthony laughs at himself.

"Alright, let's do that," says Lenny. "How about dinner?"

"Okay, but it'll have to be tonight. I fly home tomorrow."

"I see." Lenny's voice is measured.

"You sure you only just got my letter? Must have been delayed. I've been here nearly a week."

"It's in my hand now," says Lenny. He wonders if this was a good idea after all. How do you conduct a sixteen year old conversation?

"Alright then, dinner tonight," says Anthony. "My treat. But where are you, for god's sake?"

"Guildford."

"Guildford? Way out in the sticks? All civilised people live in London, Lenny. What are you doing there?"

"Living in a large house," Lenny counters.

"Touché. So where's dinner, or is that blown out of the water now?"

Lenny replies without hesitation. "Why not Lampton's?" he suggests. "For old time's sake?"

"Christ, Lenny, you haven't changed a bit," laughs Anthony. "What time?"

"I can be there in two hours."

"All-*right*," says Anthony. "You know, this is just unbelievable."

Lenny puts the phone down quickly, so does not hear a click as Michael, who is upstairs doing his accounts, replaces his extension in its cradle, a smile blooming on his lips.

Lenny drives home and has a swift, hot bath, then changes into a dinner jacket. Zoe is not in the house and he is glad. He writes her a brief note, explaining that he is meeting someone in London, and leaves it on the kitchen table, where she will find it when she returns from her charity meeting. As he drives into London, through grey and depressing suburbs which loiter at the road side, he wonders whether Anthony will expect him to have brought her. He hasn't entertained any such thought himself, from the beginning. Zoe has nothing to do with this and he wants, as far as possible, to re-create his old relationship with Anthony, the way it had been when they were first students, before women got between them. He wants none of the baggage of his more recent past to obscure it.

When he arrives at the club, he is astonished and comforted to recognise the doorman. It is the same man who ushered them in and out of this place almost twenty years ago. Older, heavier, but certainly the same man. Lenny smiles, but of course he is not remembered.

As he steps into the dark yet opulent bar, he realises with a thrill of fear that he may not recognise Anthony after all this time. His voice has changed completely, so perhaps his face and body have undergone a similar transformation. And what about himself? He likes to think that he has changed little over the years, but what will Anthony say to that?

He buys himself a gin and tonic, then allows himself to cast an eye over the clientele whilst leaning his elbow on the edge of the bar. Idly, he watches a lean, grey-haired man talking earnestly with the head waiter of the restaurant. It appears that he is asking something which the head waiter is unable to accommodate – the waiter is shaking his head with minute, fastidious gestures, a polite smile perched on his lips. Then the lean man reaches into his pocket and draws out a fifty pound note, which he slides into the hand of the head waiter with a confident and surreptitious movement. The head waiter's smile broadens and he hurriedly takes his leave, with a courteous Prussian bow towards the lean man, who laughs as he turns towards the bar.

And then Lenny realises that the lean man is Anthony. He had been thrown by the head of grey hair. An interested look passes across Anthony's face as he stares in Lenny's direction, and then it breaks into a slow, intense smile of recognition which Lenny finds familiar. For that moment it is as if the last sixteen years have not yet unspooled. Anthony could be returning from the black jack table to tell him how much of his grant he has won or lost tonight.

"You look exactly the same," says Anthony as he extends a tanned and ringless right hand to Lenny, clapping him on the shoulder with the other. "Except you grew a moustache."

Lenny touches it with an absent gesture. He has worn a moustache for at least fifteen years, feels as if he always has done. This, more than anything, underlines for him the chasm of years which lies between them. With an irrational surge of emotion, he is hurt that Anthony did not know this small fact. "I didn't recognise you at first. I was watching you for some time before I realised," Lenny admits.

"I've gotten old," laughs Anthony, running a hand through his thick and attractively greying hair. "My body rebelled. It's the Canadian climate."

Lenny studies the taut lines of Anthony's face – his perfect teeth, the fine lines etched around his deep brown eyes, those lips which could so easily break into a smile – and with horror discovers that it is a face he still loves. He spends the next ten minutes in great confusion, twisting in fear and self-revulsion, hardly able to follow the conversation. What is worse, Lenny knows that Anthony is now party to his hideous secret, from the lips of Zoe all those years ago. Why else would he have disappeared, and never even written a letter?

Later, in the restaurant, Lenny begins to relax a little. He has had three strong gins, and is now drinking red wine.

"I had trouble getting this table," says Anthony as they study the menu. "They never used to be so strict about it."

Lenny remembers that only wealthy regulars are permitted to dine in this restaurant and, with a stab of guilt, he realises that it has cost Anthony fifty pounds to secure the table.

Over dinner, Lenny asks Anthony all the questions he has

stored up over the years, and listens with rapt attention. He has not known happiness like this, the intense pleasure of simply being with someone he loves, for sixteen years. He had forgotten he could feel this way.

"It was a dumb idea to go to Canada in the first place," Anthony tells him, shaking his head. "I still don't really know why I did. I think I was trying to be different. The idea of setting up in some suburban town somewhere over here was just, you know, too boring. Plus, Helen was real keen to go."

"And how has it been going?" Lenny asks, sipping his drink.

"It just wasn't what I expected, over there," Anthony explains, ignoring Lenny's question, going back to the beginning. "I imagined a brave new world with lots of opportunities, but it wasn't like that. Actually, it was quite hostile, at least to me as a Brit. My father had given me some cash to set up a practice in Ontario, but it was hopeless from the start. I looked like something out of the Stone Age." Anthony becomes passionate, angry once again as he tells his story. "One day I went in to work, and I found the other three guys who shared the practice laughing at my equipment. And you know, they were right to. I'm here to tell you, dentistry techniques in Britain are pre-Cambrian in comparison to Canada."

The main course arrives. Anthony has ordered something bloody and unrecognisable, which oozes on to the fine white plate as soon as it is served by the waiter. Lenny has opted for the safety of sole. "So what happened?" he asks as he squeezes a slice of lemon on his fish.

"I just couldn't compete. Who was going to come to me with my box of tricks, when everybody else was offering white fillings and lazers? And this is seventeen years ago, remember. Like I say, you're way behind here. I bet you still use those cute little buff envelopes for your patients' records, don't you?" He pauses, smiling, to slice a mouthful of pink flesh, and chews it with pleasure. "So anyway, I knew when to quit."

Lenny is amazed. "You're not practising any more?"

"I haven't examined a tooth in ten years," he smiles. "I'm into the outdoors thing now. It's good money."

"But what do you do?" Lenny doesn't remember Anthony being good at any sports.

"I'm a ski instructor at Calgary," says Anthony, laughing at Lenny's look of puzzled amazement. "It seems I'm a bit of a natural. Nothing truly terrific, but good enough to instruct. Hey, I've even won some competitions."

Now Lenny remembers that Anthony used to disappear to the Alps with his family every winter, to ski. For the second time this evening he is hurt, this time at the thought that Anthony has never told him about his prowess at skiing. "Oh," he says.

There follows an awkward and uncomfortable pause, a silence as heavy as the seventeen years which lie between them, until Anthony speaks again. "It's just so weird," he says, "sitting here together like this, don't you think? I mean, we both seem so . . ." but he can't think of the right word.

Lenny's palms begin to sweat. He is still an expert on Anthony and his moods, and can tell that something is about to be revealed. He thinks he knows what it is. Briefly, he wonders if Anthony will be cruel or kind, then helps himself to more wine and braces himself for the accusation to which he knows he must admit, at last. In a perverse way it will be a relief. In fact, he wants it to happen, and even instigates the conversation.

"Tell me," he begins in a careful voice, "do you remember the night you came to dinner with us, just before you emigrated?"

"Of course. A grim day for me, that one. I'll always remember it."

Lenny feels as if he is facing a firing squad, and stares into the eyes of his friend. "Why grim?" he enquires, unable to keep his voice from trembling.

Anthony looks down, avoiding Lenny's gaze. Instead, he regards the remains of his meal, and fiddles with his wine glass. "That was the day I found out about Helen," he says, finally glancing up to encounter Lenny's uncomprehending stare. Then, in an incredulous tone: "Didn't Zoe tell you?"

"No. Nothing."

"Oh." Anthony pauses, looking at his friend. "Oh," he says again.

"What's the matter? What did Helen do?"

A pained smile appears on Anthony's face. "She didn't do anything," he says, then sighs, crumpling his napkin into the palm of his left hand. "She'd been having trouble with her hands," he begins. "Nothing much, but she'd noticed them shaking during oral exams, bumping against teeth and so on." Anthony's voice has grown heavy, older. "She was concerned about it so she had some tests done. Zoe went to the hospital with her that day, the day I came over, to get the final test results, and they told her that she was in the early stages of MS." His voice is flat, devoid of expression. He plays with the silver-topped salt cellar, sliding it across the table cloth in a tiny figure of eight.

"Helen couldn't face me herself, it was too much of a shock, so she asked Zoe to tell me," Anthony continues. "Poor Zoe. I remember her prattling on all evening over dinner, and the both of you being so enthusiastic about Monica – she'd just been born then – and all the time she knew what she was going to have to say.

"She waited until the very end of the evening, which I'm glad about because I'd have dissolved . . . And I just stormed out of there. I couldn't take it." He stops abruptly, caught by a wave of emotion. "I had no idea that I wouldn't see you again," he adds, staring at Lenny's tie. "Your face was so white, that evening . . ."

"How is Helen now?"

"She died two years ago," says Anthony, looking at Lenny with bright eyes. "That's what happens, it kills you in the end." He pauses, looking down at his half empty wine glass. "We'd been together for eighteen years."

Lenny is assailed by a cocktail of emotions: anger that Zoe has never thought to tell him any of this, and great pity for his friend. Laced through this is a huge sense of relief that Anthony did not turn his back on him in disgust, all those years ago; that Zoe did not divulge his awful secret. So deep is his relief and so grateful does he feel, that he is inclined to forgive Anthony – who sits before him like an empty husk – for the tumultuous seventeen year silence which has lain between them until this evening.

"But what about you?" says Anthony, brightening his tone in a deliberate effort to change the subject. "Are you still very much in love?"

Lenny experiences a squeezing in his heart. He feels great warmth towards his friend, who has bared to him his deepest emotions, and senses that the time is right for revelations. For seventeen years he has doubted Anthony's integrity, without cause. He has been faithless. Now, loose with red wine and relaxation, he believes that he has nothing to fear in bearing his own heart. Even so, he can't look Anthony in the face, and focuses his eyes on a point in the air just above Anthony's head. "There's only one person I've ever really loved," he says in a mild voice, "and that's you."

Anthony actually drops his wine glass. Lenny watches it slip from his grasp and make contact with the heavy linen table cloth, where it breaks into many glittering, wine-blood spattered shards. Other diners look around, discreetly, but lose interest when they discover that a waiter is not at fault.

"I'm a homosexual," says Lenny in a voice as shattered as the crystal which festoons their table. "Although I've never —"

"But what about Zoe?" whispers Anthony.

"She's known all along."

Anthony stares down at the table cloth as a pair of waiters rush over and attend to the mess in front of him. "Jesus H! I had no idea," he stammers once the waiters have retreated again. His lips are twisted into a snarl of disgust, his expression bright with anger. "I mean, Jesus . . . Is that why you hung around me all that time?"

Lenny realises it has been a terrible mistake to speak his heart. He can tell from the look in Anthony's eyes. This is not the catharsis he had hoped for, merely the brutal ending of his friendship. He almost laughs aloud. It is laughable, really. All these years he has believed that Anthony spurned him because of his inversion, and now, finally, it is true. But he does not blame Anthony. He himself finds his sexuality abhorrent, so why should Anthony not feel precisely the same? He sits immobile, with head bowed. "I'm so sorry," he says.

Anthony stiffly asks for the bill and places his credit card on the silver salver provided. Then there is silence, as each man retreats into his own thoughts.

Once out in the street, they shake hands in an over formal manner, hunching their shoulders against the sharp November wind. Lenny feels humiliated beyond measure, aware that Anthony is in a hurry to leave. As he watches his old friend walk towards his car, Lenny knows that his vile curse has caused him to lose his only ally, that he will never see Anthony again. And he resolves never to divulge his secret to anyone else. Ever.

CHAPTER TEN

Keith waits at the entrance to Alexandra Park, wrapped heavily against the weather. His baseball cap is pulled down low on his head, a thick scarf tucked into the neck of his leather jacket. He loathes being cold.

The physical warmth of the throng passing through the gates and into the park is palpable – he can feel the difference when the crowd thins momentarily. People seem to be coming in waves, he notices. After fifteen minutes spent in careful scrutiny of every passing face, searching for those of his friends, he begins to question the wisdom of agreeing to meet up with them in this way, but soon he recognises Derek's ostentatious furry hat (the one Bob says makes him look like a dignitary from the Kremlin), amid a swell of weary parents and excited children.

"A little present," says Derek with a smile, once they draw level with him. Derek is holding up an unlit sparkler, which Keith grasps with difficulty, as his gloves are densely padded and restrict the movement of his fingers. "We can light them later." Derek explains.

"Thanks. Shall we go on in?"

"Why not? Lay on MacDuff," says Bob.

Once in the park they eat hot dogs and relish, drink expensive unpleasant lager, and wave their sparklers about like children in the glow of the large municipal bonfire. The warmth of the flames reddens their complexions. Later, wedged amongst the tightly packed crowd, they watch the fireworks display, which is prolonged and spectacular (but marred by the uncontrolled shrieks of a nearby over-excited infant). Afterwards they consume more fast food, this time from a health food stall. It is gummy and almost tasteless, and Bob grumbles about it, prodding at an unidentifiable green squashy vegetable which lies in flaccid splendour in his pitta bread. He also grumbles about the stiff neck he has acquired from watching the fireworks.

As they make their way out of the park, weaving

through the thinning crowd, Keith smiles to himself, suddenly appreciating his friends.

"How about dinner on Saturday?" he asks as they make their way to the car park. "It's my turn, I believe."

"I don't believe in *turns* at that sort of thing," says Derek, looking Russian and comical in his hat.

"But we'd love to," says Bob quickly. Keith is renowned for his table, being a gifted, though somewhat haphazard, cook. "Shall we bring red or white?"

"Red, I suppose. I'm going to do something with kidney beans."

"Sounds ominous," mutters Derek as he scuffs through the layer of brown, curled chestnut leaves which carpet the pavement.

"I've invited Andrew," Keith adds. Andrew is a mutual friend, a quiet librarian who still lives with his parents. Another of The Bookends' protégés. In fact, The Bookends have tried to pair them off before now – but, at thirty, Andrew is already too old to be of interest to Keith.

"We haven't seen him for ages," says Bob, smiling. "I look forward to it."

Keith spends Saturday afternoon preparing the meal. He guesses at his weights and measures, instinctively mixing flavours and spices. Only once does he refer to a cook book, and even then only to discover how long he should boil his kidney beans. As he looks at their wrinkled, hydrated skins, he is reminded of embryos.

The meal is, as usual, a success, and the company excellent. The Bookends are witty and affable and even Andrew, usually somewhat retiring, shines.

"That wasn't bad at all, for kidney beans," Derek concedes in the respite between courses.

Keith knows that this is high praise. Derek is an expert in understatement. "Thanks," Keith says.

"Now you know why I call him Litotes," says Bob with a dry smile, winking at his lover.

Half way through dessert, the phone rings and Keith excuses himself from the table to answer it.

"Uh . . . hello? Is that Keith?"

It is the now familiar voice of Rebecca, and Keith is disappointed. Obviously, the insemination hasn't worked. He imagines she wants to arrange the next assignation.

"Speaking."

"I'm just calling about the . . . uh . . ."

Keith can hear Nin giggling in the background, and smiles to himself. There is certainly a comic element to all of this. He picks at a loose thread in the waistband of his Chinos as he cradles the phone to his ear.

"Anyway," Rebecca continues, "the thing is, you were right. It's worked! I'm pregnant!" She sounds a little scared.

Keith is stunned. The breath leaves his lungs without warning, and he can't think. He feels he should say something, but his mind is frozen.

"I found out this afternoon," Rebecca tells him. "It's confirmed. Isn't it amazing?"

"Is this normal? For it to work so fast?" asks Keith in a bewildered voice.

"I don't think so," Rebecca replies. "At least, it's never happened like this with anyone else in the SIG. Only three other people have ever managed it at all, and they took over two years to get pregnant."

"Oh."

"Maybe we're just extremely fertile people," says Rebecca.

"Yes," Keith laughs. "So what happens now?"

"I hadn't thought," says Rebecca. "I suppose we should draw up one of these contracts, like you suggested the other day, but I don't really know how to go about it."

"A friend of mine is a lawyer," Keith offers. "He advised me about it in the beginning. I could get him to do it for us, if you'd like. Then we could meet, to sign them, or whatever."

"Alright. Perfect. If you can manage that, it would be wonderful. I'll pay, of course. I'll phone again in a few weeks, to arrange to sign on the dotted line," she laughs. "It would be nice to meet, anyway," she adds.

"Okay."

"I'll talk to you soon, then. And Keith . . . ?"

"Yes?"

How can Rebecca describe the gift of this baby in words?

Mere thanks is inadequate. She wants to buy him a car, a house, and send him on a world cruise. She trusts him entirely, for something in his voice is absolute and genuine. And she is pleased that he's an older man, as this makes him safe. "Thank you so much!" she says.

When Keith returns to the dinner table, he finds that he is shaking, suffering from mild shock. The Bookends give him a worried look.

"Everything alright?" asks Bob. "Not bad news, I hope."

Keith sits at the head of the table, a strange smile dawning on his lips. "Not bad. Bizarre," he replies. He takes a gulp of wine from his glass, his expression thoughtful. "It was Rebecca," he continues, "the woman I told you about. It seems I'm going to be a father.'

"Your lesbian!" cries Derek. "That's marvellous. Congratulations."

Keith laughs at Derek's enthusiasm and runs his fingers through his hair, pushing his dark fringe back from his forehead.

"How efficient of you," laughs Bob. Then: "What do you think? You look as if you've just seen a plane crash."

"It is a bit like that," Keith admits.

Andrew, sitting opposite Derek, frowns. Derek reads Andrew's puzzled expression and leans over the table in a conspiratorial manner. "Keith has just got a lesbian pregnant," he explains.

"Oh," says Andrew in a strangled voice, sounding shocked.

"This calls for a toast," says Bob, rising from his seat, eyes twinkling. "To the new father!"

Derek choruses the toast and tips his glass towards his host. Keith smiles down at his empty plate, and Andrew shifts in his seat, embarrassed.

"At least I know I'm not sterile," says Keith when Bob has sat down again. "I suppose that's something."

"We've been trying for years," says Derek, "but Bob just won't get pregnant, no matter what."

Everyone laughs, and Bob blushes.

Later, as they relax over coffee in the sitting room,

Andrew asks the question which has been bothering him. "Aren't you concerned about getting this woman pregnant?" he demands.

"I was to start with, but now I've met her, not at all," Keith replies. He knows he will have no trouble from Rebecca. The more he thinks about it, now that he is adjusting to the reality of fatherhood, the more pleased he is for her.

"I don't think it's right for homosexuals to raise children," Andrew says.

"Not even married homosexuals?" Bob answers, keeping his tone friendly.

"That's different. A lesbian couple has no father figure. It's unbalanced."

"No more than a single parent," Derek points out.

Andrew is silent. His own father died when he was three. All he had were a few old photographs. "I suppose," he admits with reluctance.

At the end of the evening there is a general leave-taking. They all stand in the hallway, saying good night to one another and reclaiming their coats. Andrew is the first to be ready, and waits outside in Keith's small front garden. Derek tugs at the lapels of his Burberry to settle it snugly on his shoulders, and pats Keith on the back. "Good night, Daddy Lewis," he smiles.

"Thanks."

"I do believe you're jealous," Bob exclaims as he administers a gentle shove to his partner, propelling him out of the door. Then, over his shoulder, to Keith: "He'll be broody for weeks!" His breath steams in the cold November air as his nostrils flare.

Keith snorts with laughter, leaning on the door frame. The Bookends are such ordinary men that it's uproarious to see Bob so campy. The combination of the voice and expression are perfect. "Good night," he chuckles one last time, raising a hand in farewell.

Once he has gathered the debris of the dinner party, he retires to bed, but finds that he is tense and wakeful. Restless, he is plagued by circular thoughts, endlessly imagining the foetus of his child, growing imperceptibly every moment and carrying his genes. As the hours unwind and the long night progresses, these looming, stressful thoughts are superseded by a preoccupation with his clothes – which lie beside his bed, tangled and unwashed, demanding to be laundered. After a further miserable hour spent wrestling with himself, his desire for sleep at last overrides his resolve not to give in to his obsession and he gets up, scoops his clothes from the floor, and washes them in the bath. At once, he feels his stress evaporate. In his mind he imagines it rising from his body like steam. Suddenly exhausted, he returns to bed, a vague notion turning in his head that his child will be a boy. Smiling, he wonders if the child will be homosexual, having two homosexual parents. Keith hopes he will be, and with that thought, at last drifts into sleep.

※※※※※

As the weeks pass, Keith finds himself further disturbed by new preoccupations: how will he feel if the baby is deformed, or if Rebecca miscarries? His stance on abortion has also altered. Now he acknowledges that it would be murder. A part of him sincerely wishes that he had never been selected by Rebecca, or that she had not become pregnant by him. That way, he could have shown willing and done the politically correct thing without having to experience this painful re-arrangement of values. It is all very unsettling.

Most surprising is that during this time, another change has taken place. He is not certain exactly when it happened, but sometime in the last two weeks he ceased his ritual washing of clothes. It no longer torments him to leave for work with unwashed clothes in the laundry chest – he is not distracted by thoughts of their putrefying smell. He is no longer compelled to make his daily visit to the dry cleaners with his jackets, and he can sleep at night without having to soak his sweaters. It is as if a switch has been pulled, and he feels immense relief to be released from it – unconditionally delighted.

In a burst of enthusiasm born of his new-found equilibrium, Keith throws himself into work and leisure. He attempts the home-improvements he has been avoiding for months – the shelving for his compact disc collection, made of bevelled plate glass and wire; the re-plastering and wallpapering of the back bedroom; the replacement of two of the floorboards in the sitting room, which now draw the eye as they nestle anaemically between their dark-stained neighbours. He is motivated and happy, the only shadow in his heart being his solitude. But even this has been swept into the background and now occupies a small, unobtrusive corner of his mind.

One Saturday afternoon at the beginning of December he phones Simon, his lawyer friend, about Rebecca.

"I went ahead with it, and it worked," Keith explains.

"Congratulations," says Simon. His tone is unreadable. "How do you feel about being a parent?"

"Biological father," Keith answers, correcting him. *Parent* implies involvement. Then: "I don't know. Pleased for her . . ."

"But you'd feel safer with a contract, setting the parameters?" says Simon, sensing Keith's wariness.

"Yes. If you don't mind."

"No problem," Simon agrees affably. "I'll include the things we spoke about before – your anonymity, your refusal to make any financial contribution, and so forth. But remember, it won't actually be legally binding. It is merely an expression of intent." Simon is pleased to have something out of the ordinary to do. It is a welcome respite from divorce proceedings, petty libel actions, and wills. "I can get it to you by the middle of the week," he adds. "I'm quiet at present. It's the pre-Christmas lull."

"Marvellous," says Keith. "How much do I owe you?"

"Nothing at all," cries Simon, surprised. "Think of it as a Christmas gift."

"Thank you," says Keith, impressed by the kindness of this man, whom he hardly knows.

"You're welcome," says Simon.

When the document arrives, three days later, Keith is impressed. It looks extremely official and authentic, having been calligraphed in a fine hand on expensive paper, with the seal of Simon's firm at the bottom right-hand corner. His friend has clearly taken a great deal of trouble over it. Or rather, them. He has enclosed two identical copies, one for Keith and one for Rebecca, he supposes. On closer inspection of the documents, he notices that Simon has signed each copy at the bottom left-hand corner in a neat, if flamboyant hand, with space for two more signatures beneath his own. The documents feel drier between his fingers than ordinary paper, conjuring images of parchment and tallow. Excited, he makes a mental note to buy Simon a good bottle of wine by way of thanks. Then he phones Rebecca.

"I've got the contracts," he says, more relaxed with her than previously. "They look like the Magna Carta. Now all we have to do is sign them. Sooner rather than later suits me. I thought we could meet on Saturday, or is that ridiculous?"

"That's fine," says Rebecca. Then, in a tentative tone: "Could you hack coming back down to Brighton with them? I know it's a trek for you, but it feels right to meet there again, somehow. Everything went so well before. It's silly and superstitious, but I'm like that. We'll pay your petrol again, of course."

"Brighton's no problem," says Keith. "I can look my friends up again. They're fascinated by the whole saga!" Saturday is Christmas Eve. He can pop in on Gary and Paul for a festive drink and drop off their Christmas card.

"And there's one other favour," Rebecca says. "Would you mind bringing a photograph of yourself?"

"Uh . . . I don't know if I have any," says Keith, too surprised to ask why she might want one. It is a strange request. He leans his left shoulder against the wall and stares out of the kitchen window at the wintry garden beyond, shrouded in the early darkness.

"Well, if you find one . . ."

"I'll see what I can do," says Keith.

"Brilliant," says Rebecca. Then a thought strikes her: "Will that café be open in the winter, do you think? Perhaps we should meet somewhere else."

"We may as well meet there," Keith suggests, playing with the shiny phone flex. He doesn't know Brighton well enough to recommend an alternative. "If it's closed down for the season we can always look for another coffee shop together."

"Okay. See you on Saturday. Two-o-clock again?"

"Two-o-clock," Keith confirms, then puts the phone down.

Later, he calls Gary in Brighton. "I'm seeing my lesbian again on Saturday," he says. "I thought I'd drop by afterwards, around tea time. Is that okay?"

"Ah," says Gary. "That might be difficult, chuck. We're off to the in-laws in the evening. Can you make it lunchtime?"

"Lunchtime is great," says Keith, suddenly remembering that he, too, is busy on Saturday night. He's promised to go out with The Bookends. He curses himself, wishing that he'd organised the Brighton trip for another day. Saturday will now be hideously busy.

Sighing at his lack of foresight he collects his gym kit and heads off to meet his training partner, Ian. Tonight is the night he has been training for all year. Tonight he is attempting to bench-press seventy kilos, and some serious money says he can do it.

At the gym, Ian makes ribald remarks, telling Keith how puny he looks. Keith remains silent, intent on his goal. After a few warm-up repetitions, Keith loads up the bar and prepares for his lift. It is seven and a half kilos heavier than anything he has attempted before, but feels much more. With the bar now hovering an inch above his chest, Keith begins to press it back up with difficulty, and as it edges upward, he thinks of his new inner calm and the excitement of becoming a father in such an illicit, subversive manner. He suddenly feels a wave of exuberance and finds himself lifting the bar easily, then locks out his elbows, and grins. Sweat beads gather on his forehead instantly. "That's fifty quid you owe me," he puffs, delighted.

The following evening, Keith is at home watching tv, enjoying the subtle heaviness in his pectorals from his efforts the previous night, when the phone rings. He half expects it to be Gary, cancelling their arrangements for Saturday. He's famous for it.

"Hello?"

"Hello . . . Keith?" It's the voice of Nin, leaden and strange; the kind of voice that delivers bad news. "Uh . . . Becky asked me to call you. She's had a miscarriage, she's lost the baby." Nin stops, and sighs.

Keith is stunned. "My god," he whispers.

"She slipped in the kitchen," Nin continues, her voice incapable of inflection. "We laughed at the time, it seemed like nothing. But the doctor says that was probably it."

"How is she?" Keith asks, concerned. His voice is soft.

"Tired. Upset. Depressed," says Nin, as if all three epithets could equally well apply to herself. "She's resting at the moment. The point is, the doctor says she's unlikely to conceive again for a while. It's normal after miscarriages, apparently. So she doesn't know when – or if – she'll want to try again. It's all been too upsetting. That's why I'm phoning. To say it's all off for the time being. We might phone again in a few months, if we decide . . . if you're still interested . . . " Her voice trails off, running out of energy.

"I'll still be interested," says Keith, offering a sliver of encouragement.

"Thanks, Keith," says Nin.

"You're welcome."

"Obviously, you won't need to meet us in Brighton now," says Nin, sighing once again.

"No."

The conversation ends, and they do not wish one another a Happy Christmas.

Returning to the sitting room, Keith can't decide how he feels about this news. Of course, he is hugely sympathetic for Rebecca. The trauma of a miscarriage – that desperately-wanted little foetus slipping out of her like so much chopped liver when such effort had gone into it's acquisition – must be especially crushing. But he can't help feeling somewhat relieved, himself, although he is not sure why. Was the prospect of a miniature version of himself so terrifying? Could it be that he had not, in fact, trusted

Rebecca one hundred percent after all? These questions, now academic, turn and turn about in his head, filling him with an abstract sense of guilt. Guilt at his ability to remain essentially untouched by an event which, for Rebecca, is an enormous trauma. It has not changed his life in the least, except perhaps by giving him a peculiar sense of freedom that he can't quite explain. Thinking ahead, he decides not to call off his planned visit to Brighton after all. He's already geared himself up for it. Besides, he will now be able to spend more time with his friends, instead of the hurried early lunch he had anticipated.

❋❋❋❋❋

On Christmas Eve, Keith travels to Brighton by train – avoiding the heavy Christmas traffic. It takes over two hours, as the train stops at more than thirty places, most of which he has never heard of, and he begins to wish he had braved the roads after all. He is still feeling oddly released after Rebecca's news and is looking forward to seeing his friends. As he stares out of the window at, by turns, sliding winter fields and the sullen backs of grimy houses, his thoughts turn to his parents, whom he will be seeing the following day. They can never relax around him, and the atmosphere is always tense. None of them really enjoy it, and he wonders why he has arranged to spend three days with them this year, which will involve staying for two nights.

Keith arrives at his friends' flat – a small, cluttered affair above their barber shop – at twelve-thirty, and almost immediately they leave again, heading off for a pub lunch in a village nestling somewhere behind the Downs. When they arrive at the pub it is already very crowded.

"Christmas," says Gary, by way of explanation, as they squeeze through the throng. Then: "Pints all round?"

Keith, in buoyant mood, finds that the alcohol affects him more than usual. "It's a mistake to start this early," he laughs, lifting his lager to his lips. "I'm useless if I drink during the day."

"At least you're not driving," says Paul, grinning. "I'll have to keep an eye on *him*." He indicates his lover.

"So how's your lesbian thing going?" asks Gary when their meal arrives. "What's the latest news?"

Keith shrugs. "It's all cancelled," he says, and tells the story of Rebecca's miscarriage.

"C'est la vie," says Gary when Keith has finished. "If you ask me, chuck, you're well out of it," he adds.

After lunch they drive back into Brighton.

"Fancy a walk on the sea front?" asks Paul. "You can't come to Brighton and not have a troll along the prom."

The decision made for him, Keith soon finds himself walking along the Brighton esplanade in amiable silence, shrouded by a cool mist which has rolled in off the flat, grey sea, reducing the view to an ectoplasmic blur of silhouettes. After a while he begins to get cold. "How about a coffee somewhere?" he offers, hunching his shoulders against the damp.

"We ought to be getting back," says Paul. "It's a bit of a drive to my parents' place." He grimaces at the thought.

"I'm seeing mine tomorrow," says Keith, grimacing back. "For three days. I must be bonkers."

They all laugh.

"Need a lift anywhere?" asks Paul, as they make their way back to the car.

"No thanks. My train's not for a while yet," says Keith, glancing at his watch. "I think I'll walk about for a bit. Experience the sea air."

"Okay."

His friends take their leave, exchanging hugs and Christmas well-wishes with Keith. "Keep in touch," says Gary.

"I will," Keith promises with a smile. "And thanks for lunch."

"No problem," says Gary, raising an arm in farewell.

Keith strolls on along the sea front, and passes a dilapidated old pier, once white and opulent, he imagines, but now rotting and forgotten. It is severed from the mainland. Redundant supports thrust their way through the shingle like pollarded trees, with nothing but mist and sky above them. He thinks he has read somewhere that it is a listed building, but he must be wrong – clearly this pier is being left to crumble.

Further along, he encounters a large slab of metal some fifteen feet high sticking out of the pavement. It reminds him of the obelisk in *2001, A Space Odyssey*. Wondering what it is, he takes three paces backwards, to get a better view of it, and inadvertently steps into the narrow strip of cycle lane which occupies the roadside edge of the esplanade. Then he stops, staring up at the monolith, which is evidently a sculpture. A moment later a young man on a battered racing bike – approaching from the right at high speed – squeals to a halt beside him, narrowly avoiding a collision. Keith glances up, sees his mistake, and steps out of the cycle lane with a guilty look and a shrug of apology to the cyclist. The young man smiles.

Still embarrassed, Keith walks up to the sculpture and examines the brass plaque set in concrete at the foot of it: *The Kiss Wall by Bruce Williams. 1992.* He looks up at the sheet of metal, which towers above him from this angle, and, satisfied that he has now fully experienced it, he turns away from the sculpture. He decides to meander through the town centre, browsing, at the same time making for the railway station. Perhaps he will buy an over-priced glossy magazine to read on the journey home; a Christmas treat.

As he turns, he notices the young man with the battered bike leaning against a nearby railing, watching him. It is embarrassing because Keith has to walk past him. As he draws level, the young man speaks.

"You okay?" he asks. His voice is rough, late-adolescent.

Keith, surprised to be spoken to, looks at the young man. He is wearing a grey greatcoat, the kind one finds in surplus stores, but this one is holey, tattered, with smudges of oil and mud on it, and moth-eaten lapels. On the boy's hands are a pair of thin fingerless mittens, also frayed and old, and the ends of his fingers, exposed to the elements, look like raw chipolatas. "Yes, I'm fine," Keith says. "Sorry I got in your way."

The boy grins out of a tired, seriously unshaven face. "Nearly mowed you down, didn't I?" he says, and fiddles with his dirty-blond hair, which is short and spiky, solid-looking from lack of washing. "Wasn't coppin' where I was goin', me." He rubs his bristly cheek with the back of his left hand.

"Oh well," says Keith. It is a pleasantry designed to end the conversation, but he makes no attempt to leave. Keith finds the boy, unkempt as he is, wildly attractive. The element of danger which he finds so appealing in his lovers is personified in this young man, and desire wells up within him. Those glittering eyes, the angle of the youthful jaw, captivate him. He wonders if it shows. The youth, for all his charm, seems the sort to be mightily displeased at a homosexual advance.

"No broken bones though, eh?" says the boy.

"Fortunately, no," Keith smiles. Then: "I didn't realise it was a cycle lane. I'm not from Brighton."

"Nor me. Cycled here today, I have. That's why I didn't see you. I'm knackered."

Keith looks at the boy's bike, appalled. At some point in the past the frame has been hand painted olive green, but most of it has flaked off, exposing the metal tubing. The wheel rims are rusted, the tyres old and beginning to split at the walls. The front brake is held together with elastic bands. The machine is thoroughly unroadworthy and Keith is amazed that it has transported the boy thus far without mishap. "Where did you come from?" he asks.

The boy is suddenly quiet, and the light goes out of his eyes. Then he gives Keith a sly smile. "I came to Brighton because of what I've heard," he says in a measured tone, appraising Keith with a seemingly professional eye. "I heard there were a lot of queers down here." There is edge in his voice.

"That's true," Keith laughs, grasping the boy's meaning at once. "I have lots of friends here." It is the easiest way he can think of to let the boy know he is gay. In his excitement at what may happen next, he hardly notices that the boy hasn't actually answered the question.

The boy smiles again and thrusts his mittened hand towards Keith. "I'm Nick," he says.

"Keith," says Keith, shaking the boy's grubby hand. "Pleased to meet you." Then: "Have you got time for a cup of tea?"

Nick nods, and quickly chains his bike to the chalky-green railings, twenty yards from the sculpture. Then they head into the town, finding a small tea shop in an alley behind the cinema. It is festooned with Christmas decorations, the menus trimmed with gaudy tinsel, and the cake-stands circled by sprigs of holly with bright berries.

"Where do you live?" asks Nick as they wait for their order of tea and Christmas cake to arrive.

"In a place called Stubbington. You won't have heard of it," Keith laughs. "Nobody ever has."

"Course I have. Near Fareham, isn't it?" Nick replies, grinning.

"That's right. Do you live near there?" Keith asks.

Nick's expression turns hard, impenetrable, solid as a wall. "No. Nowhere near it. I just got a mate from there, is all. Fareham, that is. I've bin there a couple of times."

"What a co-incidence," Keith says.

"Yeah. Right," says Nick, sounding disconcerted. He looks down at the dark wood of the table-top, trying to appear nonchalant, and traces a swirl of the grain with his index finger. Then he raises his eyes to meet Keith's gaze.

"So where *do* you live?" Keith asks him.

"Uh. . . I live in this flat in Kemptown," says Nick, fixing his eyes on a stack of home-made shortcake in the window. "It's great."

Keith is confused. Five minutes ago Nick told him he'd cycled to Brighton today. Nick's eyes are averted, and Keith takes this opportunity to study him. His frame is slight, he looks young. "I hope you don't mind me asking," Keith begins, making a conscious effort not to sound proprietorial, "but how old are you?"

"I'm eighteen," Nick replies, giving Keith an encouraging smile. "But I don't look it, I know." At that moment their order arrives, saving him from further cross-examination.

Nick consumes his cake with undisguised voracity, washing it down with gulps of tea.

Keith sips quietly at his own drink, which is strong, over brewed, and tastes of wood smoke. "What's your flat like?" he asks in a light voice, pretending not to notice Nick's obvious hunger.

Once again Nick's expression clouds, as if forced to recall a tragic past. He clears his throat, pouring himself more tea from a red pot with tiny christmas trees painted on it. "It's not actually *my* flat," he explains in an awkward voice as he spoons sugar into his cup. "It belongs to a mate of mine. My best mate." He looks at Keith with candour, reading the lust in the older man's eyes. "I'd take you there, you know, but I can't. See, he still lives with his parents and I'm their guest. They've invited me for Christmas. Great, yeah? There's goin' to be a big party tonight. Loads of nosh and plenty of booze, my mate says. I can't wait."

Keith smiles. "Would you like some more cake?" he offers, looking at the boy. "I'm having some," he adds, making it easier for Nick to say yes.

"Alright then. Yeah. Please," says Nick with a grin.

Keith calls a waitress over and orders more cake. "So where's your friend today?" he asks Nick when it arrives, a minute later.

Nick, sidetracked by the food, is caught off guard. "What?" he mumbles, his mouth full.

Keith now realises that Nick is giving any answer to any question, more or less randomly. Suspicious yet fascinated, he wonders if he can wring a truthful answer out of him, and slides his own uneaten piece of cake towards his companion, who proceeds to eat it, unabashed. "You'll spoil your appetite for the party," Keith says as Nick takes an enormous, greedy bite.

Nick breaks off his mechanical rumination, and his gaze drops to the shiny table top. "There isn't a party," he says in a wooden voice as he flicks a stray current from the table, "and there isn't a friend." He sighs, rubbing his nose with his hand. "What it is, right, is I'm in this squat. Me and these two girls. They've both got green hair. We play loud guitars, and we've stuck a Conservative Party Conference sign on the front door. It's got electricity, and everythin'." He looks up at Keith, checking his face for signs. "And there's an old Morris Traveller parked outside," he continues. "Hasn't moved in years, by the look. It's got bin liners taped to the windows. I thought it was a wreck at first, but someone lives in there, too. An older bloke, with a goatee. And dreads. It's really great."

But Keith knows he is lying. The story is so obviously a fantasy. What disturbs Keith most is Nick's *choice* of fantasy. Is a squat something he aspires to? Something better than his present situation? And in that moment Keith pities him. Gently, he reaches across the table and puts his hand over Nick's hand, which rests on the edge of the table. "Aren't you a little young to be in a squat?" he says.

"Nineteen's not so young," says Nick.

Keith is now embarrassed by the boy's incompetent lying. "I suppose not," he says, removing his hand. Then, glancing at his watch: "I'd better hurry. My train leaves in a quarter of an hour." He is surprised at the time, suddenly anxious to be at home after the stresses of the day.

"I'll get our coats," says Nick, and he crosses to the old-fashioned coat stand by the door, whilst Keith pays for their tea with some loose change.

Then they are standing in the darkness outside the tea shop, inhaling salty mist. For a moment Keith is tempted to invite Nick home with him, but he suspects Nick would not accept. It appeals to him, in a moment of seasonal goodwill, to take in this stray and give him a home, but he recognises it as the middle-class Dickensian pipe-dream it is, and smiles to himself. "Good bye," he says. "Merry Christmas."

"Same to you, mate," Nick grins. "And thanks for the tea. Much appreciated."

"My pleasure," says Keith, and he walks off through the town, wondering where Nick will spend the night.

The streets are busy, thronging with last-minute shoppers, and Keith has to literally push his way through the crowds, all of whom seem to be moving in the opposite direction.

His progress is slow, and he barely arrives at the station in time to catch his train. At the barrier, a bored official waves him through without asking to see his ticket, and he settles himself into a comfortable corner of an eight-seat compartment, in the window seat, facing forward – his favourite position. He falls asleep after ten minutes.

At seven-thirty he arrives at his local station, and decides to buy himself a snack to stave off a sudden hunger. He selects a packet of crisps and reaches inside his coat for his wallet, but he finds the pocket empty. He tries another to no avail. Systematically, he checks every pocket in the coat, then his trousers, even his shirt, although he knows the wallet has been in his inside breast pocket all day. As each pocket proves empty, he becomes more agitated. Finally, furious, he realises that Nick must have stolen it.

When he arrives home, Keith phones to cancel his cards, then runs himself a hot bath. He wallows in the water for some time, staring at the ceiling and cursing the bad timing of the theft. The banks will not be open for two days. The most annoying aspect is that he will have no money himself over the Christmas period. He is meeting friends for drinks later on, and will now have to borrow money from someone when he arrives, something he hates to do. He toys with reporting Nick to the police, but dismisses the idea as he can't be certain that the boy was the culprit – it could have been anyone in that milling Brighton crowd. With a sigh, he hauls himself out of the bath and towels himself dry, fervently wishing the thief a miserable Christmas.

The next morning, Christmas morning, he awakes with little recollection of his evening in The Jolly Sailor with his friends. The throbbing in his heavy head indicates that he drank heavily, but how much, and what, he cannot recall. Neither does he remember The Bookends steering him into a taxi, one on either side, with him staggering between them like a broken doll, wailing about his wallet. His impressions are vague and abstract. He remembers the air of frivolity, nostalgia and genuine affection between them all, and he remembers that an act appeared at midnight which had them crying with laughter. But what the act was remains a blank, except that it involved a fairy and a melon.

Moving around the kitchen in slow motion, he prepares a small, light breakfast consisting of a boiled egg and coffee, which he consumes in silence. He does not switch on the radio, as it will undoubtedly be playing endless carols, which he detests. Revived by the caffeine, he then prepares for his journey to Faversham, where he will attend the much dreaded Family Christmas. It is the least attractive element of the holiday season.

There is a tacit understanding in the family that Keith is exempted from the event whenever he is in a relationship (partly, he reflects, because his family would regard his lover as an intruder rather than a family member – which smacks more of barring than exemption) but this year, being single once again, he has been unable to escape. As he stacks his Christmas gifts on the back seat of the car, all selected for their blandness and easy acceptability, he finds himself greatly resenting it. He wishes he could decide to go, or not go, as he sees fit – but somehow he always obeys his mother. In years when he is attached, he heeds her subtle hints that so many people would be hard to cater for, and stays away; when he is single, he rallies to her plea that it has been so long since the family was together, and comes. As he drives down the motorway, clutching the steering wheel in grim expectation, he prepares himself for a suffocating three days alone with his relatives. Again, he wonders why he has agreed to stay so long.

His parents live in a secluded hamlet deep in the Kent countryside, on the grounds of a private estate dominated by an enormous, rather ugly Georgian mansion. It reminds Keith of the Lego houses he used to build as a child, box-like and structurally simple, with no interesting features. The same is true of the owners, Lord and Lady Something, whom Keith has occasionally seen strolling in the parkland, looking for deer. For some reason his father, who runs a stable-yard for retired and broken-down race horses and lives in a modest property nearby, feels tremendously honoured to be rubbing shoulders with the aristocracy, even though they demand an inflated rent for the use of the yard and paddocks. Terminally middle-class, his father has always harboured aspirations to the higher social order, even if it means paying for it.

As he passes the whitewashed lodge house, which marks the start of the driveway into the estate, Keith admires the belt of tall firs which flank the right hand side of the road, giving way to large paddocks beyond, in which horses wander with lazy, rangy strides. To his left is a field, ploughed for the winter. Its rich brown earth is exposed, still dark from recent rain.

On his arrival at the house, which could have been transplanted from the lid of a toffee tin, he receives an expansive welcome from his mother and a firm handshake coupled with a slanted smile from his father. The cries of his two nephews can be heard from inside the house, then the voice of his sister rising above their squalling, to silence them. Stepping inside, he finds the house dark, cluttered with icons of the festive season: Christmas cards everywhere, suspended on brightly coloured strings; piles of elaborately wrapped gifts sprawling across the floor; and a large, gaudy christmas tree glowering in the corner. His brother-in-law, seemingly melted into an armchair, does not so much greet him as nod an acknowledgement of his presence. He has always acted awkwardly around Keith, and prefers to remain distant. Keith is willing to accept this, privately thinking his sister has managed to find the world's most tedious person, and married him. Keith is sure his parents feel the same.

There is a cold buffet spread on the dining table, which has been pushed against the far wall to make more floor space. His mother explains that John and Margaret – his aunt and uncle – will be arriving shortly, along with his decrepit grandmother. Keith smiles at his mother's grim expression as she mentions *Granny*. (Over the years, Granny has become deaf in her right ear due to an infection, and deaf in her left out of convenience. She is a law unto herself, casting aspersions wherever she pleases, her main function being to whip all the female members of the family, and especially Keith's mother, into an apoplectic fury.

Inexplicably, she is very fond of Keith, often palming him money when nobody is looking, although he explains that he doesn't need it. With him she drops the facade of senile matriarch, and holds proper conversations.) At Keith's elbow, his nephews grizzle that they are hungry and their mother explains that it won't be long now. At the same time, his father hands him a dry sherry, a drink he has never liked, and raises his glass to the festive season. Dutifully, Keith does likewise, swallowing the unpleasant liquid with a plastic smile. Then the rest of the family arrive in a flurry of embraces, whilst Granny shuffles through the door behind them, unnoticed, looking like a frog and clutching her ancient crocodile handbag as if someone were about to snatch it from her.

The main meal of the day is in the evening, and as usual there is far too much food. As usual, his mother, his aunt and his sister are expected to make all the preparations, whilst the four men, the nephews, and Granny vegetate in front of the television, which has provided a babbling backdrop to the proceedings all day. As the evening unfolds, Keith feels progressively more culture-shocked, wishing he could resort to drugs. During dinner, he finds himself wondering what The Bookends are doing at this moment, ruing the fact that under different circumstances he would be enjoying the company of his friends rather than his family, who, were they not related, would not tolerate one another for more than ten minutes.

Boxing Day is quiet, once all the extraneous relatives have returned home, and Keith, now left alone with his parents, finds he has nothing to say to them. He does not mention that he has had his wallet stolen, knowing how much fuss will be made over it, and, more distressing, he catches himself constantly vetting his conversation for homosexuality. He wonders if his parents are genuinely happy with this situation. They hear so little about his real life. He goes to bed that night feeling dishonest and cowardly.

The next day he takes an afternoon walk with his father, feeling more distanced from him than ever as they stroll up towards the paddocks to look at the horses. In a halting, stilted voice his father asks him about Pete. Keith explains that it ended badly, after a row over a telephone bill. As he tells his father this it strikes him as comic, for the first time. The subject is not mentioned again.

When they return to the house they are presented with a high tea of bubble and squeak, with pickles and various leftover cold meats. This is followed by a profusion of chocolate, to which Keith helps himself. Later, he accepts a cup of coffee and then, after a polite interval, excuses himself in an awkward voice, saying that he has a long drive and doesn't want to be home too late. His mother hugs him for a long time, as if this will make up for her lack of conversation over the last three days; as if she might communicate her thoughts by osmosis. His father nods, and ruffles his brown hand through Keith's hair, something he has not done since Keith was a boy. It brings tears to the eyes of both men. Uncertain what this means, Keith hurriedly turns, making for the refuge of his car. He is glad to be on his way home.

Three hours later he pulls up into his driveway and notices what looks like a large bundle of rags stacked against his front door, caught in the yellow beam of his headlamps. As he extinguishes the lights, the bundle moves, making him jump in fright. Curious, he gets out of the car and approaches it, but now the bundle lies inert once again and Keith is uncertain that it actually moved at all. But as he reaches the front door, peering down at it like some myopic nocturnal creature, he is aware of the sound of breathing. The bundle is a person, presumably a vagrant. With beating heart he stretches out his right hand, shaking him (or her) awake, and from deep within the recesses of a tattered coat, a bleary young face appears.

"You come back! Thought I was goin' to spend another night campin' on the doorstep," says a voice, slurred with the cold.

Keith recognises the voice at once. It's Nick. Astonished and also disturbed to find him here, huddled at his feet, he can find no words – just stares down at him through the darkness. He does not move.

"Aren't you goin' to ask me in?" Nick's voice is low, roughened with fatigue.

"Uh . . . yes. I suppose you'd better come in," Keith hears himself saying, but it seems like someone else, not him. "I just need to get some things from my car." He returns a moment later with his bag, now filled with unwanted Christmas gifts. It seems no one in his family knows what to buy a single, homosexual civil servant in his late thirties.

He unlocks the front door and runs to disarm the burglar alarm, dropping his bag in the hall as he goes. Nick stands in the doorway watching, the nimbus of a distant street light lending him a spectral quality. Then Keith turns on the lights and they face one another in silence. With improbable slowness, Nick steps into the hallway and closes the door behind him.

"How did you get here?" asks Keith in a bewildered voice. He is alarmed that Nick is now in his house, and feels that he may lose control of the situation at any moment.

Nick says nothing, just shrugs with his lips pressed together in a flat smile. Then he draws his left hand, which all this time has been hidden in his coat, from the warmth of his pocket, and waves a small, square object in front of him. "I found this," he says.

Keith recognises his wallet now that Nick is holding it still. "Found it? You stole it!" he exclaims, indignant. Nick, smiling, tosses it towards him and he catches it awkwardly, then rummages inside, checking to see what is missing. All the cards are there, but the cash, some fifty pounds, has gone. "What — "

"It must've fell out of your coat pocket," says Nick, cutting Keith off, walking towards him in a slow, deliberate manner. "Some bloke come out the coffee shop with it, just after you left. I was goin' to chase you, give it back. But I knew I wouldn't find you. Not with all them people." He leans on the wall, only a foot away from Keith, relaxing in the warmth. "Next day, I thought of bringing it over, but it was Christmas and the trains wasn't on. So I come yesterday. Bloody donkey's years it took me to get here," he complains. "This place is nowhere."

"You could have sent it," Keith points out in a flat voice, recognising this as another of Nick's lies. "Or handed it in to the police. You didn't have to come here."

Nick stops dead, he hadn't thought of that. "Yeah! I could of done. But I'm here now." A slow smile spreads across his stubbly face.

"Yes. You are," says Keith, wondering what Nick's motives could be. The atmosphere is heavy with desire, but he forces himself not to reach out and touch the youthful body which stands before him. Not yet, at least. He turns away. "The money . . . Was there any money in the wallet when you were . . . *given* it?" he asks.

"What do you think?" says Nick.

Keith thinks there was, but doesn't say so. He is reluctant to cast this beautiful boy as a thief, although he knows that thief he is. "How did you get here?" he demands, moving into the kitchen.

"Hitched."

"I'm surprised you could find the house," says Keith as he fills the kettle. Only people who know the area well can find their way around the warren of lanes and false turnings. He waits for Nick's reply, wondering how inventive it will be.

"I got a lift with one of the locals," Nick explains.

"Perhaps I know them," says Keith, busy with cups. "What was their name?"

"Dunno. Didn't ask."

Keith pretends to believe Nick, and pursues the subject no further. He is too relieved at the return of his cash cards to worry how Nick arrived here, but at the same time he is uneasy. Nick's actions have been most unusual, and dedicated to some strange purpose, no doubt. "Tea," he announces, handing his guest a cup.

After they have finished their tea, which Nick drinks in silence whilst his eyes constantly roam the room, Keith offers him a bath. Nick accepts at once, and Keith ushers him upstairs to the bathroom, where he lays out towels, soap, and a spare dressing-gown. Nick stays in the bathroom for over an hour, whilst Keith remains in the sitting room, looking through a fitness magazine. Nick emerges at last with his hair wet, combed back from his forehead, wrapped in the dressing-gown. He has also shaved the week's growth of stubble from his face, and now seems absurdly young, his cheeks pink.

"Used your razor. Hope you don't mind," says Nick, sitting beside Keith on the sofa. He draws the fingers of his left hand across his chin as if self-conscious of his new, adolescent appearance.

Keith feels awkward this close to Nick, partly because Nick is almost naked whilst he is clothed – an unbalanced equation – and partly because Nick seems so young, so vulnerable like this, stripped of the armour of his stubble and spiky hair. But Nick's eyes still harbour that youthful arrogance which Keith finds so attractive, and he finds himself consumed by an overwhelming desire for him. He reminds himself that Nick arrived here under his own power, driven by some private agenda, and that to act on his desire would not, therefore, be taking advantage of him. Nick does not look innocent. "Would you like to go to bed?" Keith asks at last, in a thick voice.

Nick reads the signals in Keith's face, and with beating heart, smiles. "Yeah, I would," he replies. He feels as if he's in a movie, his words and actions unreal, having no consequence. Climbing the stairs, he is astonished that it is all turning out so well. Only a couple of weeks ago he was caged in his boxy Portsmouth house, between warring, drunken parents. As he crosses the landing, he can almost hear his mother's screaming voice, her shrill soprano yammering about why can't he get a fuckin' job like everyone else. Now that he's made the break, he's too frightened to go back home. If he does, he'll be pulverised. He's had enough of his father's boots and fists. With a shiver he remembers his stay in Brighton, a whole lifetime it seems, but really only a matter of days spent sleeping rough in closed down shop fronts, hanging around on the windswept pier with other desultory youths, and begging on the street. Meeting Keith has been a blessing, he looks a soft touch. Nick feels certain he'll be able to stop here for a while.

Now they stand in the bedroom doorway. Nick switches on the light and looks around, taking in the dark wardrobes, the wooden Venetian blinds, and the large, framed, technical drawing of some unidentifiable machine which hangs on the wall above the bed. He lets his dressing-gown fall to the ground, a limp silken rag at his feet, and slips beneath the duvet as Keith undresses. "C'mon," he says in a low voice, smiling up at Keith.

"Chilly!" says Keith, shuddering in his underwear, and dives in beside him. He snuggles against Nick's warm, lean body, his conscience at rest. Nick, in inviting Keith to join him in the bed, has initiated the sexual agenda – he is merely following the lead. For Keith, the distinction is important. He has a horror of imposing himself on others against their will.

As he explores Nick's pliant, muscled form, running strong fingers over his ribs and abdomen, Keith is amazed at the position of trust he has placed himself in, the ease with which he has accepted Nick into his house, and now his bed. He knows absolutely nothing about him, except that he is a liar and a thief, yet his marvellous body negates it all. For a brief moment he imagines himself discovered in a week's time, gagged and bound, slashed to pieces in a frenzy of blood. It happens. And then the mysteries of Nick's mouth, fingers, hands, pull him deeper into himself, down into the sink of pleasure, obliterating everything.

The following morning, Keith explains that he has to go to work and Nick accepts the news with a smile, offering no plans of his own. Keith says he'll be home by six and Nick nods in a distracted manner, staring up at the ceiling. Keith isn't sure that Nick has heard. All day, as he sifts through tag-end jobs and roams the corridors of the half-empty fourth floor, Keith wonders if Nick will be there when he returns, or if the house will have been cleared, stripped of valuables. Neither scenario is very likely, Keith imagines, and he works on the assumption that Nick will just quietly slip out of the house to return from whence he came. But if he is still there, what then? He has given no thought to the future, imagining there will be none.

When he arrives home, Keith is surprised to find Nick at the stove, preparing a strange, unrecognizable meal which seems to require every pan in the kitchen. Keith watches him stir the unpromising-looking grey mulch with a long wooden spoon, and notices he's wearing a pair of his jeans, and one of his gym sweatshirts. Both articles are too large, lending him an orphaned look. "What's this?" Keith asks, his voice light, indicating the food.

"Meant to be Indonesian," says Nick, nodding towards a stack of spices ranged along the work surface to his left. "Nazi . . . something. Me dad makes it a lot."

"What's in it?"

Nick wipes his nose with the sleeve of Keith's sweatshirt. "Dunno," he shrugs. "Lentils, onion, mushrooms. Just stuff."

"Are you vegetarian?" Keith asks.

"No," Nick counters. "I like a good dollop of cow, me."

Keith smiles and takes in the scene. Nick – already so at home in his kitchen, already wearing his clothes – turns this way and that, collecting the things he needs for the meal. He exhibits no shyness, no diffidence at being in a stranger's house. His movements are blunt and confident, his left hand reaching for salt, then turmeric, whilst his right stirs the bubbling pot. He hums snatches of an old pop song, temporarily lost in his own thoughts.

Keith leaves him to it, and goes upstairs to have a bath. He lies submerged beneath the clear water with his eyes open, watching the ceiling ripple, and wonders what will happen next. He is certain that Nick has no home – his evasive answers to questions have proved that – which leaves Keith with a sense of propriety. As he breaks the surface of the water, spitting a mist of spray into the air above him as he does so, he realises that he feels trapped. He knows he can't turn Nick out on the street with nowhere to go, and is suddenly aware that Nick has expressed no desire to leave. The situation is out of control.

Once he has bathed, he dresses in casual grey sweats, and wonders if there is a future for them together. He holds little hope, as there is no point of contact between them. He seems unable to break through the wall which surrounds

Nick's secret self – a wall which is still very much intact despite the intimacy of sex last night and also this morning. With a sigh, he gives his hair a perfunctory brushing, and goes downstairs for dinner.

During the next two weeks a pattern emerges. Nick takes on the role of housewife, and Keith allows it. Gradually, they accustom themselves to one another, like neighbouring cogs in a new machine. The air of tension which at first threatened to hang above them forever, vanishes, and Keith is surprised to discover that he is happy. He goes off to work in the mornings with a spring in his step, and when he comes home at night, the house is clean and a meal is prepared.

"You don't have to do it, you know," Keith tells Nick one evening over dinner. He is talking about the housework. No household chore seems too much trouble for Nick, who tackles the washing and ironing, cleans the windows, dusts, vacuums the carpets, and polishes the cutlery as if nothing could give him greater satisfaction. This industry makes Keith uneasy, although he can't articulate why.

"It's okay," Nick replies modestly, his eyes cast down towards his food, "I like it. It's relaxin'."

"Even so . . . " Keith grunts, feeling awkward. He takes a mouthful of food. Then, chewing on a piece of meat: "If you like it, you should get a job doing it. It's silly to go to all that trouble just for me, for nothing."

Nick's face closes at this. His eyes become slits, a bloom of hate stealing across his features. "Don't you start," he mutters, just too quietly for Keith to hear.

The mood, which has descended on Nick as suddenly as a tropical storm, remains for the rest of the evening. Keith is unable to fathom what has caused it and retreats into a book, not wishing to encounter his new lover's stony glances. That night, for the first time, they do not make love. In the morning, however, Nick is back to his usual self, and Keith's wariness abates. That evening, Nick prepares his most elaborate meal to date, and the equilibrium is restored.

One night, after almost a month of undisturbed domestic happiness, Keith realises with horror that he has not seen, or even spoken to, any of his friends since the arrival of Nick – with the exception of Ian at the gym. He also reflects that he has not mentioned Nick to him, and wonders why. Usually he is crowing from the rooftops like a ridiculous peacock at the merest hint of a relationship, but this time he has retreated from the society of his friends, and he finds this interesting. Is he, perhaps, ashamed of Nick? He decides to put an end to his social exile at once, and phones The Bookends.

"The honeymoon's over, then?" It's Bob, spry as ever.

"What?"

"Your young man. Has he — "

"How do you know about him?" Keith splutters, genuinely amazed.

"I've spoken to him enough times, I should do. He always tells me you're too busy to come out." Bob's tone is admonishing and humorous at once.

"You've spoken to him?" Keith feels as if he has missed an important fact earlier in the conversation.

"On the blower, dear. Didn't he give you our messages?"

"No." Keith's voice is small. He has begun to sweat. "What messages?"

"Just invites, and so on." Bob pauses. Then: "Honestly, Keith, he sounds like an adolescent docker. Is it really a good idea?"

Suddenly Keith is more annoyed with Bob for insulting Nick than he is with Nick for not passing on his messages. "I think so," he cries, much louder than he intended, and slams the phone down. He is breathing hard, all at once aware that he is close to tears. He had wanted to share the excitement of his new lover, but has ended up yelling at his oldest friend. And now he is freshly uncertain about Nick. What other messages has he failed to pass on?

Returning to the sitting room, where Nick is lying on the floor watching a banal game show, his face only inches from the tv screen, Keith demands an explanation.

"They weren't important things," Nick shrugs, his eyes focused on the evangelically smiling game show host.

"They might have been important to me," Keith shouts,

unaware until now of the tension he has been holding back, a secret tension he has harboured for weeks. "This is *my* house, and I want — " Astonished, he looks on as Nick jumps up, strides towards him and delivers a punch to his jaw. It is a weak, glancing blow, but strong enough to make Keith's head jerk back and bang against the open door. On reflex, Keith aims a return punch at Nick, forgetting for a moment that he can bench-press seventy kilos. His fist contacts with Nick's small nose, and it erupts in a spatter of blood. Nick retaliates with a blow to Keith's stomach, and they stare at one another in hate, disgust, and fear. It is the first time Keith has ever hit anybody, the first time Nick has ever hit back. Then the tableau is broken, and Nick runs out of the room, face bloody, thundering up the stairs. Keith runs upstairs after him, worried that he has inflicted serious damage, but Nick darts into the bathroom and slams the door shut with a splintering thud before Keith can reach him. Keith tries the bathroom door, but it's already locked. "Are you okay?" he asks in a soft voice. "Your nose. Is it okay?" There is no answer. He stands outside the bathroom door for several minutes, irresolute, listening to the sound of running water inside, then goes back downstairs and collapses into an armchair.

Some minutes later, Keith pours himself a gin and re-runs the scene in his mind, but can find no explanation for Nick's behaviour. He supposes he has contravened some unwritten law, and tries to imagine what it might be, so he can avoid doing it again, but draws a blank. He sits in silence for two hours, slowly emptying the gin bottle into his glass, then goes upstairs to bed. He finds Nick curled up in a foetal position on the bed, apparently asleep, but Keith can tell from the shallowness of his breathing that he is pretending. Keith undresses and lies down beside him in silence, then quickly falls asleep, aided by the gin. In the morning he awakes to find Nick in the same curled-up position beside him, this time genuinely asleep. He leaves for work as quietly as possible, after enjoying the luxury of a breakfast he has prepared himself and eaten alone.

At the office, he finds he can't concentrate. His mind

keeps returning to the awful scene the previous night. He is aware that his relationship has run its course, for Keith cannot tolerate violence in any form, and yet, at the same time, he acknowledges that Nick genuinely makes him happy – happier than he has been for years. He wonders what to do. After hours of fruitless thought, he decides it's time for a second opinion, and phones Bob's answering machine. He leaves a halting, sincere apology for his rudeness the previous night, and then invites The Bookends over for dinner the coming weekend, ostensibly to meet Nick. He also invites Simon and his lover, Richard. He decides he will not tell Nick about the dinner in advance.

That evening, the atmosphere is one of uneasy truce. The previous evening's fight is not mentioned, and Nick acts as if it never happened, which confuses Keith. He has been expecting an apology. Instead, Nick has persuaded him to stop using the dining table. Now they sit eating omelettes from trays balanced on their laps, watching tv – something Keith hates to do. Nick says using the table makes meals too formal, and has bad associations for him.

"In what way?" asks Keith, eager to gain some insight into Nick's past life, the life he had before he came here. Up until now the subject has been closed.

"Dunno. Just . . . I don't like it. Makes me feel weird. Like I'm seven years old, or somethin'," Nick replies, spearing a mushroom with his fork.

"Unhappy memories?" Keith enquires, remembering his own family meals, especially Sunday lunches, at which he had always been afraid to speak.

"I don't want to talk about it," Nick snaps, concentrating on his food in a deliberate attempt to exclude Keith.

"Why?" Keith cries, hurt. "You live with me, Nick. Obviously I want to know about you. Why do you . . . " Exasperated, he throws his left hand in the air like a continental, lost for the right word.

Nick turns his eyes towards Keith, regarding him with a practised, patronising stare. "I don't ask you about your past, do I?" he explains. "So why should you ask about mine?"

"But I *want* you to ask about my past, Nick. I want us to –"

Nick lifts up his right hand as if stopping traffic, his palm only inches from Keith's face. "I'm not interested, right! The past doesn't count. What happened yesterday isn't happening now, so it doesn't matter." He lets his hand fall to his side, and begins to speak in a warmer, softer voice. "What I'm interested in is *now. Us, now.*" He smiles, leans over to Keith and kisses him, his lips still greasy with omelette. "That's all that matters to me," he adds.

Keith kisses Nick's ready lips as if in a dream, wondering what has happened to Nick in the past to make him so determined to forget it. In this instant he loves Nick more passionately than he has ever loved anyone. He senses an inner sadness and an intense vulnerability in his young lover, which hardens his resolve to love him more. He understands that for Nick, the hurts of one day cannot be carried over to the next, or else the accumulated hurt would become so enormous, so unbelievably huge, that it would crush him. All bad things, either inflicted or received, are therefore consigned on the instant to the past and cease to exist, requiring no further comment. In such a world, apologies are not sought, or given. Keith decides he will try to inhabit this world himself, and probes no further into Nick's former life.

On Saturday, the day of the dinner party, Keith spends the afternoon in the kitchen, preparing food. Nick accepts his banishment from the domain he has begun to consider his own with only a hint of bad grace, and lounges in front of the tv watching brightly coloured skiers hurtle down slopes flanked with brittle trees, cheering when the skiers fall. As the afternoon bleeds into early evening and Keith spreads a cloth over the dining table, sets down an arrangement of candles in the centre, and lays six places, each with many knives, forks and spoons, Nick looks on with dismay.

"They look new," Keith smiles, indicating the cutlery, planting an appreciative kiss on Nick's forehead as he does so.

"Yeah." Nick stares down at the highly-polished, glittering silverware. "So what's happening?" he asks, his voice wary.

"Some friends are coming over for dinner." Keith nearly says *the ones you've spoken to on the phone*, but stops himself in time. Instead, he says: "They're coming to meet you," and kisses him again, this time on the lips.

At six-o-clock, Keith goes upstairs to bathe and change. He decides not to dress up, as Nick has no smart clothes of his own, and might feel out of place if he's the only one casually dressed. The other alternative is to let Nick borrow some of his things, but then The Bookends – who often wear each other's clothes – might make some sort of remark about it, embarrassing Nick, or worse, precipitating one of his instant moods. Keith sighs, thinking how much easier it would be if only Nick would allow him to buy him some clothes. So far he has flatly refused all such offers, complaining that it would make him feel like a Ken doll.

After his bath, Keith checks his watch to see how he's doing for time and notices that it has stopped again. It has been in its death throes for some weeks, and he makes a mental note to replace the battery on Monday. Unstrapping the watch from his wrist, he goes into the bedroom and opens his dressing-table drawer, where he keeps his dress watch, but he can't find it. He pulls the drawer out to its full extent – rummaging amongst packs of condoms, a bottle of aspirin, a grey-looking elastic bandage from when he sprained his wrist at the gym, and various single cufflinks whose twins have been lost – but the black, velvet-lined box containing his watch is missing. He feels a stab of anxiety. The watch is the only expensive item of jewellery he has ever owned, and is precious for reasons other than its value. Trying to remain calm, he searches the shelves in his wardrobes, the chest of drawers, even the medicine cupboard in the bathroom, before reaching the obvious conclusion that Nick has stolen it at some stage. He is deeply disappointed at the thought, but the lack of surprise he feels is worse. Unconsciously, he has been wondering for some time what form Nick's pilfering might take. Flushed with instant rage and panic, he sits down on the edge of the bed, wondering what else might be missing. Then he tramps downstairs, annoyed, to confront Nick.

"Have you seen my dress watch on your travels?" he asks, trying to sound nonchalant.

"No," says Nick. "What's it look like?"

"It's gold, with four emeralds set into the face. Very slim," says Keith. He doesn't say that it was given to him by a rich Arab diplomat in appreciation for a weekend in Lowndes Square twelve years ago. "It was in the dressing table drawer."

"Never seen it," Nick shrugs. "I don't go into the drawers."

By an extraordinary effort of will, Keith allows Nick this get-out without contradiction, preferring to avoid a scene so soon before the arrival of his guests. He is determined to give the appearance of The Happy Couple to his friends, at all costs. Feeling brittle and bitter, he looks at Nick and tries to guess what they will make of him. Sudden embarrassment clutches his heart as he evaluates his lover's appearance with a stranger's eye, and he mentions, as tactfully as possible, that Nick can borrow any clothes he likes for the dinner party.

"It's okay, I'll wear this lot," says Nick. He looks down at himself – his ripped and permanently stained jeans, his stretched, shapeless black and white striped Russian sailor top, and his worn-out loafers. The stitching has unravelled all around the end of the right shoe, and his big toe protrudes from the resulting hole, like the head of a tortoise. "That alright?" he asks, straightening up and looking at Keith. There is no challenge in his voice, merely a desire for approbation.

"Quite alright," Keith smiles, his icy mood suddenly melted. He is ashamed that he wanted Nick to dress up for his friends, and pleased that Nick has refused the opportunity. "Actually, you look very good. Better than me," he admits. "Like an intellectual hedonist."

"No way, José!" Nick laughs with a slow smile as he rubs his cheek. His stubble, darker than his dirty-blond hair, rasps against his hand as he does so. "Dunno about the hedonist part, though. Maybe." It's one of his new words, one that Keith uses a lot, and now he's picked it up. "After all, what's the difference between a hedonist and a piss artist?" he says.

"Class?" Keith shrugs. He gives an inward shudder at his joke.

"Right!" says Nick with a stubbly grin. "I like it! Yeah, right!"

Half an hour later, the guests turn up. By chance all four of them arrive at once, gathering in the hallway in a festive, extravagant gaggle and waving bottles of red wine. As Keith introduces them to Nick, Simon throws him a strange, confused glance. He had expected Pete, Keith supposes, and smiles.

They move into the sitting room for drinks, which Nick ferries back and forth with zeal, before settling into a chair himself, next to Keith. The conversation is tense. The guests are aware that they all know Keith a great deal better than Nick does, and they know how insecure a new lover can be made to feel in the presence of old friends. In this fragile atmosphere, the first time Simon speaks to Nick he addresses him as Pete – which embarrasses everyone but Nick himself, who knows nothing of Pete or his place in Keith's life. It is not until they are seated at the dinner table that everyone properly relaxes.

The meal is eaten in good humour. Nick is quiet, smiling at the guests as they speak to him, giving polite but unobtrusive answers to their questions. Although most of the conversation involves things about which he knows nothing, he finds one or two opportunities to make witty remarks, which go down well with everybody. At just the right moment he offers to help with the butlering of plates, food, and drinks from the kitchen, a role he carries off with a degree of aplomb. Keith is pleased that Nick is being so much himself, and that his friends have taken to him, although he has the sensation of holding his breath for the entire evening. It is as if he is expecting the bubble to burst at any moment. And he keeps thinking about the missing watch.

Towards the end of the evening, Bob accompanies Keith to the kitchen under the pretext of fetching more wine. Bob leans on the fridge door as Keith reaches in to retrieve a bottle. "Quite a surprise," he says, looking down at the top of Keith's head.

"What?" says Keith. He is a little drunk.

"Your new man. Nick."

Keith straightens up and smiles at his friend. "He's alright, isn't he?" he says with a measure of pride.

"I have to say, we were concerned at first, when he wouldn't let us talk to you on the phone," Bob says. "What was that all about?"

Keith's expression clouds, remembering the fight. He still does not understand it. "I don't know," he admits with a shrug.

"Anyway, he appears to be charming, and devoted to you, which pleases me enormously," says Bob. "Most of your young men have been rather studied, if you want my candid view. Nick, however, seems genuine. I think he likes you."

"Yes," says Keith, remembering the way Nick has found excuses to touch his arm, or the back of his neck, whenever he passes his chair.

"At first I thought he was too young and too rough," says Bob. "But I was wrong."

"Thanks," says Keith, inexpertly removing the cork from the bottle in his hand.

Once their guests have gone home, Keith and Nick make love slowly, and for a long time. When they have finished, lying warm and sleepy in each other's arms, Nick kisses the older man's eyelids. "I like your friends," he says into the gluey darkness.

Light and happy, Keith feels as if he has passed some kind of test.

*****

Weeks pass, more or less uneventfully. Keith's friends accept his new lover into their circle, and now regard the two of them as a couple. Keith, for his part, has become anaesthetized by his happy domestic routine, hermetically sealed in an envelope containing just Nick and himself, a pleasant, almost dreamlike sensation. Even now he can't be sure how long he has been in this state. And yet, with each day, he grows more certain that the end is at hand. He has no idea why.

One Saturday morning early in March Keith decides to have all his winter jackets cleaned. It is a novel experience, he reflects, to have them processed all at once. Until quite recently he was having them laundered in rotation, on a daily basis. It seems incredible to him now that he could have spent so much time washing clothes, or having them dry cleaned. He shakes his head in wonder as he goes through the pockets of each article, checking for papers. It's a habit born of the time he accidentally destroyed an important receipt from work, of which there were no copies.

Today he has a pleasant surprise, scooping fifty pounds out of a jacket he hasn't worn since Christmas. As he stares at the money, all in crumpled five pound notes, he remembers its origin. Granny had forced it on him over Christmas dinner, surreptitiously slipping it into his pocket, under the table. At the time he hadn't looked at it, assuming it was her usual sum of five pounds. Looking at it now, as it lies on the duvet, he realises it's much too late to return it to her. She would never take it back. Instead, he decides he'll treat Nick to a surprise – a second-hand leather jacket, some shoes, or a night out. Surely he will accept this small gesture? Pleased with his idea he goes back downstairs, cradling the jackets in his arms, and looks in on Nick – who is stationed in his usual position in the sitting room: lying on the floor in front of the tv, watching the sports. "I'm just off to the cleaners with this lot," he calls on his way out.

When he returns he finds the tv dead and the house quiet. After a brief and fruitless inspection of the dining room and kitchen he goes upstairs – not expecting to find Nick there but searching anyway, as people do – and notices that the bedroom door is closed. Then he remembers that Nick complained of a headache this morning over breakfast, and opens the door slowly, expecting to find him in bed, but the room is empty. The first thing he notices is that the wardrobe doors have been carefully closed, the duvet straightened, and the pillows plumped. The next thing he notices is that the money is missing.

Keith sits on the edge of the bed, looking out at the bright, watery sky, and finds that he is not angry, but depressed. In the last two months he has come to believe that Nick has changed, that Nick really loves him, but now he knows it can't be true. A person does not steal from the object of his love. That he has deluded himself on this point thus far seems incredible to him now. His change of heart is sudden and complete.

Keith, gripped by a sense of heaviness and lethargy, considers his options. He can tell Nick to leave – now, immediately, and forever; he can confront him about the money, and warn him never to do anything like this again; or he can ignore it, pretend it never happened, as Nick so obviously will do when he returns. He sighs, his eyes cast down towards the carpet, his head throbbing with a sudden headache. What to do?

In the end, he decides not to confront Nick about the money. He fears another scene, and knows that in any case he will only receive a futile denial. He also decides not to ask Nick to leave his house, because very probably he has nowhere else to go. Instead, he decides to forget the whole thing.

He thinks he knows why Nick is stealing. He thinks that when someone has been starved of things, both emotional and material, they will naturally take whatever they can, as often as they can, in just the same way as a scavenging animal will eat all it can find in order to survive. He decides to cure Nick with affection. He will teach him to give.

CHAPTER ELEVEN

It is almost the end of the day, and Lenny and Diane are enjoying a cup of coffee between patients, an unexpected break due to a late cancellation. Lenny takes this opportunity to have a thorough stretch, with his hands placed where he imagines his kidneys to be, leaning back, while Diane sips her coffee in silence. Distantly, he can hear tiny cracking noises somewhere in his spine. He's meant to charge the woman for the broken appointment, but he can't be bothered. It's worth the coffee-break.

"So who's our last patient?" he asks Diane idly as he sits down and lifts his drink to his lips. He doesn't know why he's asking, really he doesn't care. But he likes to talk to Diane, it makes working conditions so much more pleasant. He looks at her now, sitting on a black stool in the corner, leaning on the work surface as she refers to the stack of notes at her right elbow, all in tatty buff envelopes.

"It's a Mr Elliot. He's new. You agreed to take him on last week."

"Did I?" Lenny doesn't remember. These days his life is a mechanical routine, the hours something to be negotiated, the accumulating days an ordeal to be endured. Details such as names have become entirely inconsequential.

He stares ahead at the brilliant white wall, and reflects that it's more than two months since his disastrous dinner with Anthony, yet it still crawls into his mind every day, reminding him that he is aberrant. He had hoped, somehow, miraculously, to have been cured of his obsession for his friend during the years of their separation, but it had flared so intensely before him during their meeting that he still feels raw. He knows he will most certainly never see him again. Lenny tries to comfort himself with the thought that the situation has simply returned to its original state: Anthony is gone forever. Before, he had suspected his homosexuality was to blame. Now he knows for certain. Really, nothing has changed.

"It says here that he's an actor," Diane tells him,

breaking into his thoughts. A lopsided smirk has appeared on her face.

Lenny studies her as she scans the form which his new patient has filled in. "Really?" he says. For some reason the prospect excites him. He has no idea why, as he has never had any particular interest in theatre, art, or opera – all things which people of his sort are supposed to delight in. Then he reminds himself that Mr Elliot is probably an effeminate chorus boy, and his interest evaporates.

Twenty minutes later, his preconceptions are thoroughly tested. Mr Elliot turns out to be a man of fifty, possessed of a charming smile and deft, masculine movements, and whose face is familiar. It takes Lenny a moment to place him, then he realises that Mr Elliot plays the detective in his favourite tv drama serial, and is instantly intimidated. Lenny's professional smile and handshake crumble in the face of this celebrity. Diane, he notices from the corner of his eye, is standing motionless in the corner of the room, open mouthed, a cavity form clutched to her breast. This galvanizes him. It is one thing for his nurse to be star struck, quite another for himself to be. Immediately, he regains control and ushers Mr Elliot to the chair.

He takes routine X-rays, for his files, then proceeds to run a check of all previous work that has been carried out on Mr Elliot's teeth, calling the various occlusal, buccal, lingual and palatal fillings to Diane, who notes then down on the cavity form. Lenny notices that all the previous work is excellent, and this intimidates him once again. Why is this man, who can clearly afford any dental treatment he likes, sitting here, in his chair?

"Are you having any trouble with your teeth?" Lenny asks once he has completed his check and found no obvious problems.

"Not at all," the actor replies, smiling. He looks right into Lenny's eyes. "I've just moved here, you see, from London, and needed to register with someone. So I picked you out of the phone book, being the nearest to where I live. I hope you don't mind," he laughs.

"Would you like to be a private patient?" Lenny asks. It's

a routine question.

Again Mr Elliot beams Lenny a broad smile, and a look held just a fraction longer than necessary. "No offence, I hope, but I don't approve of private treatment," he replies.

Lenny laughs. "Neither do I," he says as he looks down at Mr Elliot. Lenny finds himself transfixed by the blue eyes which look up at him from the chair, and he knows that it is not simply the famous face which is to blame. He feels a strange cloying in his throat and stomach, and is confused and alarmed to identify the feeling as sexual attraction. More terrifying is the look in his patient's eyes, acknowledging his lust. Lenny wonders how this man has recognised him as homosexual so easily, and panics. Perhaps it is obvious to everyone? Perhaps he is some hideous figure of fun, pointed at and laughed about behind his back? Sweat prickles on his forehead, which he wipes away with the back of his hand as he smiles a nervous smile. "Your teeth are fine," he says. "I'll give them a quick scale and polish, and then you'll be done." Having retreated into his professional persona he feels more secure, and ventures an allusion to Mr Elliot's celebrity. "We're very pleased to have you as a patient," he smiles.

"And I'm *very* pleased to have you as my dentist," replies Mr Elliot.

Once the scale and polish procedure is over, Lenny turns back to his patient. "That's all," he says, swinging the equipment away from the chair. "If you'd like to make an appointment for six months' time at reception . . . "

"Okay." Mr Elliot lies back in the chair whilst Lenny returns it to an ordinary sitting position, then swings his legs on to the floor and stands up. "See you in six months," he smiles, nodding first to Lenny then to Diane. For an instant his eyes fall on the picture of Zoe, then they return to Lenny. "Good afternoon," he says in a brittle voice, and walks out.

"My mum's going to be ever so upset," says Diane as she dumps Lenny's probe into the steriliser.

"What?" says Lenny, his mind still lingering over the well-made, masculine features he has been hovering only inches above for the last five minutes.

"About him," Diane explains, lowering her voice and pointing in the direction of the recently departed actor. "She'll be ever so disappointed that Detective Farrington's a pansy. He's her favourite." Her delivery betrays not a hint of disappointment. Already she is calculating the value of this piece of gossip. It will keep her in Babycham for a month.

"I didn't notice," Lenny lies, deciding that a simple denial is best, as too much explanation might give rise to suspicion.

"You can take my word for it," Diane says, busily packing up trays, stacking them away. "I can always tell."

There is no irony, no accusation in Diane's voice, and Lenny relaxes. He's sure she doesn't know about him. But he's also sure that if she ever does find out, Michael Whiting will find out two minutes later. He smiles to himself, pleased that he has negotiated this difficult situation with such success. Next time he will be on his guard.

Lenny tidies away his equipment slowly, then peels off his robe, his spirits growing heavy with the realisation that he will now have to return to his lonely, oppressive house. Once everything is put away and he can delay the moment no longer, he wraps himself in his coat – too warm for this spell of mild March weather – and heads towards his home on foot, a recent habit which has gained him two precious half-hours a day alone with his thoughts.

He has just turned the corner at the end of the street when a man, who has been leaning against a low wall smoking a cigarette, falls into step beside him.

"You're gay, aren't you?" says the man. It's Lenny's new patient, Mr Elliot. "But you're also married," he adds. It's not a question, but a statement.

Taken aback, Lenny makes no reply, just keeps walking with his eyes fixed on the grey pavement. He hopes the man will go away, but Mr Elliot continues to walk beside him, matching him stride for stride. Lenny stops and looks at him with drowning eyes. "How dare you!" he cries at last, louder than he intends. His voice is shrill, shredded with nerves.

The man holds up a hand to quieten him. "I know it's absolutely none of my business, and you can tell me to piss off if you like, but I'm right, aren't I?" he says.

It's only the second time Lenny has ever been directly asked the question and this time, like the last, he finds himself miserably conceding the truth. Although the man is a stranger, his familiar face inspires confidence. Besides, he is a fellow homosexual, and a celebrity. "How did you know?" he asks.

"Shall we say, I recognise the signs," says the actor as they resume walking, looking sideways at one another. "My name's Mostyn, by the way," he adds, drawing on his cigarette one last time before crushing the stub underfoot. Then he sees the fright in the other's eyes and smiles. "Don't worry, I'm not trying to pick you up," he laughs. "It's just that you remind me of myself, twenty years ago."

"What do you mean?" Lenny asks, growing wary.

Mostyn has never been an altruist. He can hardly believe that he has waited in the street for twenty minutes in order to give a perfect stranger advice which he will probably throw back in his face. But he has been moved today, more profoundly than he can remember being moved by anything for a very long time. The torture in those mild eyes as they hovered above him in the dentist's chair . . . He is still disturbed by that image. Only twice before has he seen that look: once in a tiger at the zoo in Munich, and once in the mirror, during the third year of his marriage. He smiles a sad smile, hoping with grim sincerity that Lenny will not have to take the undignified route to self-discovery that he himself took, conducted in unlit conveniences and on the Heath, all in an effort to protect his career. He shakes his head at the memory of it. "If you let me buy you a drink, I'll explain," he says.

Lenny is in no hurry to return home, and accepts the offer. He accompanies Mostyn to a pub he's never even noticed before, over the river at the foot of the High Street, which appears to be an isolated building standing in a car park. The walls are blackened from a fire which has happened at some time in the past.

"Arson attack, I hear," says Mostyn as Lenny takes in the scene. Then: "I don't suppose you've been here before?"

Lenny shakes his head. "I seldom come down this way," he explains.

"That's what I thought," says Mostyn with a grin. "I think you'll like it."

The pub is small and smoky, configured as three sides of a square. Women have congregated on one side, and men on the other. The middle section is more or less empty, except for two young men who are playing pinball with frightening concentration. Mostyn shepherds Lenny to the section where the men have gathered, propelling him with a light pressure to his left elbow. "You know where you are now, don't you?" he asks.

Lenny shrugs. It seems a perfectly ordinary, if down-market, bar. It's true that there are more women here than he would have imagined in a regular bar, but aside from that, there are no distinguishing features. "What's special about it?" he asks.

"What if I told you that everyone in here is like you?"

Lenny looks about, frightened and amazed. All the men around him seem so ordinary, so relaxed. Some are wearing clothes like his, others sport jeans, sweatshirts, the kind of clothes that Monica wears. There is nothing extraordinary about any of them. And so many – at least twenty!

"These men . . . " Lenny's voice trails away to nothing.

"All gay," says Mostyn into his ear, smiling at Lenny's surprise. "You really are in the closet, aren't you?"

Mostyn buys them both a gin and steers them towards a quiet table in the corner. "I hope you don't mind me bringing you here," he says, "we can leave if you like."

"No, it's fine," says Lenny, hunching his shoulders and turning his back to the body of the bar. He feels strangely conspicuous and doesn't want to be seen. A part of him is squirming at the thought that these people are looking at him, knowing that he's a homosexual, and yet at the same time another part is thrilled.

"You must think it's very odd of me," Mostyn begins, his voice suddenly serious. "I can't quite explain it myself. But I couldn't help thinking it would do you some good to come here." He makes a gesture with his right hand which encompasses the whole room, almost spilling his gin as he does so. "Now you know it exists. You can take it or leave it." He looks at Lenny, who sits opposite him, small and scared. "Now, I promised to explain what I meant when I said you reminded me of myself, didn't I?" he continues, hoping that he can help to short-circuit the painful part of Lenny's life. "You see, I was married once, too. But it didn't work, of course. You can't teach a leopard, etc . . . "

Mostyn picks up a beer mat and bends it in half, folding it backwards and forwards until it falls to pieces, as he tells Lenny about his marriage. His voice is smooth, unemotional, not like the voice he uses for his tv detective. He tells Lenny of how he was seduced into it by his agent, with the promise of more work if he masqueraded as a heterosexual; how the pressure of pretence had become unbearable; how he could not conduct relationships for fear of being discovered, resorting instead to the dangers of casual contacts; how he eventually broke free of it all, to discover that the world did not fall apart when he did so; how the world has changed so much since then; how much he regrets using and hurting Angela, the woman he married. "But remember, this was thirty years ago," says Mostyn, coming to the end of his story, more than an hour later. "You don't have to live like that now. It's quite alright to be gay these days."

Lenny is lightheaded with gin and new experience, and Mostyn's story unsettles him. But despite the advice, which seems so sensible the way Mostyn says it, he still cannot conceive of leaving Zoe, of 'coming out' as Mostyn calls it. That would spell the end of his dentistry for certain, and he can't risk that. It is the very reason Zoe has a hold over him. But Mostyn has effected a great change in him, nevertheless. He has set Lenny on the long road to self-approbation (or at least pointed him in the direction of that road), and awakened in him the possibility of indulging his desires. For the first time in his life, sitting here amongst these other homosexual men, he does not regard the idea of sexual expression with one of them as repugnant. The feeling is awesome, terrifying and exhilarating all at once.

They finish their drinks and Lenny rises, a little unsteadily, taking his leave. "Thank you for the drinks," he says. "And see you in six months," he adds, tapping his teeth.

"Or perhaps sooner, in here?" Mostyn replies, arching an eyebrow.

Lenny shrugs and leaves the bar.

CHAPTER TWELVE

Michael Whiting is preoccupied this evening as he drives home from the surgery. Preoccupied and depressed. It seems that his end of the practice is destined to sink after all, after months of teetering on the brink. He can't stand to see it all dissolve before his eyes. The sensible answer would be to let his colleague buy him out, he knows, but he can't do that. Lenny is inferior, plain and simple. Selling the business to him would be to underline his own failure. And besides, Lenny couldn't afford to buy him out. Lenny is nothing.

As he drives past trees laden with burgeoning buds, stick branches fuzzed with green, he tells himself that freak circumstances are to blame for his dire financial situation: the escalating mortgage on the premises; the government's refusal to up NHS fees in line with material costs; suddenly having to replace his X-ray machine; the exorbitant maintenance payments he has to shell out to his ex-wife. He quells an inner voice which whispers the real reasons: that he is spending more than he earns on gear; that he has only half the patients Lenny does; that he is, frankly, losing it. Just this afternoon he dropped his probe during an oral exam and was unable to focus enough to pick it up. He is scaring his patients away, and they are running to pathetic little Lenny instead.

He crosses lanes, feeding himself into the one way system, and reflects bitterly that Lenny has even acquired a celebrity patient, of which there are many here in the heart of the Home Counties. He know this is good for the practice and that it should please him, but it doesn't. It only makes him more jealous of Lenny. Why does he seem to have everything?

As he slides through the city streets his thoughts turn, as they so often do, to the fabulous Zoe, at whose temple he worships in solitary devotion every night. Why does Lenny have a beautiful, desirable wife when he, Michael, must make do with unsatisfactory one-night-stands? (He's given up on relationships completely now – all his girlfriends complain that he loves his gear more than them.)

He stops for a red light at the foot of the High Street, aware of his tumescent member. To his right is a picturesque cobbled stone footbridge, which spans the river and leads to the notorious queer pub which has withstood three arson attacks in as many years. Michael glances down the road and sees a small, dapper figure make its way from the pub to the footbridge, then watches with senses dulled as the lone figure trots across the road just yards in front of his bonnet. As the lights turn to green, Michael notices that the queer has a moustache, of course, and sneers derisively. He also notices that he is wearing a coat a lot like Lenny's.

Michael continues to snake slowly through the one way system, cursing at the traffic, as if he has a god given right to congestion-free passage through the city, where others do not. Then he awakes with a jolt to a sudden realisation. The man in the road! It didn't *look* like Lenny, it *was* Lenny. Surprised, he thumps the palm of his hands against his padded steering wheel, and lets out a high, triumphant shout. "Lenny's a queer," he says aloud as he slides past the darkened shopping precinct. "Lenny Jeffries is a fucking faggot!" Suddenly everything slots into place. The look of sublimated terror, which Michael has seen on Lenny's face every day for the last eighteen months, is the look of a queer in hiding – the abstract air of sadness which surrounds him is their trade mark.

Michael smiles, his mood lifting perceptibly by the second, and runs a slender hand through his greying hair. This new theory makes sense of the more recent past, too: He remembers Lenny's letter from Canada, and the phone call he overheard that same evening, to a man named Anthony.

Lenny has been depressed for months, coinciding precisely with this phone call and the resulting dinner date in London. This is not mere chance. Michael decides that Lenny has been jilted by a lover, or else this Anthony is an ex-lover who won't come back. Michael lets the idea run in his head for a while, and it pleases him. It seems solid, plausible, and he decides to adopt it as fact, wondering if patients might be persuaded that a queer dentist poses a health risk, and that he, Michael, would be a safer choice.

Recalling that Lenny and Anthony arranged to meet in a club called Lampton's, Michael is suddenly struck by an idea, a way of testing his hypothesis. He pulls over to the side of the road, grabs his cell phone, calls Talking Pages and secures the number of the club. Then he dials the number he's been quoted, sure of his hunch.

"Lampton's gaming club, how may I help you?" The voice is cultured, with a trace of a Middle Eastern accent. Michael smiles to himself. All Arabs are queers.

"Hello, I'm in London for a couple of days, and I've been recommended your club by a friend, a very good friend," says Michael.

"Yes?"

The voice is completely non-committal, and Michael tries another tack. "My friend tells me your club caters for certain tastes. For men who enjoy other men?" Michael tries to keep the disgust out of his voice.

"I'm afraid your friend is mistaken, sir. We are a gaming house. A casino."

"I see." Michael is disappointed in the extreme. The man is certainly not lying.

"But there are places in –" Michael presses a red button and cuts off the cultured tones in mid sentence. He doesn't want to hear about the delights of Lenny's grubby underworld.

As he cruises the last few yards to his house, he realises he could be entirely wrong about Lenny – he doesn't exactly conform to the stereotype. Then he decides he doesn't care. A few salient hints dropped in the right ears around the surgery will cause plenty of damage, irrespective of their truth. He's not certain how it will affect business, but at least he will feel happier knowing that he has exacted his revenge on Lily White Lenny. If he's going to sink anyway, he might as well smile whilst doing it, and take Lenny with him.

Later, as he lies in bed, fantasising as usual about Zoe and the touch of her magnificent body, a further triumphant thought occurs to him. If Lenny is queer, then Zoe may become available. All he has to do is tell her that her husband has a sordid secret. In the same moment he realises that Lenny may be prepared to part with money, possibly large sums, to keep this information from her. His eyes widen in the darkness. Perhaps there is financial reward in this after all? A way to save himself? With a contented sigh, he continues to masturbate, thinking how much Zoe must want the touch of a real man. He knows he is the one she needs.

CHAPTER THIRTEEN

Monica has been home for less than ten minutes, having just arrived back from Cambridge for Easter vac. The house is empty, and she lounges in the kitchen waiting for her father to come home, leaning her left arm on the old farmhouse-style kitchen table. It is an ostentatious monstrosity which dominates the room completely.

Monica sits in her favourite position, with legs stretched along the length of the polished bench – purchased as a companion to the table – and her back to the cold wall. She stares down at the table as she cradles the mug of coffee she's just made for herself, and reflects that Zoe has no taste. For a room to successfully support this monstrous product of de-forestation it would have to be twice the size it is, with stone flags, not pukey cushioned hexagonal tiles. And the table would have to be covered by a gingham cloth, with home baked bread heaped on it. Over the years she must have got used to it through exposure, but now that she's at college Monica sees it with new eyes. Her verdict is that it's gross. How come she didn't notice when she came home for Christmas?

Monica shudders to recall that dreadful month at home. The house had been unbearable, her father more miserable than ever, as if someone had died. The forced gaiety of the season had underscored the whole period with heavy irony, highlighting her father's inner torment. Her Campaign of Love had made no impression on him. She had smiled at him as often as she could, through tight lips drawn carefully over her acid-raddled teeth, but he had been oblivious. She has bigger plans for this vac. She will cure him with love, and the Strong Goddess will help her. She has prepared a special mantra. All she needs now is a photograph of her father, and she can begin . . .

Monica is jolted from these thoughts by a sudden hunger pang, which stabs her insides like a laser. Sitting where she is, she faces the clinical white door of the refrigerator, scene of many uncontrolled gorging dreams, and she crunches her eyes shut to blot it out. She presses her head against the rough brickwork behind her and tells herself that she will not succumb, and recites the Litany of Power in a rhythmic voice, drawing her knees up to her chest and cradling them in her arms as she jabs her head back against the wall with increasing force. A light sweat breaks out on her forehead, dampening her dark fringe, which sticks in strands to her clammy skin, and she calls on the Strong Goddess to help her: *Oh Em, give me power over food. Let me withstand this test as you withstood the Testing Trial. Strength is everything, I want your strength. I want to continue your work, but I can't in a weak body. Let me grow strong, let me not be a slave, let others be my slaves. Let me rise above this to reach your heights.* Her lips flutter, yet utter not a sound.

But the prayer goes unanswered. Unable to resist the Siren call of food, Monica rises from the bench and pulls open a cupboard, rummaging through packets of dried goods until she finds the one she is searching for. Semolina. Nothing else will do right now, it has to be this. As she pours milk into a pan and sprinkles the fine speed-yellow powder over it, she tells herself she won't binge, that she'll eat sensibly tonight. She grabs an oversized wooden spoon, stirs the milk and watches it thicken from the consistency of water to hot mud. The pudding shudders with the vibration of numerous tiny volcano-like explosions, making noises like a phoney sound effect.

Before long she realises that in her haste she's made it too thick. Trying to pour the mixture out of the pan, she sees that it has become almost solid, sliding into her waiting bowl as a homogenized lump. She returns it to the pan, adds more milk to thin it, and stirs the concoction with wild, rapid jerks. Gradually it thins to the right consistency, only now there is much too much of it. Shrugging, she pours herself a bowl, ladles on some sugar, and slops it into her mouth with frenzied mechanical movements.

As she finishes her third bowl, she realises that she's left her weighing scales at college. This is disastrous, there are none here at home. She will not be able to monitor her weight on a daily basis now. How could she have forgotten to bring them? She will have to go out and buy some more in the morning – if she doesn't she will begin to feel out of control. Even now she is seized by an abstract dread, the insurgence of a crazy panic. Unable to weigh herself immediately, an overwhelming desire which obliterates any pleasure she has derived from eating the food, she runs up to her room, her most calming environment, and stands motionless in the dark, absorbing the special atmosphere it possesses. This room, more than anything, is what she misses from home whilst up at Cambridge, for it contains the True Shrine and all her Icons.

She has tried to build a Shrine in her room at college, but it has no power. Knowing that it would be black sacrilege to remove any of her Icons from the True Shrine, she has inscribed her Mantras and Litanies in cloth-bound books, along with the more common interpretations from the Book of Truth, and she has erected another picture of the Strong Goddess, together with a snapshot of the Holy Bird, but despite any number of candles, and wreaths of incense hanging above her head like ectoplasm, the atmosphere just cannot be recreated. Monica suspects that the True Shrine faces Hollin Brow. That must be what gives it its special power.

Feeling in need of immediate guidance, she flings open the doors of her wardrobe and gazes in pure joy at the Holy Shrine. Tears spring to her eyes. The Strong Goddess crowns the altar, dispassionate and calm, staring down between two wooden candle sticks with spiralled double helix stems. Beneath Her is the centrepiece of the Holy Bird, beautiful even in death, which emanates calmness as it lies across the Book of Truth, its wise glassy eye looking into eternity. Next to the Book of Truth are the gathered remnants of the Testing Trial, Monica's most precious possession. She kneels in the wardrobe doorway and reaches out to stroke the yellowed pages with loving fingers, giving a reverential nod to the Goddess as she does so. This moment is beautiful, and so holy it makes her catch her breath. Then she lights a candle, this time purple for healing, and places it at the foot of the Shrine. The uneven flame casts a mysterious glow over her Icons, and Monica smiles. Surely no one could fail to be moved by this sight? A sense of inner stability comes over her as she absorbs the power of the Goddess, lets Her hard gaze bore right into her soul in the flickering candlelight. She sighs, and feels a wave of calm, knowing that the Living Goddess, in her mercy, has absolved her for her semolina binge.

Newly purified, Monica is about to throw herself on the bed, to lie inert, staring at the ceiling, when she remembers her mission for her father. She walks down the narrow stairs which lead from her eyrie to the second floor, and moves quickly into her father's bedroom with the stealth of a thief, having first checked that he is not inside. The room is sparse, containing a wall of built-in wardrobes, like her own room, and a dressing table. *Give me a sign, Em. Show me where the photos are,* she asks the Goddess as she looks around the room for clues. Then she sees a penny on the carpet, just below the bottom drawer of the dressing table, and knows where to look. Pennies are significators, like arrows in the woods. They show you the way. A penny is never there by accident. And they must never be touched by the right side of the body. That's intense bad luck. It can ruin everything.

Sliding the drawer open, she finds it full of magazines – gory dental journals showing step by step guides to operations, and advertisements for new kinds of drill. Monica digs deeper into the drawer, stacking the magazines on the floor beside her until she pulls out the last one, revealing the pale pinkish wood of the drawer bottom beneath. She smiles as she regards the few remaining articles in the drawer: Three paper clips; two receipts in faded purple dot-matrix print; an old glasses case, misshapen after being squashed beneath so many dental journals; and a strip of Photo-Me pictures, which lie face down, wedged into a corner. She knew she would find them here, the penny predicted it. She cradles it in her left palm now as she squats beside the drawer. The left is the good side of the body. She can feel the positive energies of the coin rippling through her, and she knows these photos will be excellent.

Monica picks up the strip of pictures and looks at them for some time. She is surprised to see that they are black and white. Her father looks very young in the photos, and he has no moustache, which makes him look silly. In the first picture he is smiling hard into the camera, all teeth, a smile which includes his eyes and proves that he was happy at the time the photograph was taken. This is perfect. He is wearing a dark suit, a wide tie, and no glasses. Monica then studies the other man, the man crammed into the booth next to her father. He is making a stupid face into the camera, like a monkey, whilst trying not to laugh. His hair is as dark as her fathers, only there is more of it. This man has his arm round her father's shoulders, she can see his right hand resting on her father's right shoulder. Monica then looks down the strip of pictures, noting the sequence of events with interest. Lenny's friend squeezes Lenny's shoulder more tightly – she can see the tension in his fingers – whilst his expression resolves from monkey into pure laughter. Her father's face changes from laughter into something soft as he turns towards his friend, giving the camera his right profile. In the last picture, Monica can see her father's lips beginning to pucker into a kiss, whilst his friend, oblivious, stares ahead at the camera.

As she turns the pictures in her hand, wondering if her father's kiss ever reached it's target, she notices some writing in blue biro on the back of the strip of pictures: *Me and Anthony. 1976.* She smiles. Her godfather, whom she has never seen because he lives in Canada, is named Anthony. She wonders if this is him.

Lost in her thoughts, she faintly hears the front door click shut two floors below her, and hurries to replace the journals in the drawer, still clutching the photographs. She runs upstairs to her room, places them at the foot of the Shrine, then descends to the ground floor to welcome her father home. She knows it won't be her mother, she left a note on the kitchen table to say she's at another of her fakezec charity binges.

Monica returns to the kitchen and stations herself on her bench once more, the place she's claimed as her own for the last ten years. At the other end of the room Lenny is fiddling with the kettle, filling it, switching it on. Then he turns towards her, smiling, and it almost bursts her heart to see it. It's the first smile he's given her in ages. She notices his white, straight teeth, the bunching of his cheeks, the light in his eyes. It seems familiar and she doesn't know why. Then she remembers. His eyes look the same way in the Photo-Me shots she's just been looking at – happy and alive. Unable to stop herself, she gets up and hugs him for a long time, something she hasn't done since she was a child.

"Hello," she mumbles into his chest. Inside, she praises the Strong Goddess. The photographs have begun to work already, and she hasn't even done her mantra yet.

"Coffee?" Lenny asks.

Monica nods. "You're looking good," she smiles. "How is everything?"

Lenny puffs out his cheeks as he makes them both a drink. "Fine. Everything is fine," he replies.

Monica sits back down at the table and rummages in her shoulder bag, an ethnic, embroidered affair made of a dark canvas-like material and decorated with layers of gold and silver sequins. Finally she draws out her cards. She knows this is the right moment for the Tarot. "Cut the pack," she tells her father. "I've got a good feeling about this."

Lenny, quizzical and self-conscious, sits at the table, places his mug to his right, and reaches for the pack of cards which Monica has positioned in front of him. He smiles at the intense expression on the face of his daughter.

"Use your left hand," Monica blurts just as Lenny's fingers reach the cards. Lenny stops and picks up a portion of the pack with his left hand. The card he picks, the cut card, is the eight of Swords. Monica takes it from him and places it on the table in front of her. They both stare at the card. It depicts a person wearing a blindfold, with his hands tied behind his back. All around him is a cage of swords. Lenny is impressed. "What does it mean?" he asks.

"It means you feel trapped. No. You *think* you're trapped, but really you aren't. You see here?" Monica indicates a gap in the fence of swords, directly in front of the figure. "This person is free to go. He can walk away, if only he knew it." She looks up at her father, whose expression is strange, his jaw loose. "So what it means is, you think there's no way forward, but there is. You just haven't looked yet. Does that make sense?"

"Yes. Perfect sense," exclaims Lenny, amazed, his voice small and strange. "Where did you learn all this?"

"Someone called Jade at college is into it. She says I'm psychic."

"Perhaps you are," Lenny says. Then, indicating the cards: "Your mother wouldn't like it."

"What *does* she like?" Monica shrugs. She says this to show Lenny that she's on his side. It will come to sides one day, she's sure of it.

They drink their coffee in companionable silence, smiling now and then, until Lenny asks her about her second term at Cambridge.

"It was alright," Monica replies. What she wants to say is that it was scary. She didn't realise how scary until she got back home, to her safe existence in the house she's known all her life. She gives her father a huge, brave smile, hoping to ward off further questions. Lenny's eyes linger on the smile, and Monica knows he's studying her worn teeth with their ruined enamel.

"Would you like me to see to those over the holidays?" he offers in a diffident voice, the voice he habitually adopts when bringing up this delicate subject.

"Once a dentist, always a dentist," Monica laughs, embarrassed, as she brushes her fringe out of her eyes. He must have asked the question a million times. But lately her teeth have been getting worse. Yellower, more stumpy. Monica's worst nightmare is for Zoe to bulldoze her way into Monica's private life, telling her she's sick and in need of treatment, and her freshly massacred fangs might be the cue her mother needs. "Okay. But don't tell mum," she whispers, and they both smile. Now Zoe will never know her secret. Her naive father will give her perfect, uncorroded teeth. Excellent.

As Lenny rises from the table, making his way to bed, he

turns and winks at her. "Mum's the word," he says.

His expression reminds Monica of the old Photo-Me poses again. She watches his retreating back as he leaves the room, and decides that now is a good time to test her theory, when there is no eye contact. "Did you love Anthony?" she asks. Her father is hidden in the shadows of the dining room, but she sees him stop dead, and knows she's right.

"Why don't you ask your cards?" he replies, his tone light. Then he hurries upstairs.

Monica does not wait up for her mother. She wants to avoid the standard stilted, over formal conversation which they'd undoubtedly have concerning her academic progress at Cambridge. There's nothing she can tell her mother. All she has achieved this term has been the completion of her xeno-collage. She has stuck the photographs into books, a page for each picture, and named the subjects. She has given them histories, occupations, relationships. They seem more real this way, and more powerful. Their life-force is a reservoir for her to use whenever she needs to, now that they are named and can be called upon. But of course, she can't tell her mother about that. Instead she writes her a brief note, saying that she's home, and leaves it on the kitchen table.

Monica goes up to her bedroom and undresses, then sits naked before the True Shrine, cross-legged, staring hard at the old picture of her smiling father. She lights some incense, two purple healing candles, and recites the Litany of Power ten times. Then she begins her Mantra of Unconditional Love, a composition of her own in French, with the Photo-Me strip pressed to her Third Eye with the fingers of her right hand, and her left palm on her psychic energy centre, in the region of her solar plexus. Smiling, she can feel the healing vibrations flowing out of her, through the floor, and into her father in the room below. She will cure her father's sadness, his lack of love. Now she knows its cause, it will be easy. And she has one hundred and eleven body energies to help her.

CHAPTER FOURTEEN

Keith is lying in bed next to his lover, smiling. They have just made love, passionately, slowly, and now Nick is dozing in his arms, his body turned away, facing the wardrobe, his buttocks pressed against Keith's warm groin. Keith rolls over and sees Nick's new clothes, the ones they bought at the weekend, lying in a heap on the floor by his side of the bed. His own clothes, hastily removed last night, are lying nearby. The legs of their jeans are entwined, a blue and black tangle of denim. The shiny zip of Nick's leather jacket has caught a brilliant shard of sun, and projects a dancing reflection on to the ceiling above him. It is seven-thirty on a Tuesday morning.

Keith is so happy, so full. He is immensely pleased that he didn't throw Nick out, didn't cause a scene for the sake of fifty pounds. Even though he doesn't trust Nick, he loves him, and this is what has silenced him. In the light of what Nick has given him in return these last few weeks, it would seem churlish to haggle over money.

He stretches his arms above his head, trying to persuade himself to get up, and remembers with a tinge of sadness that it is not just fifty pounds. It's fifty pounds, and a watch worth several hundred, plus the money from his wallet that first day. He has mentioned not a word about the thefts of his watch and money to his friends, and feels awkward about it. He is sure they would disapprove, The Bookends especially. They would tell him to get rid of Nick at once. But he can't do that. One reason is that a part of him already depends on Nick, is scared that he can't do without him. He ignores the other part, which feels used, ridiculous.

As he slides out of bed and dresses quietly, he rationalises his position: Keeping Nick and giving him a home is really no more than what The Bookends did for him in the past. They saw him right, helped him put his feet on the ground, and now he's doing the same for someone else. He knows it's a delusion but it holds up, providing he does not scrutinize it too much. How has this happened? Keith wonders, looking down at Nick, who is feigning sleep on the other side of the bed, emitting cartoon snores. Why are relationships always so complex?

Keith clicks the bedroom door open and steps outside on to the landing. Nick, hearing the sound, turns to him with clogged eyes and a weak smile. "I'd murder a cuppa," he says. "Do us one, why don't you?"

"Alright," Keith smiles. "But I'm not bringing it up here."

"Go on!" Nick groans.

It's one of their areas of conflict, and Keith doesn't want to get into it now, so he says nothing. He beams a level stare at his lover instead.

Nick relents. "Okay, I'll be down in a sec," he says.

Keith goes downstairs to the kitchen, thinking about what Nick said last time they rowed about it: that Keith wanted to turn him into someone else, someone like Keith, who went out to work and did middle-class things, like not having breakfast in bed. Keith shakes his head, refuting the accusation, but a nagging thought clings to the back of his mind. There are whole areas of Nick that he does not understand.

Nick soon appears in the kitchen, dressed in his new clothes, his limbs awkward. Keith wonders, as he looks at Nick's new Levis, if he's moving too fast by buying him clothes. But Nick needs them, even he can't deny that. Once again, Keith shudders at the coldness of Nick's reply when he'd suggested it.

"I'm not a doll, or a kid," Nick had said, flying into an instant rage. "It'd make me feel under control, under your thumb."

He had not even tried to listen to Keith's response, and had remained sullen when Keith went ahead and bought the clothes anyway – jeans, T-shirts, DMs, and a second-hand biker's jacket.

Now, wary of the subject, Keith resists the temptation to tell Nick how good he looks, sitting there on the other side of the table, all stubble and attitude. Instead, he eats his breakfast in silence, whilst Nick slurps his too-hot tea like a noisy chimp, then gives him a perfunctory kiss on the head and leaves for work.

On arrival, he finds a memo on his desk reminding him of the up-coming meeting with his superiors this afternoon. He is not looking forward to it. They are due to discuss the complicated issue of the accuracy of the census procedure. His bosses want to believe the figures, especially the politically useful ones, and will not hear of possible inaccuracies despite the fact that many figures are extrapolated from elsewhere.

Keith spends the morning reading through useful documents and reports, doubtful if even the basic head count of the population is accurate. He personally knows of two enumerators in the central London area who simply dumped their entire quota of census forms in the lobbies of the giant tenement blocks that they were supposedly serving, and when the time came to collect the forms, they discovered that the whole lot had been torched by the resentful occupants. Thus eight hundred inner city dwellers had been expunged from the statistical map. Keith knows this is not at all uncommon.

The meeting goes badly. His superiors suggest that any inaccuracies are inconsequential, the figures erring if anything on the small side. So in fact, they say, if inaccuracies do exist there are probably *more* single mothers, for example, than the statistics show. Everyone seems pleased by this, especially the man from Whitehall who sits in the corner, saying nothing. Keith wants to mention that this logic also means there are more people in general, more children, requiring more hospitals and more schools, but he doesn't. Instead, he thinks of Rebecca and Nin, and wonders how they are getting on.

When he arrives home that evening, he knows immediately that something is wrong. Everything looks normal, but it feels different, and he doesn't know why. He calls out for Nick, but he's not in the house. When he enters the living room he understands, and his stomach sinks. The sitting room has been burgled. The entire music system – CD player, turntable and DAT machine – has been removed from its shelving in the alcove, along with the tv and video, as well as numerous cassettes and CDs. Keith leans on the door frame, his right hand pressed to his forehead. He actually feels physically sick. He's read that people feel like this when they have been robbed, but has always thought it was exaggeration. They talk of feelings of violation, uncleanness, and of not wanting to touch anything. This is exactly how he feels now. He forces himself to look round the room again, checking to see what else is missing, but everything else seems to be untouched. He inspects the drawers which contain his silver cutlery, and finds that it has not been disturbed. Neither has his artwork, which still hangs on the walls, figures peering out of frames like tacit witnesses to the crime. He makes himself tour the entire house, careful not to touch anything in case he smudges a useful fingerprint, but discovers no further thefts. It is clear that Nick, for surely he is the culprit, knew what he wanted, and this makes Keith feel even more peculiar. He is not yet capable of anger. He only feels a sense of disbelief that Nick, whom he has nurtured, loved, and cared for, could repay him in this way.

Descending the stairs, Keith discovers that his legs are weak from the shock. He makes a cup of strong coffee in an attempt to revive himself, and leans back against the work surface in the kitchen as he drinks it. He glances up at the kitchen clock, matt black with chrome edging, and notices that it's six-ten. He memorises this, it may be useful to the police. Then he dumps his mug in the dishwasher, and goes next door to talk to his neighbour, Mrs Pugh. She is eighty-seven, the same age as his grandmother, but she looks much younger. She and Keith get on well.

"Were you in at all today, Mrs Pugh," Keith begins when she answers the door, "because I've been burgled, and I wondered if you heard anything?" His voice is high, his throat constricted with nerves. He hadn't meant to blurt it all out like this. Obviously he's more affected than he thought.

Mrs Pugh's frail, tanned hand flies to her mouth, masking the silent Oh! that she forms with her lips. Her brow darkens into a frown, the skin becoming almost translucent at her temples, where it is stretched tight. The lines between her eyebrows deepen. "Burgled, you say? My dear, that's awful.

You must . . . " Her voice trails off in mid sentence, her eyes clouding.

"Are you alright, Mrs Pugh?" Keith asks, worried. She looks as if she is about to cry.

"It's my fault," she says, her voice quavering, eyes brimming with tears. "It really is my fault. I'd no idea. I thought it was alright."

Keith isn't following what the old lady is saying and tries to calm her by making soothing noises. He leads her back into her house, steers her into the sitting room, sits her down in her favourite chair, and then perches on the arm. "What did you see?" he asks. "Did you see something?" Mrs Pugh nods, her eyes focused on the wall. Her sitting room is smaller, darker and much more cramped with furniture than Keith's. It seems untouched by time, although Keith knows it has been decorated more recently than his own. He helped to do it. "What did you see?" he asks again, but Mrs Pugh seems too frightened to speak.

"It was the young man who lives with you," she announces at last, her voice suddenly strong. "He was with another boy. A scruffy type. I saw them taking things from your house, and putting them into a white car. No, wait a moment, I think it was a van." She places her right hand on the arm of her chair, palm downwards, as she remembers. "I asked him – Nick, isn't it? – I asked him what was happening, and he said you were buying some new equipment. He said you'd told him to get rid of the old things today." Mrs Pugh looks up at Keith, her face pale, a tear trickling down her left cheek. "I'm so sorry, dear. He sounded quite genuine."

"It's not your fault," Keith smiles. He is fighting back tears of his own as he says this, feeling violently sick, his head pounding. As he suspected, Nick is the culprit! He has been robbed by his lover, and betrayed again. "Thanks Mrs Pugh," he stammers, rising from the arm of the chair in a sudden movement, "I think I'd better go now." And he rushes out, fleeing to the sanctuary of his own, violated, house. All that matters is that he gets home before the tears come.

As he runs up to the bedroom, Keith wonders where Nick is now. Surely he won't have the gall to return after this episode? Furious, Keith hurls himself across the bed and flings the wardrobe doors open with such force that one of them cracks, and peers inside. His suspicions are confirmed – all Nick's clothes have been removed. He won't be back. Suddenly exhausted, Keith sits down on the edge of the bed, staring into the wardrobe but seeing nothing. He feels completely empty. As he falls backwards on to the bed and covers his face with his hands, the only thought in his head is that he is alone again. The idea makes him feel hot and ill, yet also there is a strange sense of relief. Nick and his complicated mysteries will trouble him no more. He is free. With this relief comes the knowledge that he is not surprised it ended this way. It was inevitable. Then he begins to laugh, with no clear idea why. It seems the most inappropriate emotion, yet the most cathartic. His whole body is gripped in convulsions of a dangerous, brittle kind.

He lies on his bed for some minutes, wondering what to do next. More clear headed now, he realises that Nick is trouble and that he's better off without him. He hopes never to see him again. His instinct is to forget the whole calamitous affair, pretend it never happened and start all over again. But the bitter pangs of rejection, of love spurned and unreturned, give him enormous pain. As he lies there, in his darkening bedroom, he realises he can't ignore it, he can't pretend that nothing has happened. He has more pride than that. It is not acceptable for someone to do this to him, he does not deserve it. He must take some action.

PART TWO

THREE YEARS LATER

CHAPTER FIFTEEN

Lenny stands in his chilly hallway wrapped in a burgundy towelling bathrobe, and stares down at three letters which lie at his feet on the carpet. Two are bills, but the third is a large, swollen buff envelope. The package has clearly caused the postman problems. Too big to fit properly through the letter-box, it has been folded in half – a difficult task considering its thickness – and brutally shoved through the aperture. It has torn open in the process. Lenny can see portions of regular sized envelopes inside the larger one, revealed through the ragged gash which obscures his address.

As soon as he sets eyes on the envelope Lenny knows what it is, and his heart bangs in his chest with a surge of illicit excitement. It's the replies to the personal advertisement he placed in *Time Out*. Two months previously, Mostyn had suggested that he place the ad, half as a joke, and to the surprise of them both, Lenny did. Now he stoops down and picks up the results in a clammy hand, feeling a twinge in his lower back as he does so. He straightens up, rubbing his lower vertebrae with a gentle circular motion of his free hand, and grins at the envelope. Feeling it with his fingers, like a child trying to guess a Christmas present, Lenny reckons he has about twenty replies.

The last three years have been a revelation, Lenny reflects as he carries the envelope through to the kitchen and makes himself some breakfast. Through Mostyn, he has met people from many walks of life who share his sexuality, and each one has enabled him to slot into place another piece of the jig-saw that is himself. Now, at last, he is beginning to see a whole. If he is still ashamed, at least he is no longer disgusted; no longer paralysed into inaction by his own self-hatred. So what if it has taken him three long years to reach this point, to be able to place a simple advertisement? He is proud of himself, it is a watershed. Lenny knows he has Mostyn to thank for it.

He has described himself as 'inexperienced' in his

advertisement, and as he sips his coffee he wonders what kind of replies this has generated. He imagines his notice must have seemed unbelievably twee to most readers, but then he decides he doesn't care. The free publications Lenny has seen lying about in the *Spotted Dog* depress him mightily, striking him as trite, superficial, and extraordinarily phallocentric. Looking at the pictures in these papers, and reading the articles, Lenny feels like a different species to these men, and is therefore glad that his advertisement will have seemed so different. He knows he is repressed. He knows that he will never be 'out' – if it means being like the men in these papers, he doesn't want to be. All he hopes is that his advertisement will help him to find someone who will understand that he really is a beginner; that he must be allowed to proceed at his own pace. He hopes to find a discreet companion sensitive to his situation, outside the public glare of the *Spotted Dog*. There is no way he would ever have the confidence to talk to someone in a bar, even now.

Lenny decides to take the replies with him to the surgery. He doesn't have time to sift through them all before work and besides, Monica, recently returned from Cambridge for good, might appear at any moment, wafting into the kitchen like a Dickensian somnambulist. He knows that she suspects him of homosexuality, and he doesn't want to feed her any definitive evidence. For three years he has expected her to raise the subject – after the night she asked him outright about Anthony – and for three years she has kept her silence, smiling at him with her new, perfect smile. Perhaps the adult thing to do would be to talk to her and explain everything, but Monica is so strange that he can't begin to guess how she might take the news. Now, she drifts about the house like something from another world, awaiting the results of her finals. She hardly speaks, hardly ever goes out, and spends most of her time in her room, or poring over massive, complex Tarot spreads on the dark dining table. Even Zoe, it seems, is too frightened to ask her to stop. Monica has expressed no interest in any career, and appears to have acquired not one single friend from her three years of college life, or her year spent teaching in Paris as part of her course. She has grown thinner, androgynous, her make-up more severe. And perhaps strangest of all, she appears to be growing no older. All this has given him a creeping sense of uneasiness about her.

Lenny walks from the kitchen, grateful that today he has been able to breakfast alone. Usually, he is confronted by the sight of his daughter, huddled sideways-on to the table with her back against the wall, her knees drawn up tight to her chest. She never looks up when he enters the room, just chews on the end of her pen as she scribbles notes in a mid-sized black hardback book which she balances on her bony kneecaps. He, in turn, does not ask what she is writing. The first morning he found her there, he asked this same question and was answered by a shrug and a terrifying smile – a smile that told him not to ask again. He never did. Once, he managed to glimpse a portion of one of the crammed pages over her shoulder, and found it was written in a kind of impenetrable code, full of Greek characters and numbers. He assumed it was a diary, and saw no harm in it. In fact, thinking about it now, the keeping of this journal seems the most normal thing about his daughter, aside from the bizarre language she has chosen to write it in.

With an involuntary shudder, Lenny goes back upstairs to his room, and dresses for work. He chooses a pair of casual navy blue trousers, a light short-sleeved shirt, and does not put on a tie. Scanning himself briefly in his large, full length mirror before he goes downstairs, he wonders at the subtle change that his appearance has undergone of late. Gone are the formal suits, the cufflinks, the buttoned down collars and ties. A new, relaxed Lenny has emerged from somewhere, at least outwardly. He hopes this will percolate through to his deeper self with time. Already he is feeling more confident, happier. He no longer feels quite so much as if he is on stage, wearing an uncomfortable costume.

Hitching up his trousers around his slimmed-down waistline, he smiles at his reflection. He will be forty-three soon. That, of itself, would have depressed him three years ago, but now he feels that his life is burgeoning with possibility. The old cliché 'life begins at forty' runs through his mind as he leans closer towards the mirror, extracts a tiny comb from a small leather wallet which lies on the dressing table, and carefully combs his moustache. Despite the discovery of some new grey strands in the otherwise dark hair on his upper lip, he reflects that the cliché is, for him at least, a truth. The combing motion both soothes and excites him. Mostyn has told him that moustaches are icons in homosexual society, something of which he had been quite ignorant, but now he is keenly aware of it. If he sees a man with a moustache in the street Lenny sees him with new eyes, innocently imagining him to share his sexuality. He has allowed his own moustache, previously well-clipped, to grow much larger. Studying it in the mirror now, he doesn't think it looks attractive, but it does give him a sense of security. Something to hide behind. Perhaps his new-found confidence can simply be attributed to this?

But not all things have changed, Lenny reminds himself as he walks to the surgery. He is still working for the despicable Michael Whiting. And every day is torture – the atmosphere at the practice, hardly ideal when he first arrived four years ago, now being almost intolerable.

This new era of bad feeling began two-and-a-half years ago, when Michael tried to turn the staff against him in a sort of coup, by circulating undisclosed rumours about him. At the time Lenny tried to persuade Diane to tell him what these rumours were, but she refused, tearful and upset. All she would say was that she didn't believe them, that no one else did either, and that they originated from Michael Whiting. But Lenny didn't find it hard to guess what the rumours might be, and grew afraid. His constant, desperate efforts to appear normal since that time have put him under enormous strain.

Oddly, Michael's attempted toppling of Lenny has backfired – the staff are far more loyal and supportive of him now than ever they were before the incident. But this, in turn, has thrown Michael into a silent, towering rage. If he was contemptuous of Lenny before, he is now openly rude and hostile on a daily basis, and regularly makes lascivious remarks about Zoe. Frankly, the old Lenny would have collapsed beneath the weight of this relentless oppression. It is only his new belief in his own worth that has protected him.

All the while Lenny has dreamed of escape. He had hoped, at one time, to build up a large enough clientele to buy another practice for himself, like the old days, but that is clearly a chimerical ambition. As his earnings have increased, so has Zoe's spending. He half suspects that she's doing it deliberately, a calculated move to subjugate him. Recently, in an attempt to rid himself of Michael by other means, he tried to find another chair in another practice, but it seemed there were none available and he has now reconciled himself to his unenviable lot. There are moments when he feels as if he is staring up at an unreachable sky from the bottom of a black, slippery well.

Today, work is routine – check-ups, a few fillings, some referrals to the newly hired hygienist – until the arrival of Mrs Piggott. She is a frustrated, flirtatious housewife in her forties, and Lenny hates treating her because of her outrageous behaviour. Today she is wearing a tight, lime green minidress which slides up her thighs as she reclines in the chair. Lenny tries not to look and pulls on a fresh pair of rubber gloves, snapping the elastic round his wrists with a professional air. But Mrs Piggott, single-minded in her mission of seduction, will not be deterred, and sucks Lenny's fingers lasciviously as soon as he inserts them into her mouth, her eyebrows rising in a suggestive come-on as she does so. She flicks her tongue in and out of her mouth like a reptile, and Lenny feels deeply embarrassed. Then she caresses his index fingers with her fat tongue. At this, Lenny asks Diane, in a loud voice, to place the suction tube in the woman's mouth, even though suction is unnecessary (he is only performing a routine examination). Diane does so, allowing the suction tube to attach itself to Mrs Piggott's roving tongue. Diane glances up at Lenny for approval, and they exchange brief smiles. Once again Lenny is reminded of the value of a good, reliable nurse.

At the end of the day, Lenny pretends that he has some accounting to see to and loiters around, waiting for everyone to leave. This takes some time. Wendy and Diane are going out this evening, and they stand in the lobby deciding what to do. Eventually, as they shrug themselves into their lightweight summer jackets and adjust the straps of their shoulder bags, they elect to visit a yuppie pub round the corner for a drink before going on to the cinema, where they will see a much hyped thriller in which Lenny has zero interest. They have chosen this film because it stars Diane's favourite actor, Richard Gere. Lenny smiles at them. "Have a good evening. Enjoy yourselves," he says.

"We will, don't you worry, Mr Jeffries," Wendy replies over her shoulder as the two young women push their way through the double glass doors, and exit into the summer evening. Her cheery smile is confident, assured.

Alone in the building now, Lenny returns to his surgery, collects his coffee mug, extracts the envelope which contains his precious replies from the far reaches of a private drawer, and makes his way down the narrow corridor which separates his room from Michael's. At the end of the short corridor is a small kitchen area containing a sink, draining board, kettle, and coffee making equipment. Shelves cling to all four walls, from eye level to the ceiling, on which are stacked the dental notes of every patient.

Lenny makes himself a drink, then sinks into a raggedy old armchair in the corner of the room, beneath some of the shelving. Soon he will get down to the business of the evening, a task which he is anticipating with both trepidation and delight. Will he find himself a lover amongst these hopeful suitors? As he sips at his coffee, his eyes roam the shelves of dental notes above him in a casual manner, noticing several bundles encased in transparent yellow plastic sleeves rather than the usual buff paper. With idle curiosity, Lenny reaches up for one. It's a patient of Michael's, and Lenny can see from the enclosed questionnaire, visible through the plastic, that he's a single man in his late twenties. He replaces it amongst its neighbours, and pulls down a second one. Another single male over twenty-five, Michael's again. Inspection of a third and forth yellow plastic envelope reveals the same pattern – it seems Michael has earmarked all unmarried men over a certain age. But why? Then Lenny figures it out. They are all potential homosexuals. Lenny wonders what possible use this information can be to Michael, at the same time sensing danger for himself. He feels his scalp tighten and prickle at the thought, a light sweat breaking out on his hair line. Perhaps, with his new-found confidence, he has become complacent and let slip some vital clues about himself?

He is about to slide the small yellow folder back into place when he is disturbed by footsteps in the corridor outside. Intensely surprised, he lets out an involuntary cry, and drops the folder on the floor. His heart beats fast as he watches it slide across the shiny tiles, and with frightened eyes he stares at the door. He had been so sure he was alone in the building.

Michael appears in the doorway. His eyes lock with Lenny's, then follow his gaze downward, finally resting on the folder which now lies a few inches away from his right foot. Once again he looks up at Lenny, his expression a mixture of curiosity and alarm. Slowly, Michael bends down and retrieves the folder, then walks past Lenny without a word and replaces the notes in the waiting gap on the shelves.

"It fell out," says Lenny, aware as he says it that it's not in the least convincing. "I knocked the shelf with my head when I heard your footsteps," he adds, desperate to recover face. "I thought I was alone."

"But you weren't," says Michael with an unpleasant smile. He looks hard at his colleague, whose forehead is now beaded with perspiration, and establishes eye contact. "They're the queers," Michael says, nodding towards the folder he's just put away. "I put all their notes in yellow folders to remind myself."

"What for?" asks Lenny. His voice comes out controlled and even.

"To remind myself that I'm at greater risk from them," says Michael. He's now only inches away from Lenny, watching his face for signs of fear or indignation.

"Oh," Lenny replies, turning away to pick up his coffee mug. "I don't bother with that."

"Perhaps you don't think it's necessary. For you," Michael purrs.

Lenny turns back and stands, transfixed, before his tormentor, his heart thumping out of control. What to say? "It doesn't worry me, to be honest," he ventures, surprising himself with the coolness of his delivery. Then he swigs the last of his coffee, forcing himself to make slow movements when his basic instinct is to flee as fast as possible. "Well, that's me for the day," he says, remaining nonchalant, as he rinses his mug and dries it with a small gingham dishcloth. "I'm off." Then he scoops up his envelope of replies from the arm of the chair, says a polite, formal good night to Michael – who stands motionless in the room, staring at the armchair in an odd manner, saying nothing – and makes his exit, careful not to make it seem like a retreat.

As he leaves the surgery, his heart still booming in his ears, Lenny feels annoyed. His plan to examine his replies in seclusion has been thwarted. Still jittery, he decides not to risk going through them at home and instead elects to go to the *Spotted Dog*. He hardly ever goes there, for fear of being marked and known, but it seems a fitting environment for the task and besides, Mostyn might be there to give him some help. His spirits and excitement rise at this prospect and, happier now, he makes his way through the early summer streets, a light breeze blowing away the memory of those few awkward minutes with Michael.

The pub is relatively quiet tonight, which suits Lenny. He doesn't feel guilty about taking up lots of room with his letters, which he has spread out across the small round table in front of him. Sipping demurely at his gin, he reads through each letter, and scrutinizes the photographs which some of the respondents have enclosed. (Lenny didn't ask for photographs, and is surprised to receive them.) Most of the replies are from married men, and Lenny at first decides that these are quite unsuitable. Then he remembers that he is married, too. Stabbed by twinges of guilt and hypocrisy, shocked that he could have overlooked this essential fact, he begins to reconsider these applicants. Perhaps, he reflects, it is a sign of how far he has come that he no longer *feels* married to Zoe.

Lenny discards several suitors right away, as being too frightening, too overpowering, too different from the discreet, understanding professional for which he has advertised, and places their letters in a pile on his right. Then he stares down at the next photograph in the pile before him, attached to a letter by a pink paper-clip. It depicts a man named Terrence, who appears to be pulling another man around on a lead, in a busy bar. The lead, a three-foot long stainless-steel rod, is attached to a studded, spiked collar that the second man is wearing round his neck. Terrence sports a pair of tight, shiny trousers, possibly made of rubber, and a bechained leather harness. His chest is white and shapeless. His partner, the man on the lead (also shapeless), is wearing nothing but a pair of army boots, and is on all fours at Terrence's feet. Alarmed, Lenny forces himself to read Terrence's letter, which explains in great detail what he wishes to do to Lenny and how he will be initiated, stressing how good Terrence is with 'inexperienced' men. He goes on to say that he is the soul of discretion. But not, Lenny reflects with a smile, discreet enough to avoid having his picture taken in a crowded bar, wearing a fetishist uniform! With one swift movement of his arm Lenny consigns Terrence and his friend to the pile of letters on his right, all destined for the waste paper basket.

Once Lenny had sifted the 'Definitely Nots' from the 'Possiblys', he buys himself another gin and lets his mind wander for a few minutes before going back to his work. As he casts a hopeful eye round the bar, checking to see if Mostyn has entered since he last looked up, the juke box plays an old song from the Seventies which is currently popular, and it reminds him of college, of his youth; of when he had a blank slate in front of him on which to sketch his personal life. The free associations that the song induces seem entirely apposite now. He feels that he is again at the beginning of his emotional life. Take two.

After some further study of the 'Possiblys', his judgement only slightly impaired by the gin, Lenny manages to whittle the contenders down to three and lines them up on the table in front of him. In the end he decides to go for Brian, a quiet, dark haired doctor of forty-two. He's married, with three children. His wife doesn't know he's homosexual. Lenny feels that Brian is likely to be discreet as he is in a sensitive position similar to his own, and feels good about the choice. But he keeps Jack and David in reserve, in case Brian doesn't work out. Jack is a forty-five year old builder who has had homosexual feelings all his life but never acted on them before, and David is a lawyer of almost sixty who still lives with his mother in Epping.

Pleased with his evening's work, Lenny folds the letters from the three successful applicants with great care, making sure to pair them up with the correct photographs, and slips them into a pocket. Then he finishes his drink, largely melted ice by now, and gathers up the remaining letters and photographs, which he carries through the bar in both hands. Once outside, he deposits them in a large metallic industrial bin which stands in the far corner of the car park, and walks home happy.

CHAPTER SIXTEEN

In his office upstairs, Michael is smiling to himself. Finally, he has something solid to hang on his bumbling Goody Two Shoes colleague, and he is delighted. As he crosses the room, he performs a victorious boxer's salute to his reflection in the darkened window, and sits down behind his desk, feeling immensely powerful.

It could so easily have been an awkward moment for himself – Lenny discovering his unethical yellow folders like that – but as usual he has turned defense into attack, this time with spectacular effect. Replete with pleasure, he raises his legs and rests them on the desk next to the small, incriminating envelope which he has just tossed on to the desk top, then leans back and exhales with satisfaction. So fragile a moment has led to this.

※ ※ ※ ※ ※

Michael and Lenny face one another in the small, highly-charged file room. Lenny is trying hard not to look as if he is making a hurried escape and attempts a smile as he grabs a large buff envelope from the battered armchair, in a fake-casual manner. Then, as he elevates the package and slots it beneath his left arm, a small white envelope tumbles from a rip in the wrapping and falls back into the armchair. Lenny doesn't notice, just keeps on walking, saying good night, at last leaving the surgery altogether. Michael says nothing, just stares at the envelope.

As a profound silence settles about the small room, Michael moves over to the chair, picks up the envelope and examines it. It is not addressed to Lenny. The letter simply carries a box number in the top left-hand corner, written in uneven blue capitals. With racing heart, Michael slips his little finger into a small opening beneath the flap of the envelope and rips it open, curious as to its content, sensing that it may be useful.

Michael sinks into the armchair and studies the short letter inside. It has been scribbled on shiny ruled paper which resembles a page torn from a school exercise book. The hand matches the capitals on the envelope – shaky, childlike:

> Dear 'inexperienced',
> My name is Lance and I'm writing in answer to your ad. in Time Out for a 'Friend'. I'm 6ft. 3ins, 52 inch chest, nine inches of meat. I work out regularly. I like to fuck and be fucked, am into yellow, occasional red. My hobbies are fitness and dog breeding. If you like my photo, send me one of yourself, and phone me (0181-342-2175).

Michael is both shocked and excited. There are parts of the letter he doesn't understand, but he can make enough sense of it to know that Lenny is inhabiting a sordid netherworld. This is a situation he can exploit. With his mind overrunning with possibilities, his eyes fall to his lap, where a snapshot lies face down. Turning the picture over, Michael studies it: a full-length photograph of Lance totally naked, the over-developed chest and genitals verifying his vital statistics. He is standing with his feet apart, a Pekinese dog clamped under each arm. Lance is smiling into the camera, trying to look sexy; the Pekinese dogs look bewildered and uncomfortable, both sporting elaborately tied red bows in their hair. Their eyes are pink in the photograph, because of the flash.

Michael slips the letter and photo back into the envelope, and taps his pursed lips with it, his eyes bright with ideas.

※ ※ ※ ※ ※

Now, as he sits back in his black and chrome office chair, he considers his options – a task he warms to, like a hungry man viewing an appetizing menu. There can be no doubt about Lenny now, he is certainly queer. The question is, how best to use the information?

He recalls the previous occasion that he tried to convince his staff that Lenny was homosexual. He had been surprised to find that they flatly disbelieved him, silencing him with laughter and dismissive tones, their eyes reflecting their diminished respect for Michael and his slanderous untruths. This had happened because Michael had furnished them with no hard evidence – even he had not been sure of the truth of his claims – but now, with this letter as emotional collateral, he feels sure he'll be able to convince them.

He reminds himself to be more cautious this time, to tread carefully. He has learned from his previous effort that Wendy and Diane, and even his own nurse, are much more fond of Lenny than he had imagined. This time, he must not appear underhanded or they will begin to question his motives. Ever since his previous, abortive attempt at character assassination, his superior status has been under threat – and Michael knows that being king of the hill is no fun without the domination that goes with it.

He rises from his chair and stands at the window, looking out over the car park in which his new, grey top-of-the-range BMW stands alone. He's hugely proud of it – this schoolboy status symbol which signals to the world that he has *arrived* – despite the fact that the money has come from his late mother's estate rather than through his own success. No one else knows that, he reasons, so the respect it commands is undiminished. Now, regarding the unchallenging lines of his vehicle with pleasure, he feels not the slightest tug of guilt that he does not view the death of his mother as a personal loss so much as a massive financial gain. He had never been close to her – when she died, he hadn't seen her for six years. And she couldn't have shuffled off at a more convenient moment in his life; his business was on the brink of disaster when she had the stroke. The sale of her house, together with her savings (considerably more than he'd anticipated), has left him with enough security not to have to worry about the practice, and not to need Lenny's financial contributions in order to keep afloat. In short, Lenny has become dispensable.

Michael rubs his hands together with pleasure at this prospect, and returns to his chair. Wondering how to proceed from this point, he pushes against the carpet with his right foot and swivels his chair in slow anti-clockwise circles, his hands clasped as if in prayer, his forefingers forming a steeple and pressed tight to his lips. He is enjoying himself immensely. The sensation of power over the fate of another individual is better than sex. Revolving slowly, he decides not to blow the whistle on Lenny just yet. Wendy and Diane will have to be primed before the wheels of Lenny's big exit can be set in motion, and besides, there is much fun to be had out of the situation first.

Michael smiles a slow smile, opens the top right-hand draw of his desk with a small key and withdraws a shiny black box, also locked. He opens it with reverence, and stares down at the fine white powder inside with hungry, dilated eyes. Another boon from his late mother. She always said she'd see him right. Thanks to her, he'll be flying for years.

CHAPTER SEVENTEEN

Lenny walks to the surgery full of hope this morning, clutching his letter to Brian. He wrote it the previous evening on his return from the *Spotted Dog*, sitting up at the dressing-table, bathed in the yellow waxy light of his bedroom. He has enclosed a photograph of himself, and a more detailed description of his circumstances.

Now, as he slips the letter into the waiting rectangular mouth of the post box, vibrant in the morning sunlight, he feels a rush of excitement. The metal mouth is cold against the side of his hand as he drops the envelope inside and hears it rattle down into the empty cage within. Looking down at the collection times, he notices that he has missed the first post. His plea for love will lie inert in the enclosed darkness for the next three hours, just a few yards away from where he will be working. The thought pleases him, makes him feel clandestine and different.

He steps into the waiting room and greets Wendy with a smile, which she returns as she arranges her appointments ledger, pens, ruler, and telephone on her desk. "You look cheerful," she says as she sits down, rummaging in her handbag. Then she draws out a slender metal file and begins to work on a ragged nail.

"It's the weather," Lenny replies, his face smiling of its own accord, no longer under his control.

"Oh yeah," Wendy deadpans, unconvinced. The summer thus far has been notable for its high winds, low temperatures, and rainfall. Today, although sunny, is decidedly chilly and more consistent with the weather in early October than June. She looks up from her nails and regards Lenny, whose smile has become enormous. "If you say so," she concedes. Then: "Would you like a coffee?"

Lenny nods yes, and wanders into his surgery thinking that Wendy is an exceptional sort. She has stayed with the practice for more than four years now. Most receptionists leave after a year, or two at the most. Some only stay a matter of months. Lenny doesn't blame them really. They are paid an ungenerous salary, and their functions are simple and tedious. He knows he couldn't do Wendy's job for more than five minutes without becoming bored to extinction, but she seems to enjoy it. She is good with people on the phone, and also when they come into the surgery for treatment. She appears to sincerely enjoy meeting and calming them. Perhaps it is her *métier*.

Lenny slips on his robe and checks his appearance in the small mirror on the wall opposite, patting a few stray hairs into place. He registers with pleasure that he appears slimmer, sleeker. The garment no longer tightens around his waist, and looks almost flattering.

"Coffee," says Wendy as she enters the room with a gentle knock. She has caught him admiring himself in the mirror, and smiles. Lenny blushes scarlet. "You carry on. Don't mind me," she says, and retreats into her own domain.

The morning passes without event. Diane is subdued, suffering from another of her regular bouts of boyfriend trouble. Between patients she tells him snippets of information – wrongs done, lies told, promises broken – and Lenny can do no more than nod in sympathy. He is not good at handling such situations, has never been one to confer advice. But despite all this, his own mood remains buoyant and untouched.

After lunch, however, things take a dramatic turn for the worse. He has just picked up his probe, to treat his first patient after the break, when he sees a message lying in his instrument tray. It's written in tiny letters, executed with the finest of Rotring pens, on a piece of paper no larger than a postage stamp. Lenny is curious, and, feigning a change of heart over his choice of instrument, he turns back, replaces the probe in the tray, and quickly reads the note. He has to lean down to be able to make out the tiny words, his nose only millimetres away from the paper. The message reads: I HOPE YOU'RE USING RUBBER GLOVES. YOUR SORT NEED TO.

Lenny is suddenly terrified and finds he can't breathe, breaking out in an immediate profuse sweat, partly from fear and partly from shock. His underarms are slippery with moisture, his brow wet. His day has been shattered with these poisonous words, and in an uncontrolled movement he knocks the tray with a shaky hand, making it rattle. He darts a surreptitious glance towards Diane, but she has seen neither the note nor his reaction to it, busy as she is with work of her own. This comforts him a little, and he quietly retrieves the note and slides it into a pocket, trying not to communicate his fear and discomfort to his waiting patient, who stares up at the ceiling like a docile captive animal.

As he continues to examine the patient, his mind wanders down avenues of accusation. Who has written this, and why? Have they witnessed one of his infrequent visits to the *Spotted Dog*? Or is it a guess? Suddenly, as he picks at the tartar behind the lower front teeth of his patient, he stops dead, his probe poised only inches away from her open mouth. He knows who it is! It's Monica! Thinking back, he remembers leaving Brian's letter open on the dressing table the previous night, in full view. It would only have taken one of Monica's strange perambulations through the house – something she has done habitually since she was a child – for her to discover his secret. He curses his lack of thoroughness. He has not been careful enough.

Unable to properly concentrate on the job in hand, he fears this oversight may well prove disastrous on both a personal and professional level. He has no way of knowing what Monica's motives might be, but guesses they are not benign. Sad and unprecedentedly bitter, Lenny continues his work without enthusiasm, wondering what her next move will be. Probably, she will inform Michael that her father is an invert.

CHAPTER EIGHTEEN

At two-thirty on Saturday afternoon, Keith finds himself on his way to the reception area. As he walks the cool corridors, his hears his heels clack dully against the hard, shit-coloured linoleum which covers every inch of flooring in the building. With distant voices echoing behind him, he trails an idle finger along the uneven brickwork of the wall, painted over with a thick covering of chip-proof, graffiti-proof shiny paint, and looks up at the narrow windows, set high in the wall, only a few inches from the ceiling. He glimpses a clear, open sky – a portion of which is covered with mackerel clouds which suggest an indolent sun, balmy conditions, and the middle of summer – but Keith is cold. No matter how intense the sunshine, it seems that Mortonlake absorbs all heat, refusing to let any of it through to those within. Or perhaps, in the depths of its castle-thick walls, the building converts the solar warmth into a clammy cold which it then releases into the interior.

It is this permanent coolness (not actually damp but suggestive of it, with the resulting niggling discomfort), which has deepened his depression over the last few months. Nothing can shake him from it for long, not even, as now, the prospect of visitors. The degrading and humiliating loss of his freedom has cut too deeply; the wintry, underwater quality of the light does not allow it.

What had he expected it to be like here? he asks himself. He doesn't know. But the reality has been an unpleasant shock. Here, time seems distorted. Hours in Mortonlake are as long as whole days in the outside world, the counting of which is impossible to bear. Much better not to contemplate the days, weeks, months that must elapse before his release. He decided to give up counting long ago. As he winds through the labyrinthine complex he shakes his head, freshly bewildered at his predicament, his once purposeful stride now reduced to a lethargic amble.

As he nears the reception office, Keith finds that he is looking forward to seeing The Bookends again, and his step lightens. He hasn't seen them in six weeks. At the end of the corridor, he catches sight of his unshaven face in the mirrored window of a locked door, and feels a mess. He runs his fingers through his hair, now grown long and greasy, and sighs. His mood is punctured. In an attempt to smarten himself a little he hitches up his blue denim trousers, now hugely faded, and tightens his belt one further notch. Then, checking his appearance in the large, wired window of the office which stands next to the visiting booths, he tucks in his work shirt. With another tiny sigh, a mixture of anticipation and dread, he places his hand on the elongated steel handle of the visiting room door, depresses it, and walks in.

Facing him are five booths, all in a row, clinical and impersonal. The booths are not entirely private, there is merely a thin partition between each chair, extending a meagre four feet from the thick perspex window which separates the visitor from the inmate. In addition, the partitions only run three quarters of the height of the white formica-clad room, and this fosters a distinct lack of intimacy. Conversations can be easily overheard. Taking in the primitive facilities with renewed dismay, Keith is struck by the similarity between this room and any one of dozens of housing benefit offices he has visited during his time in the civil service. It almost makes him smile.

When he glances towards the windows, Keith sees The Bookends waiting like a pair of nervous birds, sitting behind the glass of the end booth. He catches their eye, and they smile, gesturing for him to join them – Bob beckoning with a crooked finger, Derek cocking his head. As he approaches, Keith notices how similar they look now. Twin haircuts, twin moustaches, twin forced jollity in their glinting eyes. Or is it simply that he's forgotten how much they operate as a two-cylinder machine, now that he sees so much less of them? He smiles at his friends, a genuine smile full of gratitude that they continue to visit him without fail, and sits down in the uncomfortable orange plastic bucket seat provided.

For some moments nobody says anything, they just

smile, and this communicates their love for one another eloquently. Then Derek raises his hand to the circular perforated area low down in the window, which bellies out on both sides, through which one is supposed to speak. With determination, he inserts his smallest finger, the little finger of his right hand, into one of the tiny holes, pushing it in as far as it will go. Keith, on his side, does the same, and manages to make contact with his friend. The tips of their little fingers are now kissing in full view, here in the middle of this terrible, austere room.

"How are you?" Derek asks. His voice is quiet, gentle, as if he is in a library or a hospital. He presses his little finger harder against Keith's.

"You're looking well," adds Bob, with an emphatic nod designed to disguise the lie. "How's life?"

"I'm okay," Keith shrugs. What can he tell them of his life in prison? What has happened since their last visit? Nothing. Merely the passing of time, the slow, inexorable progress of seconds towards his release. There is a strained pause. Why do these visits hurt so much? Keith wonders. The pain of seeing his friends is greater than the pain of not seeing them, and yet he can't ask them not to come. He won't do that to them, it would be a cruel rejection. And in a very real sense, somewhere deep inside, he knows he needs them. They are his stability, his lifeline to the normal world – a world so far removed from his life in Mortonlake, where things are fast slipping out of control. "So what's going on with you two?" Keith ventures at length. Then, to Bob: "I see you've had a haircut."

In the last couple of years Bob has begun to lose his hair, his greying curls giving way to an astonished, pink scalp. Refusing to give way to camouflaging measures, which fool nobody at all and are acutely undignified, he has finally taken the sensible step of cropping his hair. He is still self-conscious about it, he only did it a week ago, and his neck still feels chilly and exposed. At Keith's mention of it he runs his palm over his skull, which now has the texture of suede, and grins. "Yes," he smiles. "Now every one will think I'm a clone."

"Or trying to look like me," adds Derek, who has kept his hair short for similar reasons for many years.

"It looks good," says Keith, privately thinking it rather accentuates the roundness of Bob's face, and makes him appear foolish. Keith hopes he'll get used to it. And suddenly, as he regards his friends through that dehumanising quarter inch of perspex, an ethereal reflection of his own face superimposed on Bob's, he is appalled by the thought that when he was first sent here, Bob had all his hair. That's how long he's been wasting away in Mortonlake – long enough for his best friend to go bald. How much else has changed in the outside world, which he is not party to? How much more of life has been ripped from his hands, never to be returned? It's a familiar whipping post, his regular night-time companion as he lies awake in his narrow, uncomfortable bunk willing the hours of night to pass quickly and without event. The thought depresses him utterly, quietening him, like a sudden freak fall of snow. He wants his friends to go away this minute, but he also wants them to hug him, to hold him close between them. As he sits in his rumpled, stinking clothes, he feels quite beyond help or hope, bombarded by this mass of contradictory emotions.

On the other side of the window, The Bookends continue to converse in a slow, tentative manner, regaling Keith with stories of work; of their friends; of the parties they've been to; of the clothes they've bought; of the new bin man, whom Derek finds extremely humpy. It's a litany of trivia, an attempt to make Keith feel a part of their lives, even if he is physically out of it for the present. But they find it excruciating, like knives in the gut, especially given Keith's recessive mood. Derek has to fight hard to control his voice, fearing that a choked cry might escape his lips at any moment if he is not vigilant. This vision of their strong, handsome friend, now reduced to a lifeless, disconsolate shadow is the worst sight imaginable.

They stop talking for a moment, and overhear the woman next to them telling her husband that Charlene has been caught shoplifting again. In a toneless nasal voice, she is blaming him for her daughter's lawlessness. She says he's set a bad example. The husband bangs the perspex wall with his fleshy palm and tells her to shut the fuck up. Derek shudders, knowing that Keith has to exist in this environment twenty-four hours a day, and flashes him a watery, sympathetic smile.

Some minutes later, a bell rings three times – three short, muffled bursts which signal that visitors must now leave. Derek looks down at his finger, still wedged into the hole in the perspex window. The last segment has gone white and numb. He removes it, then looks up at his friend. His imprisoned friend. "Hang on, Keithie. We're all thinking of you," he says.

"When you get out of here, we're going to throw a huge party," Bob adds, smiling. "The biggest fucking party you've ever seen. Just watch." There is an edge of defiance in his voice.

Then they are all standing. Bob presses his palm to the window, his fingers taking on the look of something vacuum packed, and Keith does the same, resting his forehead on the window as he does so. There are wobbly smiles, whispered goodbyes, and then The Bookends turn away.

Keith remains still for some time, his forehead and right palm firmly pressed to the window, watching his friends depart. They walk slowly, cowed, like old people. And then, when they are half way across the still-crowded room, they do something Keith has never seen them do before. They reach out, each finding security in the touch of the other, and leave the room hand in hand, like refugees walking from the bombed rubble of what used to be their home. And it occurs to him then, for the first time, that he is not the only one who has been punished.

He leaves the white room feeling exhausted. Visits have this effect on him. It's getting more and more difficult to face his friends as time passes, and Keith has a vague, unformed sense of panic lodged somewhere in his gut that he will not be able to rejoin the outside world at all when the time comes. Perhaps, strange and unpleasant as it is in Mortonlake Prison, it would be easier to remain here for ever than to begin life again, to reforge those friendships and connections outside. It frightens him that he feels this way – it is not rational, not controlled. He still has six months to serve, and feels sure that these feelings of separation will have become unmanageable by the time he is released. And what will he do with himself, anyway? The civil service will not have him back, not after the furore surrounding the messy details of his case. Not after the gutter press, in an evangelical purge of those in public places, claimed it was a 'Hot-bed of Homos' on account of it.

Keith returns to his quiet cell and flings himself down on his bed, freshly indignant at the gross injustice done him. It is something which has grown no easier to bear with the passage of time. He feels as angry, powerless and bitter about his sentence now as he did the day he received it. His mother, in moments of emotional crisis, has always resorted to the old cliché that time heals, but she has never been thrown unjustly into prison for a victimless crime – a crime which should not be in the statute books at all. There are some wounds which even time cannot salve, Keith reflects as he punches his pillow in a renewed outburst of fury. Exhausted, he stares up at the low, cracked ceiling, and through clenched teeth moans the eternal question into the musty air above him: "How did this happen?"

*****

It begins in the gloom of his bedroom, as he lies contemplating the ceiling, feeling broken and abandoned. Nick has left him. No! Nick has robbed him, betrayed him, ***then*** *left him. There is an enormous difference. For the first time Keith recognises that he is suspended in a cycle of abuse; that his relationships always follow a pattern, and that the pattern is destined to repeat itself time and again unless he breaks it. The Bookends have been telling him as much for years, but only now does it make proper sense to him. And the power to change it all is, quite literally, to hand. A moulded black plastic Mercury telephone, which sits not two feet from his unquiet head, can redeem his sense of self-worth, can heal his blighted love life. Slowly, but with the precision of one* whose mind is already quite made up, Keith lifts the receiver and phones the police to report the theft.

Two hours later, Keith is sitting in an austere interview room at the Stubbington police station. He has been given a plastic cup of tasteless coffee. Wary after his first scalding sip, which burnt him, he cradles the cup in his hands, waiting for it to cool. On reflex, he runs his tongue over the rough burnt patch on the roof of his mouth, which still hurts.

The interviewing officer is sympathetic, and tells Keith that he's been burgled in the past himself, that it's a rotten thing to happen; that he's sorry to say it, but – what with funding being so tight these days – domestic burglary is placed fairly low down on the priority list and Keith shouldn't hold any expectation of the villain or villains ever being apprehended.

Keith mentions that he knows, or rather thinks he knows, who the culprit is. There were two of them, in fact. Actually, he adds, speaking too fast and correcting himself, he doesn't know both of them. Just one. The ringleader. He's certain the other boy was a mere lackey. But he definitely knows who did it. Then, after this outburst, he retreats behind his cup of coffee, sipping at it with careful lips.

The interviewing officer suddenly becomes more interested. This is unusual, not a regular burglary after all. There is a subtext. He asks Keith how he can be sure who the villain is, and notices the silence immediately after the question, the thoughtful expression which has settled on the face of the punter. He discards the interview form that he was about to complete and rests his forearms on the table top, leaning forward a little. It has been such a dull day. Perhaps this will prove diverting.

Keith tells the officer that his neighbour witnessed the theft, could identify the young man in question if necessary.

The officer wonders why, in that case, Keith's neighbour didn't report the theft herself?

Keith explains that, at the time, she didn't realise a theft was taking place.

The officer points out that this would be obvious, surely? A pair of strangers walking out of the house next door with arms full of electrical goods is rather suspicious, wouldn't he agree?

Keith then explains that the neighbour knows the offender

slightly, because he has been living with Keith for the past six months, and therefore did not seem suspicious at the time.

The officer relaxes, disappointed. Now the subtext is all too clear. Domestic trouble. Lover-Walks-Out-With-Stereo-Equipment. He'll probably be back in a week. The officer has seen it all before, and it's not worth the paperwork. With a degree of tact, he asks Keith if the departed young man is likely to return, and adds that in his experience of such cases there is little point in filing charges. He lowers his eyes to the table top, where the index finger of his right hand is lightly tapping the stained pine.

Keith informs him that this is the last in a series of thefts, and insists that a proper investigation should take place. And yes, he wants to press charges. His neighbour has already agreed to make a statement, he adds. He takes a swig of his coffee, which has cooled rapidly in the small chilly room, and they proceed to complete an incident form. The officer makes slow, weary pen strokes as Keith supplies him with the relevant information, which makes him feel as if he's trapped in a Kafka play.

They are both as surprised as each other when, much later on, they discover that Keith only knows Nick's first name, and more surprised still to discover that Keith has no idea where he came from, or where he might have gone. At this, the officer arches a cynical eyebrow, his Parker poised in mid air above the form, and suggests that Keith has been raising a cuckoo.

Nothing happens for several weeks, and Keith tries to readjust to his new, solitary existence. To his surprise, he feels as though a burden has been lifted from him, rather than the familiar sensation of someone having ripped his innards away, as is usually the case when left by lovers. His friends remark upon the turn of events with vague astonishment, adding that the two of them had seemed such a good couple in the end.

One day Keith's neighbour, Mrs Pugh, is invited to an identification parade at a police station in Portsmouth. Keith takes the morning off work to drive her there, and afterwards she tells him that his young man was amongst the suspects in the line up. She says she hopes she's done the right thing to identify him.

Keith moves his left hand from the gear stick, where it has been resting as they drive homeward, absorbing the gentle vibrations of the engine, and pats Mrs Pugh's frail, papery hands, which lie in her lap. He tells her she has done exactly the right thing. Although he does not feel it himself. He is simply regurgitating what everyone around him has been telling him for the last two months: That he is doing the Right Thing. He hasn't told The Bookends, or Simon, that he feels, unaccountably, like an appalling traitor. Neither does he tell Mrs Pugh. He doesn't need to. He can tell she feels the same.

Two evenings later Keith receives a phone call from a man with a heavy, slurring voice. He says the police have been round, snooping about and asking questions. The voice continues in this vein for some time, despite Keith's request for it to identify itself. Then it abruptly stops – the tirade severed in mid-sentence.

Four days later the man rings again, whilst Keith is cooking his supper. He tells Keith that Nick has told him everything: how Keith kidnapped him, forced him to go and live with him; how Keith used to creep into Nick's room every night and bugger him despite his pleas for mercy; how he threatened Nick with the heavy mob if he ever breathed a word of it. He rounds off by calling him a filthy pervert.

Keith is astonished and leans against the kitchen wall for support. The beans he has been preparing for his evening meal are forgotten as they bubble and spit on the gas ring. Smoke begins to rise from his untended cutlets beneath the grill. At last he summons his tongue into action and demands to know who he's talking to, and is further astonished to hear the familiar, yet now so unfamiliar, voice of Nick suddenly at the other end of the line.

Keith stands in the kitchen doorway, transfixed by the wreathes of smoke which now curl up towards the ceiling like an acrid mist, as he listens in disbelief to Nick's demand that Keith drop all charges against him. Nick's voice is shaky, as if troubled by the ghost of recent tears.

Keith, now roused into genuine anger, asks in a loud voice why on earth he might want to do that?

Nick tells him that if not, he may be forced to bring charges of his own. He reminds Keith that he is only sixteen after all, and that what Keith has done to him is still very much against the law; that there are stiff sentences for predatory older men who prey on young boys.

Furious, Keith screams into the tiny mouthpiece that blackmail is also an offence, and hurls the phone back into its cradle with such force that it wrenches free of its wall fastenings and drops to the floor like something murdered. He stares at the plastic apparatus at his feet in abject horror as the smoke alarm on the kitchen ceiling lets out a piercing, modulated shriek. With a lunge, he retrieves his obliterated cutlets from beneath the grill and slings them into the red flip top bin in the corner, staring down at them as they nestle amongst the debris of other meals – empty cans, vegetable peelings, the unnecessarily bulky packaging of recently consumed convenience foods. In the background the smoke alarm continues to wail, a Cassandra shrieking her warning of impending doom. He'd had no idea that Nick was only sixteen.

Eleven days after that phone call, Keith receives a letter from the police which informs him that, due to a counter claim of indecent assault from Mr Nicholas Marley, which throws into question the validity of his own allegations against Mr Marley, his case has been suspended. Furthermore, investigations will be carried out to ascertain the validity of Mr Marley's allegations against him.

Keith is distraught at this terrible news, hardly able to take in the words, which are printed plainly in thick black letters on expensive paper that crackles between his thumb and forefinger. He drives to work cocooned in numb shock, heedless of the traffic. His mind is elsewhere, concocting dark and unpleasant futures. Later that morning, still reeling, he phones Simon from his constricting office. He has done nothing since his arrival at eight-fifty. He has remained slumped in his chair, immobile, staring miserably at his desk top for more than two hours, wreathed in an anxiety so acute it hurts his stomach.

Simon listens without comment as Keith proceeds to tell him the whole story, without varnish and, remarkably, without self-pity. He is too stunned at present to register this emotion. It will slip into his consciousness, like an insistent needle, much later.

When the tale is told Simon informs him, in a smooth, calm voice, that he would be happy to defend him in court. Unfortunately, he explains, this means he will be unable to testify as a character witness himself, either for Keith or Nick. But The Bookends can be called separately for this purpose, so nothing is really lost.

Keith, unfamiliar with the niceties of the law, is soothed by the authority and genuine concern in Simon's voice, and trusts his judgement. Besides, he would prefer to have Simon, a friend, defend him rather than a stranger, however well recommended.

Events quicken their pace. The local paper runs a front page story on Keith's involvement 'with an innocent teenager', which is taken up by a salacious tabloid two days later. By now the story has become more sinister, the tabloid version screaming revenge on behalf of the 'Youth Cruelly Raped By Wicked Pervert'. No one seems interested in his side of the story. For three terrible days, Keith finds himself besieged by seedy men with telescopic lenses wherever he turns. They lie in wait outside his house and outside his place of work, slouched low in the driver's seat of their cars, eager fingers ready to press the cruel shutter. On the fourth day the Senior Principal requests an interview with him.

The Senior Principal is a large, embarrassed man, who shifts in his seat as if the tenor of the conversation causes him physical pain. His eyes rove the unadorned walls of his office throughout the interview without once resting on Keith. Keith, by contrast, is on a high from all the stress, the incredible pressure from all sides. He feels focused and direct, winnowed by the scorching wind of blame which is currently tearing through his life, and finds it easy to resign, which he does eloquently and without ceremony.

The Senior Principal becomes more relaxed at this, telling Keith he's sorry to see him go, but the press have got the scent of blood in their nostrils; that they've begun to point awkward fingers in all directions. He's sure Keith understands; he doesn't like the whole business any more than Keith.

At this Keith laughs, loudly and quite openly, before walking out of the building for the last time, towards an unknowable future. As he steps into the light outside, a part of him is honestly relieved to be leaving these unfriendly corridors, together with the whisperings and furtive glances to which he has been subjected over the last weeks. No one has dared speak openly to him for fear of contamination, especially his so-called gay brothers and sisters. He has become a pariah, and the whole thing makes him sick.

During this period, Simon and The Bookends prove the most loyal of friends, always calling in on the pretext of some errand or other, to keep an eye on him. He sees through the pretence, and they know he does, but nobody says anything about it. Keith can see the concern which has settled in their faces and is greatly touched by it. Simon is particularly affected, it seems.

And then the nightmare proper begins, the trial – which exceeds all theatrical expectation, outdoing every court-room drama Keith has ever seen on television. It takes place in a large, wood-panelled room which reminds Keith of the inside of a cigar box, peopled by black-clad figures whose archaic robes flap like raven's wings as they turn this way and that to deliver their remarks. To one side sit the jury, whose implacable eyes hide a thousand prejudices: doe-like women and wide faced men whose gazes are periodically turned on him, idly, in the same casual manner that they might glance over their pie and chips at a tv documentary about the famine in Africa. The public gallery is full, teeming with those eager to hear the juicy story, highlighting the absurd, brief notoriety which has been foisted on him. He feels as if he is taking part in some grotesque pantomime, where the 'oh yes he did' and the 'oh no he didn't' will, crazily, determine his future. Constantly, he has to fight the urge to vomit from fear.

From where he stands, in the box reserved for the accused, flanked by two police officers, Keith can see just four familiar faces: Simon, whose confident smile does little to quell his somersaulting stomach, despite his lawyer's air of passive authority; his parents, who sit grey and rigid, as if hewn from granite; and Nick. The presence of his parents confuses him. Should he feel grateful, or ashamed? The faces he most longs to see are those of The Bookends, but they are not here. As witnesses they are excluded from the court room, and must wait to be called. He thinks of them now, nervous, huddled together in an austere box-like room, and is grateful beyond words for their love.

Hardest of all to bear is the sight of Nick, who will later stand in the witness box to testify against him, distorting the truth, reinventing it. From the moment Keith catches sight of him, by accident, he knows he is lost. Nick has arrived in court looking impossibly young, and sits between two adults that Keith presumes to be his parents – a bloated woman Keith's own age and an older, angular man who looks Portuguese. Nick is motionless, staring directly ahead, seeing nothing. The spiky, *dirty-blond hair has been tamed with a light oil and is neatly combed across his head, parted on the left. He has shaved closely, his cheeks fresh-looking, and wears a white shirt with a blue striped tie, topped off with a black blazer bearing an insignia on the breast pocket in gold and maroon braid. All this conspires to make him look vulnerable – a mere schoolboy. The effect is devastating, and Keith knows that no one here will believe in the other Nick, the hard, seductive, adult Nick, who inveigled himself into Keith's life and then his bed. Keith watches the boy's jaw tighten as his Portuguese father says something to him, then lowers his eyes. He would like to believe in god now. Not in order to be saved so much as to have something to pray to – that act of impassioned hope, that sense of doing **something**.*

And the ordeal becomes more unbearable with each passing moment, each phase of the ritual more excruciating than that which preceded it. As Nick finally takes the witness box and spouts his unbalanced 'truths', Keith finds he must occupy himself with pain, to suppress the urge to leap up and scream denials, or to point accusing fingers. So he curls his hands into fists, pushing his strong nails into the fleshy pads of his palms, and chews the inside of his cheek – actually biting off tiny lumps of tissue which he swallows in a warm wash of blood – as the lies, Nick's re-arrangement of the facts, continues unabated. His performance is near perfect, a mixture of confusion and vulnerability, his voice faltering for effect at difficult moments. From time to time Nick's smug lawyer smiles a sad, compassionate smile, then turns to the impassive jury who look on with distaste, believing everything.

Then Simon stands, unhurried, shuffles some papers which lie scattered on the small desk before him, and turns his eyes toward Nick. It helps that he has seen Nick in his true state, at dinner with Keith, but even he finds it hard to impose the real truth over the convincing schoolboy disguise he sees before him now. He knows the jury have had no such advantage, and may not be persuaded to believe it, but hopes the real facts will speak more powerfully than the clever costume the boy is wearing. Briefly, Simon wishes he could testify, could tell the jury just how sexual and adult Nick can appear when out of lamb's clothing. But The Bookends will have to do it for him.

First, Simon makes Nick tell his story: how Keith would come into his room every night and, being so much stronger than himself – a bodybuilder in fact – hold him down, his face pressed into the pillows until he could barely breathe, and make him submit to sex against his will. It is a word-for-word reproduction of the monologue Nick delivered earlier for his own lawyer, clearly learned by heart and recited again now for the benefit of the jury. Simon hopes this is not lost on them. As a lawyer, he knows a learnt answer means fear – fear of having to deviate from one version of the facts, in case flaws and inaccuracies appear. Immediately Nick has finished, Simon delivers the court a potted history of how Nick came to be living with Keith – how he turned up on the doorstep one night, and subsequently stayed for several months – then dares Nick to deny it. He doesn't. Simon then asks Nick why, if he was being abused in this terrible way, he didn't leave, run away one day whilst Keith was at work?

Nick says Keith threatened him with the heavy mob if he ever left, or breathed a word of it.

Simon, with a cool flip of a sheet of paper, to which he pretends to refer, then tells Nick that it is on police record that Keith neither knew where Nick came from, where he went after he left, or even what his second name was. It is impossible, Simon argues, for Keith to have followed up any such threats, and Nick knows it. The reason Nick did not leave Keith, Simon suggests, was because no abuse was taking place. In fact, he and Keith were having a successful relationship, and had been for many months. Nick is now denying this for some unfathomable reasons of his own, and has brought this action against Keith merely to deflect the original allegations of theft against himself.

Nick says nothing to this, and for the first time hangs his head. The jury become more animated. Nick's parents exchange astonished looks, his mother phlegmatic, his father dark and furious, brows pulled into a disturbed frown. He spits into his hand like a pagan warding off the unlucky spirit of a solitary magpie.

Nick is replaced in the witness box by Keith, who then tells the unvarnished tale from beginning to end with care, and attention to detail. He clings to the shiny chrome handrail which runs across the front of the box as he speaks, is surprised at the coolness of it, except for two warm patches where Nick's desperate hands *have also clutched. His voice is low and husky, his throat dry. From time to time, he sips from a glass of water which he finds on a tiny shelf below the lip of the box, as he tells of his relationship with Nick, of his growing affection, and the pain he felt each time he discovered one of Nick's thefts. Then he tells them of his decision to do and say nothing about it; of his decision to cure Nick with love. And he tells them of the sex – the gentle, consensual sex with a man who knew what he wanted from Keith's body. Keith realises that two small tears have slid down his cheeks during the telling of his story, and, looking round the room at the faces of the jury, his parents, and Simon, he dares to hope. His account is so obviously true that all present are moved. He knows they believe him.*

The Bookends, in turn, tell their story of the dinner party when they first met Nick, stressing the affection Nick showed towards Keith on that occasion, and his adult appearance. Derek testifies first. Then Bob repeats the story, adding that he spoke to Nick before this, on the phone; that he seemed strange, sounded aggressive, would not let him talk to Keith.

Simon is no longer concerned that he cannot testify – The Bookends have done well – and he sits back down, quietly confident, once the testimony is over.

But the judge, a desiccated, pallid man of middle age, soon delivers a swift and killing blow to the burgeoning optimism which has risen around the court room. In summing up, he suggests to the jury that there may indeed be reasonable doubt as to the charge of sexual assault, but points out that there can be no doubt that sexual acts have indeed taken place, as admitted by both parties. He remarks that this second charge – buggery of a minor – is a grave one, which must be considered carefully. The jury then retire, and return swiftly, the verdict unanimously reached.

Keith stands as the judge turns to him and declares that he has been found guilty of the charge of buggery and indecent assault brought against him, and that punishment for this crime carries a maximum sentence of seven years in prison. But, he adds, arching his right eyebrow to demonstrate his considerable leniency, given the mitigating circumstances he will sentence Keith to a shorter term. Three years. He will serve three years in prison for his crime. Then, the terrible pronouncement made, his mouth shuts like a trap, his lower jaw snapping upwards in a jerky motion resembling that of a ventriloquist's dummy.

And this is the last image which burns into Keith's brain: the sinister, slit-like mouth of the judge, with his wooden, puppet lips pressed tightly together, having unalterably sealed his fate for the next three years.

❊ ❊ ❊ ❊ ❊

Keith's breathing has become rapid and shallow, as it always does when he dwells on this subject. A familiar knot of anxiety, his uneasy bedfellow over the last two and a half years, squeezes his stomach like an acid fist as he shuts his eyes, trying to blot out the stark reality of his austere surroundings: the staring white ceiling and its bare bulb, the shiny chip-proof bricks, the basin, the slop bucket beneath it, and the tiny far-up window which lets in so little light. The coarse blanket which covers his bed has rubbed a raw patch at the back of his neck whilst he has been lying here, torturing himself with memories. Fresh tears well up behind his tightly closed eyelids as he tries to blot that out too. Then his chest tightens and an involuntary shuddering sigh escapes from his mouth. Utterly wretched, Keith rolls over on his stomach, burying his face in his cool, musty pillow, and feels that he has sunk as far as he can go.

Later, he drags himself up, swings his legs over the edge of the bed and moves to the wash basin, where he runs a small quantity of cold, yellowish water. It is the colour of very dilute urine, and Keith is suspicious of its purity. Nevertheless, he scoops it from the basin with cupped palms and splashes his hot cheeks with it, rubbing fiercely with his hands as if this action might expunge the memory, make it go away. In fact, he half succeeds. Or rather, his obsessive thoughts concerning the trial are replaced by further, different thoughts. Now he's activated his major obsession: his child.

Over the last two years, Keith has come to believe that Rebecca lied to him about her miscarriage, and his aimless mind has latched on to this like a limpet. Martin is not dead. He is a healthy two year old. Rebecca has fed him foul lies to throw him from the scent, to keep him away from his child. He is sure of it. For Keith, Martin is now the main focus of his life, the solitary illumination in his otherwise dark world.

    Keith moves from the basin and walks across his cell, thinking fondly of his son, and reaches for his diary. He keeps it on the single shelf in the small alcove in the corner, along with a biro, a bible (prison property, not his idea), and a small wooden sculpture he made in a woodwork class last year, now recruited as a paperweight. The diary is in fact a series of exercise books, their covers made of pale green sugar paper. He doesn't like these flimsy covers as much as the sturdy, almost shiny card he recalls from his own school days. He runs his fingers across the front of this, the second volume, and looks down at the large printed letters which take up the whole cover. He had intended to call it 'DIARY', 'JOURNAL', 'MORTONLAKE', or something of similar literary pretention, but somehow his hand had disobeyed, instead inscribing the word 'MARTIN'. His son. His boy.

    Keith takes the diary and the biro over to his bed and sits down. With peculiar reverence he opens the book and stares down at the grey envelope affixed to the inside of the front cover. It contains a letter from Rebecca, written more than four years ago, which marks the beginning of Martin. Keith slips his hand inside the envelope, pulls out the letter, and stares down at the familiar faded print. As is his ritual before writing in his diary, he re-reads the letter:

Dear Mr Lewis,
I am a member of the SIG, my name is Rebecca Kilbride, and I have seen your details on our files. I am interested in you as a father. Even writing this feels weird. Perhaps we could meet to discuss?
Yours,
Rebecca K. (01483 175654)

And then he closes his eyes, conjuring the face of the child he will never see. In his imagination, Martin looks almost Oriental, with enormous black eyes and thick black hair. Keith's hair. Martin's skin is dark, so he will not have his mother's problems with the sun. Keith holds the image in his mind with intense fondness, a fondness which he would not have believed himself capable of three years ago, imagining a strong resemblance to himself in the face of his son. Then he opens his eyes, replaces the letter in its envelope, turns to a fresh page somewhere near the back of the book, and begins to write.

CHAPTER NINETEEN

For the past few weeks, Monica has been awaiting the results of her finals with a kind of dull impatience. Essentially a formality (she has already been told, off the record, that she's won a First), she knows it will be a ticket into the media – journalism, publishing, a job in television as a translator – but none of these options fill her with purpose, as they require action on her part. She knows that none of these possible lives are the big IT she's been waiting for. One day, she is convinced, a prettily wrapped package which is her destiny will arrive on her doorstep, clearly marked MONICA, eclipsing her shapeless desires and silencing her family, who will have been baying at her heels for months, wanting to know what she's going to *do*. How can she explain to them that her future will find *her*, that she will recognise it when it appears and not before?

In the meantime she has returned home, in the absence of any better plan, and taken up her role as Daughter once again, proceeding from the point where she left off four years ago. It has been easy to slot back in, like picking up a long discarded piece of knitting in which the stitch is simple and the pattern familiar. Sometimes it seems that her years at college have never been, that they exist only in her imagination, experienced in some realistic, lucid dream. Jade, her only acquired friend from university, has told her of such things. Jade has projected her Astral body through walls, flying through the stratosphere to planes where people dream whole lives in a single night, and Monica would be willing to believe that this is what has happened to her, were her very knowledge of Jade not to disprove it. Perhaps, in fact, she is still only sixteen, and her life has not yet begun. Or better still, twelve, before she started bleeding.

Her existence at home is unstrenuous, undemanding, peaceful. She enjoys having the house to herself during the day, whilst her father picks at anonymous teeth and her mother feigns industry, flitting amongst her vacuous friends like a mindless butterfly. Monica seldom ventures outside, except to search the streets and gutters for Sign and Icons. She spends her days drifting from room to room, undisturbed, snacking on bowls of semi-dried fruit and double cream which she carries about with her as she perambulates the house, the lip of the bowl suspended only inches below her craving mouth the way the Chinese eat noodles. She has discovered that the fruit, in large doses, acts as a natural laxative, for which she is grateful. It's a much more pleasant way to exercise control over her little body than the handfuls of laxative pills to which she has grown accustomed whilst at college. She doesn't particularly like this new mode of evacuation, she prefers the emetic method, but since the acquisition of her new teeth, courtesy of her father three-and-a-half years ago, she has tried to limit herself to two heweys per week in an attempt to preserve her smile. Actually, she thinks she's read somewhere that porcelain is resistant to stomach acids. She could probably return to her regurgitative method with no worries.

Today, having experienced the vibrations of every room in the house from her morning tour, Monica stands in the back garden, shovelling dried fruit down her throat from a large flower-patterned bowl, allowing the heat of the early summer sun to percolate her black clothing. The silver identity bracelet which her father gave her last birthday rattles against the side of her bowl as she spoons the food into her mouth. She is thinking of nothing in particular, finds the view of the hill rising in bright beauty before her uninspiring. The clinking of her identity bracelet, the only sound in the otherwise still morning, begins to annoy her, and she raises her arm above her head to shake it further up her forearm, where it wedges against the sleeve of her roll-neck and is silenced. Two drops of cream drip from her spoon and into her newly beaded hair as she does this. She doesn't bother to wipe them off.

Monica feels the sun on her pale face, a good feeling, and stares up into the shadowy branches of the cedar tree which looms at the far end of the garden. The tree has dark power, a kind of magnetism, and in some way Monica feels that it has dominated her whole life. It seems to have remained a constant size throughout time, neither losing branches in the frequent gales which whip across the North Downs, nor growing new ones. Lately, she has been spending many hours in this tree, the tree of her childhood. Two weeks ago she rediscovered the crook she used to settle in as a child, some twenty feet off the ground, where the trunk separates into three large branches, creating a natural seat large enough to sit in. She had not visited the spot for fourteen years, not since the ghost of Darren's falling body burned itself into her mind, but now she feels able to. In fact, she likes it there.

She used to call this secret domain The House. As a child she had sometimes explored still higher, climbing first one, then another, then the last of the three trunks which grew on up from The House, finding other child-sized nooks in which to hide herself. As she chews her last mouthful of prune and apricot, Monica recalls her huge excitement on one occasion as she placed her sandalled foot on the topmost branch, which bent even under her inconsiderable weight, and, clutching at other fronded branches with palms sticky with resin, pushed her head out through the very top of the tree and felt, literally, on top of the world. Higher even than the horrid, bricky cathedral, whose golden top winked at her from across the city.

Her more recent arboreal adventures have led her only as far up as The House; her older, larger body feels unsafe higher than this. Here she has read French classics, in the original; works by Aleister Crowley, and other, more interesting works *about* him (she is amused, for example, that such a man was born in a place as vacuous as Leamington Spa); books on self-hypnosis, with accompanying cassette tapes; and others about psychometry, telekinesis, and ley lines. She has studied all these things in the strange twilight gloom of her cedar palace, idly fingering the thick strands of her wooden-beaded hair, which clatter against one another as she does so. She loves this place almost as much as she loves her bedroom, enjoying its unnatural coolness, hidden as it is from the direct rays of the sun. If only she could have her Icons with her in The House, it would be perfect.

Mesmerised by the green-black depths of the tree before her, Monica is reminded of the night, now four years ago, when she crept into the garden and begged the stars by the power of the One Eleven to rescue her from university, from her drab life. The memory comes to her whole, as if projected on to a spacey film screen in her head. She also remembers that nothing had appeared to happen at the time, her life had trickled on as before, but she takes this vivid memory – strangely in colour, although it had actually happened at night – as a sign that at last the hour has come. Propelled by a sudden urge to visit her hideaway, she bends down to place her bowl of fruit, now empty, on the lawn beside her. Then she steps up to the tree and places her hands on the bole, enjoying its rough texture against her skin as she presses her cheek to it. She looks up at the unblemished trunk – no branches sprout for the first eight feet – and grabs at a length of rope which dangles from the lowest branch. The rope is old, has taken on the colouring of the tree. There is a large knot tied at the end of it. Even now, as an adult, Monica can barely reach up to it. As a child she had to jump.

She clambers towards the safety of the lowest branches by slowly advancing up the rope, hand over hand, with her feet walking up the trunk, and wonders which father slung this rope around this branch, and for what child? What was he or she like? Or was the father Lenny? and is the child herself?

Above the first branch, which is so thick Monica can't get her arms around it, other branches are arranged at convenient intervals. For an adult, the climb is as easy as the scaling of a ladder, and less exposed, and she is soon ensconced in her private shady tree-womb, her back against the thickest of the three trunks which surround her, her knees drawn up to her chest. A fleck of bark has lodged in her left eye, making it water, but otherwise she has arrived without incident and, once her breathing has returned to normal, she gets down to the business of the morning.

Monica pulls at the zip of a small canvas pouch which dangles from a coloured braid around her neck – she wears the pouch at all times – and draws out a diminutive red biro (which she found on the pavement outside the bookmakers in the High Street), and her Book of Signs. The book, a small A5 hardback note pad, contains all the potent Signs, both good and bad, which she has encountered of late. In her private code she has noted down all the details of these Signs, together with the dates of the sightings: A succession of lumpen, heavy stools – all week; a gathering of seven magpies – May 29th; two pennies – no dates; a white feather which alighted on her fake-fur jacket – June 2nd; six pieces of thistle-down, of which she managed to catch four – June 2nd; two falling leaves, unfortunately diseased – June 6th; three rabbits, on separate occasions. No dates; a dead river-rat – June 9th.

Chewing on the plastic end of her biro, now dented with tooth marks, she considers these Signs. Something is certainly about to happen, but it seems the meanings are confused. The rat and the diseased leaves clearly portend failure, malpractice and bad endings, as do her recent misshapen stools – but the feather (such an excellent sign) and the rabbits suggest new projects which are well-starred. Monica is perplexed, until she realises her mistake. She hasn't taken the pennies into account! Clearly the pennies, her divinatory guide at all times, are telling her that the Signs speak of *two separate* events. Both loom large in her life, and one will end well, the other badly. Unfortunately there is no clue as to the nature of either event, but this is typical of all her divination at the moment, it's all clouded by the negative influence of Pluto, which is in retrograde.

Monica decides to clarify the meanings of these Signs further, and fishes out a small photo of the Strong Goddess, which she cradles in her left hand whilst reciting the Mantra of Coincidence for seven minutes. Then she dips her hand back into her canvas pouch, feels with her fingers for one of her gritty Rune-stones, which are cold to the touch, and withdraws Othila, the Rune of Radical

Separation. Reverentially, she lays the rune on her thigh, and contemplates its meaning, her beaded fringe clattering against her forehead as she bends her head in thought.

Othila, part of the Cycle of Initiation, is like the Lightning-Struck Tower from the Tarot, and calls for a laying down of the old ways for a new beginning, in order to claim rightful destiny. This is truly exciting and, like the dead rat, portends something momentous. *It's starting, Em, I'm going to do something, like you did. I can feel it,* she murmurs, and the breeze smudges the words away as soon as they leave her lips. The lethargy which has clung to her for weeks melts away like mist rising from her soul.

Monica is convinced that her life to date has been a preparation for what Othila is now predicting, even if the events themselves have not been revealed to her, and her mood soars. The element of bad endings does not deter her, as it does not directly mean bad *for her.* No, whatever it is will set her apart from others, will give her her heart's desire! It will make her special! The combination of the Signs and the Rune put it beyond doubt.

Monica collects up her things and slides down from the tree, then dusts herself off, retrieves her bowl from the lawn, and goes back inside the house. She is full of purpose. She wants to capture today forever, and decides that a photo is called for. It is only two weeks since her last four poses (she has gone to a booth to take photos of herself on the first day of every month, without fail, clearly marking the date of each on the back, since her thirteenth birthday), but this, she feels, is a special occasion. She wants to see her soul captured beneath the emulsion, wants to be able to read the marks of this day in her photographed face, in years to come. She'll have it enlarged, displayed prominently on the wall for all to admire. Everyone will marvel at how *obvious* it was, even then, that she was going to be famous.

Monica walks slowly through half-empty streets, and makes her way to the Photo-Me in the newly erected, posh shopping precinct off the High Street, as the one at the station has been vandalised by thickies with DMs, who have no respect for the miracle of photo-sensitive paper. She doesn't like this precinct, it's even worse than the other one at the bottom of town. Here, the shops are even more crowded with disgusting Lipos cooing over off-the-peg C&A frocks in size eighteen, the music even more eerie, and the whole thing makes her feel as if she's on a spacecraft headed for Jupiter.

As she coasts through the temperature-controlled mall, she observes various forms of manic behaviour which interest her: women who constantly check their handbags to make certain they're securely fastened, looking down again and again, as if they expect to be the victim of some invisible bag thief; people who look for their reflection in every shop front they pass, their eyes glued to themselves rather than the goods displayed within; elderly ladies with fluttering mouths, evidently engaged in some internal dialogue, usually accompanied by a faint whiff of urine.

As Monica reaches the Photo-Me booth, she sees two uniformed attendants approach a middle-aged crustie wrapped in Oxfam rejects, bin-liners and string, who has the audacity to be eating a sandwich in an area clearly marked as a No Food zone. They each take an elbow and escort the crustie to the nearest exit, oblivious to his articulate remarks concerning the innocence of sandwich eating in public places. With a slow, clattering flick of her bead-adorned head, Monica reflects that uniforms make people lose their sense of logic.

Slipping into the unearthly glow of the booth, she decides on a muted background and pulls the orange curtain aside, drawing the grey one across in its place. With a practised glance, she calculates that the stool is set at exactly the right height – someone with her body length has recently used the booth, or else a taller person has been rewarded with a disappointing photo of themselves minus the top of their head. (Monica calls these Egg-heads, resembling as they do the decapitated stumps of boiled eggs, and has found some excellent examples over the years, dropped casually to the ground by persons too embarrassed to use them for their passport, rail, or ID cards.)

Before inserting her money into the waiting vertical slit, Monica dons the red beret she has brought with her for the photos, and piles her heavy fringe on top of it, where it sits in an appealing necklace tangle. Then she makes the sign of the Triangle and concentrates on her future, at last pushing the chubby pound coins into the machine, which gulps them down like a hungry bird. She gives the lens both profiles and two head-ons, smiling and unsmiling, then steps outside to await the results, which will emerge in a few minutes like a cardboard tongue. Outside in the mall, subjected to the scrutiny of all those brain-dead Guildford ladies, she feels compelled to remove her beret. She feels their hate stares bouncing against the back of her head, and reflects them back at their perpetrators using techniques she has learnt from her books.

The photos are good today, the emulsion unblemished. Monica stares down at herself and is delighted at her angular cheek bones, her translucent skin, and the dark bruised circles around her eyes. They conspire to make her look other-worldly, and powerful. She looks like a magician. Her face is androgynous, as is her torso, still unencumbered by discernable breasts, and this pleases her also. Once the photos are properly dry, Monica folds them with great care, along the border between the second and third pictures, and tucks them inside her pouch, where she can feel them resting against her heart.

She meanders home at her usual dawdling pace, taking random turns to either right or left as the fancy takes her, and soon finds herself in the street where her father works. She studies her watch and decides that she will pay him a surprise visit – at lunch time he is unlikely to be treating a patient unless there is an emergency of some kind. As she walks, she runs her fingers along the black painted railings which separate the pavement from the parkland beyond, collecting old city dust on her fingertips – the kind that doesn't come off right away with soap and water. The park houses a cricket ground, an athletics track, and nearest to the railings a small play area for young children, dotted with colourful slides, swings, roundabouts, and strange, unrecognisable creatures which bounce up and down on giant springs. The play area is deserted and looks eerie, like something post-nuclear, the last remnants of civilization after the final plague has ripped the life out of everyone on Earth.

Arriving at the surgery, Monica steps into the reception room and approaches the desk. It's the first time she's ever been here when anyone else is around, during normal hours. On the two occasions in the last four years that she's let Lenny look at her teeth, he's done it after hours, whilst on call. "Is my father in?" she asks the latent Lipo at the reception desk, plastering on her best daughterly smile, the more easily to display her father's handiwork.

Wendy looks up from her magazine, sandwich poised inches from her lips. "I don't know, I'll check for you," she replies, finding it hard to place the gaunt teenager standing in front of her. She is sure Mr Jeffries' daughter has been to university, yet this child looks far too young for that. Perhaps it's another one she doesn't know about. As she buzzes through to Lenny's surgery she reminds herself to ask Diane, who knows Mr Jeffries much better than she does.

"Nobody there, I'm afraid," says Wendy, after several buzzes have gone unanswered. "Can I take a message?"

"Oh, don't bother. I was just passing, and I . . ." She trails off as a handsome, severe-looking man enters the room from a small corridor on the left. He's older than her father, slighter, and has a confused aura – unusual in one of his age.

"So you're Lenny's brilliant daughter," he begins without introducing himself, flashing on a druggy, dislocated smile. Monica doesn't like his tone. "I must say, you take after your mother," he adds.

Monica is horrified. She would rather tear the flesh from her face with her crimson nails than bear a passing resemblance to her mother, who everyone says is so beautiful. Her fake-zeccy mother whom she never sees, always so busy with her cliquey charity meetings and dinners. Anyone would think it was a real job. "I think I'm much more like dad," she replies, her voice pleading with them to agree.

"You've certainly got his eyes," Wendy concedes.

Monica gives her a weak, thin-lipped smile – her old smile, the one before she got her new teeth. "Thanks. Will you tell him I called? And tell him not to get excited – I haven't had the results of my finals, or anything."

"Okay."

And Monica turns, begins to leave the surgery. But before she reaches the door, her father's partner (she assumes) calls her back. Hearing him use her name is weird, and makes her feel strange and uncomfortable. "Yes?" she says, turning back to the man, whose face is now wearing a gross smile.

"I want to give you something," he says. "Wait here a minute." And he disappears into his surgery, leaving Monica and Wendy to exchange baffled shrugs. A minute later he re-emerges with a small white envelope, which he proffers to Monica. "Give this to your father when he gets home," he says. "You can tell him it's from me."

"Why don't you give it to him yourself?" Monica asks, surprised, careful to keep her tone polite.

"I think it would be much more effective coming from you," he replies mysteriously, a salacious smirk playing on his lips. "Let's just say it's a surprise for your mother."

Monica realises that no further explanation is being offered and leaves the room, clutching the envelope in her hand, and walks back out into the street. As she turns towards the children's playground, she decides to recite extra healing prayers from now on to protect her father from this awful person, who, just by standing close to her, has made her want to run home and have a bath. Poor Lenny has to work with him every day! Briefly, she imagines how terrible it would be to be his patient, pinned beneath him in that chair, those fierce eyes staring down her throat.

Several mothers with small children have entered the playground since she passed before, making it seem normal again. Two of the children are seated in swings with little box seats, whilst their mothers stand behind them, gossiping with each other. A third mother stands alone, whilst her little boy rocks manically back and forth on a giant yellow duck which is, unfortunately, impervious to his desire for movement. The mother seems bored, is examining her nails, heedless of her son's mounting frustration.

Monica enters the playground via the self-closing wire gate, and folds herself into the slatted wooden bench which faces towards the various apparatuses. The envelope falls to her lap, forgotten, as she watches the children on their swings, their little legs kicking out and back. She remembers swings as being her favourite childhood pleasure, her desire to describe a complete circle – swinging right up over the bar and round again – intense. She never achieved it, seldom even got higher than the horizontal, but there were whispers at school that it was possible, and Monica spent her entire childhood trying.

And it is at this moment, as she watches these children swinging to and fro with such obvious delight, that she first has her idea. Strangely, it enters her head quite formed, seeping up from her unconscious perhaps, and fills her with excitement. This is the IT she has been waiting for all her life, the destiny which her Rune, Othila, has predicted. But the plan is complex and will need much preparation.

Smiling to herself, she lowers her head in a silent prayer of thanks, and sees the envelope in her lap. As she fiddles with her identity bracelet, still blank and unengraved almost a year after her father gave it to her, she stares at the envelope and is seized by the urge to open it. Then she notices that it's not stuck down in any case, the tongue is just folded into the body of it, so Monica pulls up the flap and draws out the letter inside. The first thing she sees is a colour photo nestling between the folds of the letter. It's a picture of a large, naked muscle-man with a tiny dog under each arm. He is staring directly into the camera. The accompanying letter, written in hurried capitals, reads:

Dear 'inexperienced',
My name is Lance and I'm writing in answer to your ad. in Time Out for a 'Friend'. I'm 6ft. 3ins, 52 inch chest, nine inches of meat. I work out regularly. I like to fuck and be fucked, am into yellow, occasional red. My hobbies are fitness and dog breeding. If you like my photo, send me one of yourself, and phone me (0181-342-2175).

Monica lets the letter drop back into her lap, surprised. She has always thought that her father was homosexual – and has been quite certain of it since she found the photos of him and Anthony – but she always assumed that Lenny was unaware of it himself, or at least aware only on some deep level. This letter, however, unless a silly prank of his partner's, seems to suggest otherwise. Intuitively, she feels the right course of action is to confront her father about it. Besides, he has to be told now for his own sake – his awful partner has obviously read the contents of the letter too, and may be planning a surprise of his own. What astonishes Monica most is that her father has been indiscreet enough to allow this letter to get into his partner's hands in the first place.

By five-thirty she's installed on her bench by the wall in the kitchen, waiting for her father to get in, praying that her mother won't be home until much later, as usual. Zoe would complicate everything. Monica is nervous, and drinks a mug of camomile tea to calm herself, made with fresh camomile from Pewley Down.

Her father comes home at six-ten, shutting the front door in his usual quiet way. In fact, everything about him is quiet, Monica realises. This fits in with her private image of Lenny in a way that Lance, the muscle-man, doesn't. Just thinking about Lance makes her wonder if she hasn't got this terribly wrong, that it really might be some slimy joke of her father's partner. Perhaps she's going to embarrass them both to extinction.

When he enters the kitchen Lenny adopts his standard routine, smiling hello as he steps over to the kettle. He fills it up and plugs it in without a word. Then, the ritual complete, he turns around to talk to her, leaning back against the work top. Monica used to wonder why he was always so desperate for a cup of tea when he came home, but now she's met his gross partner she's not surprised at all. She'd need a couple of vodkas.

"How was your day?" he asks, his new, thinner face smiling at her. "You do anything exciting?"

"Nothing much." As she shakes her head, to emphasize

the point, her head clatters. "I called in on you, actually," she adds, wishing to draw the conversation to its meatier content right away. No point in skating all around it for hours.

"Oh?" Lenny raises his eyebrows, cocks his head to one side. Then, trying to seem nonchalant, but failing to keep his voice under control: "Did you get your results?"

"No, nothing like that," Monica replies, smiling. "Didn't they tell you I called? I told them to tell you. And I told them to say that it wasn't about my finals."

"Fatal, I'm afraid. I never get messages," says her father, now busy with the kettle as he makes his tea. "So why did you call in?"

"No reason." Monica stares down at the smooth, pale table top on which her palms are spread. How to do this? "Look, I want to ask you something," she says in a thick voice. She does not look at her father, and keeps her eyes fixed on the backs of her hands. "Is this anything to do with you?" She pulls out the now battered white envelope and slides it down the table to where Lenny has perched with his tea.

Lenny stares at the envelope without touching it. He knows what it is without looking inside. It's the tell-tale hand-written number in the top left-hand corner, in a script he does not recognise, which gives it away. But where did Monica get it? Did it arrive late, separated from all the others by some fluke? "Where did this come from?" he asks at last, finding, contrary to his expectation, that he's relieved Monica knows. At last the mystery has been solved; it was surely she who wrote the poisonous note in his surgery. Much better this way. Perhaps he can persuade her not to tell his work colleagues. Unless that was the purpose of her visit today? A light sweat breaks out on his forehead at this thought, which he wipes away with the back of his hand. His monster daughter come to destroy him . . .

Monica turns to look at her frightened father, and smiles. "It's all right," she says, "I've known for a long time. Or thought I did. But this clinched it."

Lenny has covered his face with his hands, adopting an

attitude of despair. He is breathing noisily through his nose, snuffling, fighting against tears. "I'm so sorry," he stammers. "What must you think?"

"I don't think anything," she says, hushed. Then, in a firmer voice: "But I do wonder how you could have been stupid enough to let your greasy partner get hold of it." She indicates the envelope.

Lenny's head snaps up, eyes wet. "What do you mean?"

"That's where I got it from," Monica tells him. "He gave it to me today, when I came to see you. I think you should know that it was already open when I got it. He's read it."

"Oh god!" Lenny cries, and buries his head in his hands again.

Monica makes a fresh pot of tea, with cinnamon, and pours them both a cup. Her father has recovered somewhat by this time, and is reading Lance's letter when she returns to the table. He looks up at her as she places the mug in front of him.

"I don't even know what half of it means," he smiles.

"I can guess," Monica says as she sits down next to him. Then she launches into the questions: "So how long have you been gay?"

"Always," Lenny shrugs.

"Was Anthony your boyfriend?" Monica remembers the smiling pictures of the two of them. They seemed so happy.

"Anthony is normal," Lenny replies in a voice of stony resentment.

"So are you," says Monica, placing her thin hand on her father's larger, browner one, and stroking it. They sit this way, silent, for some moments. "But you loved him?"

"Yes." Lenny's voice is a whisper. He's never talked to anyone like this before, not even Mostyn. How strange that he's now unburdening himself to his fragile daughter. But it feels good. He lifts his free hand and presses it on top of Monica's, sandwiching it. "Yes, I loved him," he repeats.

"And what about Zoe?" Monica has always called her mother Zoe, never mum. It's part of the distance between them, or at least the measure of it. "Did you ever love her? I won't tell her, I promise."

"She knows," her father says, his eyes tired. "Before we were married, she knew."

"So why did you do it? Get married, I mean. Was it me? Was she pregnant with me?" Monica's eyes are wide with wonder.

"No," Lenny says, and stares into his tea. "It wasn't you."

"Why, then?"

Lenny shrugs. How can he speak of a different time, a more repressed time; of self-hatred so strong it's like a poison; of a desire to conform so great that it makes you willing to compromise your soul for ever; of a delusion that a life of lies is nobler, more acceptable, than a life of difficult truth? "She asked me to," he answers simply.

Monica takes this in, then leans across and kisses her father's wet cheeks. "Thank you for telling me," she says, meaning it. "I've always been on your side. I hope you know that."

"How extraordinary. I always thought you hated me," says Lenny in wonder.

"There's enough hate in this house without me adding to it," Monica replies.

She goes on up to her bedroom without eating dinner, her head full of thoughts. So her mother has known about Lenny all along! Why, then, is she so hostile? Rather than draw closer to understanding her mother through this revelation, she feels the chasm between them widening by the second. Then the realisation hits her: Zoe has dedicated her life to punishing Lenny for being homosexual. Such a futile and vindictive endeavour. And what will happen to her poor father, now that his partner knows his secret? Bad things, she can tell.

As she thinks it all through, it becomes clear that her father's fate is one of the events predicted by the Signs earlier – the one with the negative outcome – and she recites heartfelt prayers of healing for him, sending him strength and love and harmony before an array of purple iridescent candles.

Later, switching to the Litany of Power, her thoughts return to the brilliant idea she had in the park during the afternoon. This is clearly the second event, the one destined for shining success, as predicted by Othila. The one that will change everything. *Oh, Strong Goddess, I feel my destiny calling. I shall emulate you and continue your strange work,* she chants as she fiddles with her fringe and smiles at the Holy Bird.

Her devotions complete, she climbs into bed at last, with only the red pin pricks of two sticks of incense for illumination in the darkness, and lies awake imagining the future, impatient for it to begin. She's far too excited to sleep.

CHAPTER TWENTY

Another Sunday at Mortonlake and Keith, as usual, spends most of it alone in his cell, reading back over his book. The book he now calls 'MARTIN'. He's decided it's going to be a novel, a hybrid of autobiography and diary, but he has told himself this merely to justify the effort, pain and long hours he's put into it. He knows, rationally, that he has no skill as a writer, that the words do not cohere into a whole. He knows that what he is really doing is turning himself inside out and reflecting it on paper; that this book is, and shall always remain, only of interest to him.

The manuscript now fills three exercise books, neatly executed in a precise hand. It begins as a series of more or less random thoughts and feelings, fragments of lucidity, gradually coalescing into a kind of confessional diary as it proceeds. As he reads through the second volume, leaning back against the uneven brickwork, legs stretched out over the brown blanket which covers his bed, he is fascinated by its revelations. By the beginning of the third, the manuscript has evolved again, from diary into a series of open letters to his son. Letters revealing everything about himself; letters outlining his hopes for his child; lengthy tracts on the iniquity of the penal system, the breakdown of morality, his own loss of self-esteem. In short, the manuscript describes the grim journey of one who has fallen, in his own eyes, outside of society and into some inky depth which will leave him forever stained.

Keith stops reading and leans his head against the wall, eyes shut. He doesn't remember feeling half of the things these pages describe so forcefully. But what he does remember, and still feels acutely, is this obsession with the boy he has never seen, which rises almost palpably from every page. The boy and the book (somehow they have become fused into one in his mind) are now his passion, his *raison d'être*, his sole occupying thought for much of the time. Every night he agonizes over his exercise book, not able to sleep until he has captured in words the precise quintessence of his feelings for his son. Often he works far into the night, and sometimes, unable to articulate himself, he stares frantically at the blank page before him until morning. Lately, he has taken to carrying the book around with him, rolled into a scroll and squeezed into a pocket, forever afraid that someone might sneak into his cell and read it if he were to leave it unguarded for a moment. This would be unthinkable. Martin is his special secret.

Constantly, he tortures himself with visions, forces himself to play the awful game of What If? What is Martin doing now? What does Martin look like now? Does he, too, lie awake at night, conjuring the image of the one missing from his life? These thoughts are not pleasant, and whir perpetually in his brain, night and day, with unstoppable momentum. At times it gets so bad he entertains thoughts of going to the prison psychiatrist, once even found himself marching down the corridor to the medical office, but at the last moment, as his hand curled round the dull brass door handle, he thought better of it. He could not be sure that the information would not be passed on and used against him at a later date. So he is alone with his problem. A problem which, from time to time and for no reason at all, escalates to an excruciating plain of torment, like a cheese-wire tourniquet wrapped around his heart. A cheese-wire called Martin. And there is no end to this pain.

Disquieted by these thoughts, Keith drops the manuscript to the floor and lies face down on his bed, letting the silence press down all around him. He tries to calm himself with the thought that he has only to survive another six weeks at Mortonlake, and then he will be free. But this, too, makes him uneasy.

Later, after a bland evening meal of translucent goulash with mashed potatoes served on a moulded tray which doubles as a plate, Keith meanders through the communal area, adrift. Groups of men huddle together, playing cards, watching television, or muttering quietly to one another, all dressed alike in their drab prison uniform. It's a scene he's got used to over the years, bleak but not without security of a sort. He supposes some people, an outsider, might even consider it comfortable, cosy. But it isn't. Loss of freedom might be many things, but it is certainly neither comfortable nor cosy. A television set is no salve for the austerity, darkness and violence of this place. There are areas he dare not visit, where drugs are rumoured to abound, and serious criminals swap skills for future use. Areas where he, as a sex offender (and here, everyone mysteriously knows what everyone else is in for, even if, like Keith, you have told no one), is far from welcome. He has been subjected to verbal abuse on a regular basis, and the threat of physical harm has been ever-present. And this at Mortonlake, which, he has been reliably informed, is a 'soft' prison. He could easily have ended up somewhere far worse. Never again will he tolerate anyone who claims that prison is no punishment, a view usually espoused by those who have known only privilege. It is terrible. Terrible, frightening, and boring beyond measure.

Keith is proud of the way he has negotiated his way through these three years. He has gritted his teeth, kept his head well below the parapet, and hung on. At first, setting his sights on his eventual release had been too painful, it being too far ahead to seem either real or to offer any comfort, but recently it has proved a tremendous help. He has clung to the date, September 11th, with the tenacity of a man who is offered an outstretched hand as he hangs from the top of a tall building by his aching fingertips. Although sometimes he wonders why. The idea of returning to the bomb-shattered life he left outside these walls is not the rosiest of prospects. He doesn't even have a home to return to any more. That disappeared long ago, repossessed when he stopped paying the mortgage. Life will never be easy again, he reflects bitterly. But then, at least it won't be *here*.

He is deep in these thoughts when he feels a hand on his chest, palm outstretched, blocking his path. He looks up at the owner of the hand, into a face which has, at some point in the past, been ravaged by acne.

"If it isn't Keith Lewis!" says the man slowly. The voice matches the face.

Keith says nothing, now seeing three other men ranged

behind the one who's talking to him. He recognises two of them as hard cases, people he has been recommended to avoid, and feels uneasy as he registers that they are alone in the corridor. In his thoughtful wanderings he has strayed far from his cell.

"Keith Lewis. Otherwise known as The Child Fucker," says the man. "Now why do they call you that?" he muses, his smile melting into a pantomime of thoughtfulness. He turns to his friends who stand close behind him, smirking.

"Because he fucked a kid, Dave," offers the man standing at Dave's right elbow. He speaks slowly, giving each word equal weight, his voice filled with undisguised loathing. "That's why they call him The Child Fucker."

A dread cold creeps over Keith's body. This is dangerous. It feels unlike all previous verbal assaults. Somehow it's more calculated. Keith senses that something appalling is happening, but he can't decide what to do. Should he lash out? Should he turn and run? Or should he lash out, *then* turn and run? But these thoughts have barely formed in his mind when two of Dave's henchmen step over and grab him by the upper arms, large hands squeezing his biceps.

Dave moves in close, his breath steaming Keith's glasses. "And soon you'll be leaving us, Mister Lewis," says Dave, his face a parody of sorrow. Keith still says nothing, and jerks his head away from Dave. But Dave reaches out a strong hand, and, applying pressure with fingers and thumb, presses hard into Keith's cheeks and slowly turns his head back to face him. "Full of beans now, aren't you? Now that you've got grown men to deal with. Eh? Not as easy as with little boys, is it, fagboy!" Then, into the deepening silence: "Nothing to say for yourself? Then I'll tell you what we've got in mind. You're leaving us next month, ain't that right? Being let loose again. So me and the boys thought we'd organize a going away party for you." He glances to his sidekicks, who stand smiling around him like terrible apostles. "Thought we'd give you a little leaving present. Didn't we, lads?"

At this he gives a sharp nod, and Keith is pushed backward on to the floor in a swift movement, whilst Dave wraps a handkerchief tightly round his mouth. Struggling, terrified, Keith is picked up by the four men and rapidly dragged through blurred corridors – he can't tell where he's being taken – then finally thrown down on the damp, knobbled tiles of an unfamiliar shower room. One of his captors then ties his wrists together with a piece of biting nylon cord, knotting it again and again, each time with increased violence, each time forcing the cord deeper into his flesh. The pain makes him see purple. Then he is rolled over on his stomach, his face pressed to the cold floor by a boot. Keith turns his eyes upward, and sees the face of Dave leering down at him. Dave has stuck his hand inside his trousers, and is masturbating. At the same time, Keith feels hands tearing at his clothes, pulling both trousers and underwear right off with a violent tug, exposing his buttocks to the chilly air.

"Like I said, we're going to give you a leaving present to remember," says Dave, producing a large erection from his flies. He spits on his hand and rubs the saliva over himself. "I'm sure you're going to like it."

And then Dave disappears behind him whilst another boot keeps his head pinned firmly to the floor. Keith shuts his eyes tight. This is what he has feared most for the past three years. As he feels Dave forcing his way inside him, Keith decides to stop bucking, thinking that this will lessen the pain. But Dave is rough, very rough, and the pain is appalling in any case. All around him he can hear sounds of masturbation, cries of encouragement, and worst of all, Dave's triumphant grunts in his left ear. All he can feel is the heat of pain in his innards, and the crushing cold of the floor against his face. There is nothing else. Finally, Dave stops moving, his withdrawal as painful as his entry, and Keith tries to regain control of his terrorised body. But before he can properly breathe, there is someone else on top of him, inside him, screaming, 'fucker, fucker, fucker.' When this second man withdraws from him, Keith feels something warm and sticky running between his legs – blood or semen, he doesn't know which. The pain this time is much greater, the ignominy deeper. Then, as other hands jerk his hips upwards, he realises with a mind dulled by agony and terror that he is to be raped by all of them. And he passes out.

❁❁❁❁❁

He awakes in the infirmary. Here, everything is white, and comfortable. A nearby nurse, seeing his eyes open, comes over to his bed.

"How do you feel?" she asks.

Keith can't answer that right now, because he can't remember anything. Physically he feels bruised, his wrists and face mostly, but inside he feels broken in pieces.

"Try to rest," she says, and leaves.

Keith sleeps, wakes, sleeps some more, then wakes again. He eats a meal of lightly scrambled eggs, which he vomits back up half an hour later, then falls asleep again. As he slips off, he thinks they must be giving him something to keep him sedated, because his body weighs tons, feels enormous.

The next day, the third since he was admitted to the hospital wing in deep shock, badly beaten, Keith feels a little better. His wrists still ache, and he looks at them now, drawing them out from beneath the crisp covers for inspection. They are bandaged. He peers beneath the gauze, and sees the rainbow hues of ageing, severe bruises. Oddly, he has no memory of how he came by them, or what he is doing here. Then, as he stares down at the strange scored marks on the inside of his left wrist, which resemble a failed suicide attempt, it all comes back to him, quite suddenly. Every dreadful detail. With a shuddering sigh, he leans back against the soft pillows, wishing the memory away.

Later, the psychiatrist, Dr Endicote, comes to talk to him, asks him how he feels. Keith finds he can't speak and lets his anger flow out through the medium of tears, more tears than he has ever shed before. When they finally stop he feels cleaner.

"It wasn't your fault," the psychiatrist tells him. He sounds so certain that Keith almost believes him.

Two days later, the doctor in charge calls Keith into his

office for a talk. He has news to break to him before sending him back to Mortonlake proper. The doctor's face is grave, his manner typically hippocratic, all so as not to betray his feelings. He looks directly at Keith, clearly dreading what he has to say. "I'll come to the point, Mr Lewis," he begins, opening the buff folder which contains Keith's notes and staring inside. "There are some issues we need to discuss with regard to . . . to what happened to you."

"Being raped, you mean?" It's the first time Keith has said it out loud. It sounds terrible.

"Yes," the doctor says, trying to sound matter-of-fact. "Now, the men responsible have already been identified and dealt with — " Keith looks at him, surprised, cutting him off. "It wasn't hard," the doctor continues with a shake of his head, answering Keith's look, "they were actually bragging about it!" He stops, pulls a nervous hand across his forehead. "Sorry, you don't need this. The fact of the matter is that at least one of these men is known to be HIV positive. Drugs."

"Now, I don't know how much you know, but you'll be aware that you're at risk of infection, so perhaps you should think about having a test. Of course, you can't have one right away, it takes roughly three months for antibodies to appear in the bloodstream. But I suggest you think about testing after that time."

Keith is dumbfounded. He is due to be released before then. What a way to start the rest of your life. "Are you sure?" he says. He has to force the words out of his mouth, otherwise he might never speak again.

The doctor nods. "I think it's a good idea for you to continue seeing Dr Endicote for the time being," he says. "It will be especially important, in the light of what's happened."

Keith, who has sat motionless in his chair throughout this, face rigid as cardboard, eyes fixed on the moving lips of the doctor, feels his shattered life disintegrate completely. It will be more than Dr Endicote can manage to piece it together again.

CHAPTER TWENTY-ONE

Lenny walks to work this morning, in keeping with his new, leaner self, and feels good. As he strides through streets the colour of pale gold, the sun already warm on his face, he feels that he has won a small battle in the war against deceit. Telling Monica about his homosexuality has erased a cloud of doubt from his mind. Now she knows. Of course, she claims she knew before, but now *he* knows she knows. And what a confidante she turned out to be! No reproach, no disgust, not so much as a raised eyebrow. And this morning, during a bizarre encounter over the breakfast table, she informed him with the same equanimity that she had received her official notification of her degree. A First. The news seemed actually to bore her, whereas he, even now, is thrilled. Doors will open for her, great opportunities will arise. She will be one of those fortunate enough to choose. Lenny hopes that she will soon think of something to do with herself – her lack of motivation, of interest in anything, is exasperating. But she has always been like this, languorous and strange, slightly frightening. That's why he is so surprised to discover that, in the matters of the beating of his own heart, she is a stalwart ally.

This morning, Lenny is expecting some sort of confrontation at the surgery between himself and Michael, and he wonders what form it will take. He is still impressed with Monica, and grateful, that she averted a potentially dreadful scene yesterday. With a remarkable degree of sensitivity, she took the incriminating letter home with her, rather than confront him with it at the surgery, as so many outraged daughters would have done. This was clearly Michael's plan. And what will Michael do, now that Monica has thwarted him? In what way will he terrorize him? Is his ultimate plan to tell the rest of the staff, or to extort money from him? All these old terrors rise up before him again, only this time in the full knowledge that Michael is acting on information rather than conjecture. It's a difficult, stressful situation. All he can do is immerse himself in his work and wait, but it will not be easy.

He arrives at reception at eight-forty, and, after a brief conversation with Wendy, who is already stationed at her desk, Lenny enters his surgery, dons his white robe, washes his hands and prepares himself for the day ahead. He smiles at himself in the mirror, straightens his hair, examines his moustache for grey hairs, and shrugs. Another day peering down ungrateful throats, he reflects, then switches on the steriliser and flexes his fingers.

As he turns to face the room, he notices a white note sellotaped to the headrest of his dental chair, and his heart sinks. It's begun. Whatever war Michael has planned, this is surely the opening shot. Peeling the yellow tape from the headrest, which makes a soft swooshing sound, Lenny studies the note. Scarcely a note even, just two words, but the spiteful implications are clear to Lenny: HOW'S MONICA? it says.

Lenny decides that he won't give Michael the satisfaction of domination and ignores the note, neither seeking nor avoiding his colleague as the day wears on. At the end of the afternoon they meet, briefly, in the communal record room, but Lenny gives nothing away. He tells Michael how proud he is of his daughter.

"Her results came through from Cambridge this morning. She's got a First," he tells him.

"Congratulations," Michael replies in a terse, dry voice.

On arriving home, Lenny decides he wants to celebrate Monica's success, even if she doesn't. He'll invite her out for a meal, or to the theatre, or a film. Besides, he wants to talk to her about Michael. Lenny is uncertain what to do next, fearful of confronting Michael openly lest he reveal his secret to the whole staff, but afraid of blackmail. Perhaps clear-headed Monica will have some good advice to give. Lenny hopes Zoe will be busy again tonight. He can hardly take out his daughter without inviting her along too, but her presence would make any talk of Michael impossible.

Not finding Monica at her usual station by the kitchen table, and not knowing of her recent rediscovery of The House, Lenny climbs the two flights of stairs to his daughter's bedroom, nestling in the eaves of the house. As he climbs, he realises that he hasn't been up here for years. Monica's is the only room on this top floor, and it has been long accepted that this is her private domain, entered by invitation only. He knocks at her door. No answer. He knocks again, and the door, which has not been properly closed, swings open to reveal his daughter's room. The curtains are drawn, and it's dark. She is not there.

Temporarily distracted from his search for his daughter, Lenny flicks on the lights and takes a few moments to look around. Old sheets, dyed purple, have been slung from the roof. They billow down, lowering the ceiling by several feet, and give the impression of imminent thunder. He also notices several half-eaten Mars bars lying on various surfaces, all dusty, with their wrappers torn off. But what catches his eye and stills his heart is the wardrobe. The doors have been flung wide open and reveal a strange shrine which has been built inside, made of brick and plaster. Small, jagged pieces of mirror have been pressed into the plaster like mosaic, casting crazy, fragmented images of all they reflect. In front of this shrine lies a book with a mummified bird resting on it, along with a vast number of spent and half-spent candles, and beside them a stack of old and yellow newspaper clippings. Crowning this horrid tableau, set between two wooden candle-sticks with double helix stems, stands a large portrait of Myra Hindley.

Lenny is struck by an alien fear, steps backward out of the room, and stumbles down the stairs in his haste to get away. He has no idea what the shrine means, he doesn't want to think about it, but it feels bad. Grabbing his coat from a peg in the hallway, he leaves the house as if pursued by fire, quickly thrusting his arms into the sleeves and banging the front door behind him. As the air hits his face he realises he's sweating.

He paces the streets for hours, aimless and with no destination in mind, realising that this is the proof, if proof were ever needed, that he doesn't know his daughter at all. Above him, the stars look down just the same.

CHAPTER TWENTY-TWO

On the morning of his release, a uniformed prison officer lets Keith out of his cell for the last time and escorts him down the long bleak corridors which lead to the reception area. Here he is handed his clothes, all in a neat pile, which he changes into behind a small screen. He lets the prison uniform fall to the floor and makes no attempt to pick it up, such is his contempt for everyone and everything at Mortonlake. He is sad, but unsurprised, to discover that his own clothes no longer fit him.

Keith steps round the screen and returns to the counter where the issuing officer stands, and awaits the return of his personal effects – some keys, a five pound note, and some loose change which was in his pocket when he arrived at Mortonlake, three years before. One of the coins is now obsolete. He stares at the money, which sits in a small plastic tub on the counter. The officer pushes it towards him, and Keith scoops it out, dropping it casually into his pocket. Keith is then escorted to the door, a small studded wooden affair set into a much larger barrier, and at last steps through it a free man. No one has said anything to him throughout this – not 'sorry', not 'goodbye', not even 'good luck'.

As he stands alone in the sunlight, a light breeze playing against his face, he tells himself it's over, that it's the moment he's been awaiting for the last three years, but the taste is not so sweet. Freedom? What is that exactly? He does not feel free. The three exercise books which he clasps beneath his right arm will always remind him of that, will always bear witness to his darkened future.

Keith feels dazed and fragile as he slowly makes his way to the car park. The Bookends are waiting for him there. He can already see them in the distance. Bob is leaning back against the car, smoking a cigarette, whilst Derek paces back and forth, throwing glances in Keith's direction. Keith is unaccountably nervous and feels awkward. Then Derek sees him, and, finding that he can't stop himself, Keith begins to walk faster, breaking into a run before finally crashing against Derek's chest like a re-united lover, and kisses him. Then he turns to Bob, who hugs Keith like a wild man, as if he's trying to fuse the two of them together with sheer force.

Bob drives them home in silence. It's a sombre occasion quite unlike the one he had imagined, in which they would all shout, sing, and whoop in exuberance. Bob knows there will be no party now. Instead there will be endless patience and understanding. As he pulls into the driveway, Bob wonders what it will be like having Keith staying with them. Not like the old days, when they first met him. Keith was young, green, happy, then. Now he is so changed that Bob can barely recognise the man who sits huddled in the back seat as the same person. What must it be like, Bob wonders, to have first your freedom, and then your home, taken from you? How often does it happen this way? And what if there are no friends or family to help? At least Keith has some capital to fall back on . . . Inwardly, Bob shudders to think how easy it is to sink below the horizon of ordinary existence.

"We've put you in the big room upstairs," Derek explains later as they sit drinking coffee in the sitting room. "Some of your things are there, too. Not all, of course. Some's in the loft, and Mike's got the rest in his garage."

"Thanks," says Keith. He's overwhelmed to be back in the real world, in this familiar house with his two best friends. "It's very good of you."

"No it isn't, it's bloody easy," smiles Bob. Then: "Stay here as long as you want, treat it as your own home."

"I . . . I can pay . . . How much rent —?" Keith begins, but he's cut off by Derek's silencing hand.

"We don't want any," Derek says, kissing the top of Keith's head.

And with that, the matter is closed.

✽ ✽ ✽ ✽ ✽

Over the next month, Keith tries to adjust to freedom, but finds it strange. He does not follow Dr Endicote's recommendation to seek psychiatric help outside Mortonlake. Instead, he spends the long hours of the afternoons shut away in his room, poring over his exercise books, re-reading the details of his prison life with something like nostalgia. But something about the first volume begins to bother him, and soon he is unable to read it at all without developing a violent headache and feeling nauseous. One particular afternoon, as he re-reads those first traumatic entries, he realises what is wrong: it reads as if Martin were dead! Distraught, confused, and with head pounding, Keith rips up the flimsy book in a frenzy of paper snow, runs out into the back garden clutching the confetti of lies in his arms, and burns it.

After this purge he feels happier, and makes new, lengthy entries dedicated to his son, and makes bargains with god. During this time he is increasingly tormented by fear that he is HIV positive, and spends hours peering at himself in the mirror, searching for signs. Of course he mentions none of this to The Bookends, whose patience and hospitality he does not wish to tax beyond reasonable limits. Already he knows he can never repay them for their help. Instead, he prepares lavish meals for them when they return from work, he smiles and laughs, and tries to give the impression that he is coping splendidly.

One afternoon, feeling as if he is liable to explode, he phones the National Aids Helpline. After a brief consultation in which he explains his situation, he is given the number of a clinic in London which conducts same-day HIV tests, with a promise of a result by five-thirty that afternoon. He phones the clinic and is told to turn up the following morning. No appointment is necessary. That night he sleeps badly, dreaming of a small dead child wrapped in a blanket, whilst all around there is the sound of engines. He wakes at seven-thirty with a pounding headache, drenched in sweat, to the sound of Bob taking a shower in the bathroom next door.

The train fare to London is breathtakingly expensive, much more than it would have cost to drive up, but the train is a lot easier, given his state of mind. Besides, he feels it's worth it at any price. He's reached the point where he's got to know his status, one way or the other. Armed with sandwiches and a book (which he will be too keyed-up to open all day), Keith makes the journey to the clinic in a kind of fear-induced catatonia, inwardly plotting his future. If he's positive he knows exactly what he'll do: he'll track down his son, somehow, just to see him before it's too late. He won't have anything to lose by that stage. On reflex, he feels in his coat pocket, draws out the letter from Rebecca, which he now carries with him at all times, and stares at it fondly, stroking the page with the pad of his index finger.

When he finally arrives at the clinic, after a claustrophobic tube journey, he finds the waiting room full of miserable-looking people. The atmosphere is heavy with fear. If he were an animal, he'd be able to smell it. Feeling like an automaton he reports to reception, where he is given a red card bearing a code number and is told to take a seat.

Keith has had two previous HIV tests in his life, once for insurance purposes and once for Rebecca, but in both cases the results had been academic. On each occasion he had known that he was negative. There had, therefore, been no stress; it had been as simple as a visit to the dentist. But this time it is different. This time there is a very good chance that he will be told he's going to die. He feels literally sick with fear, and soon becomes just another terrified, miserable-looking person littering the waiting room, staring at leaflets about hepatitis, drugs, and blood.

Finally, his number is called, and a sympathetic woman with large glasses ushers him into a small white room. On her lap she has a form.

"I'm going to ask you some questions," she says in a smooth voice, "Okay?"

"Okay," Keith agrees.

"Right. Are you gay?"

"Yes."

"And why do you want an HIV test?"

"I think I've been at risk."

"You've practised unsafe sex?"

"Yes," says Keith. "Actually I was raped. By four men."

He is surprised at how easily this comes out. It's as if he's talking about some other person, not himself. His voice is dispassionate.

The woman's jaw loosens somewhat, her face a mask. "I see." She swallows hard, and Keith is pleased that he has managed to shock her. "Did you report this incident?" she asks.

"I didn't have to. It happened in prison, four months ago. One of the men who raped me is HIV positive," Keith replies.

The woman dispenses with any further questions. They both know he's at risk. Instead, she sends him through to a nurse who is waiting in an adjoining room. "They'll take a blood sample in there," she says.

Keith sits down on a blue plastic chair whilst the nurse snaps on a pair of rubber gloves and takes a syringe-full of startlingly red-looking blood, which she decants into a small plastic container. "That looks healthy," she smiles, and sends him back in to the counsellor.

"If you'd like come back at five-thirty, we'll have the result for you," she says with an encouraging smile. "It'll be more or less definitive. Four months is certainly a long enough period for you to produce antibodies, and false negatives are extremely rare. If it comes back positive, we'll run a double check on it, just to be sure, but our failure rate either way is a fraction of a percent."

Keith spends the rest of the morning riding the tube, fretting about what he's going to do if he's told he's going to die. To him HIV and Aids are the same. Everyone he's ever heard of who was HIV positive has died, or is now in the process of doing so. He's certain that no one survives. He visits Hyde Park around lunch time and tries to eat his sandwiches, but he finds he can't swallow them. Although he took great pains to make them moist, with plenty of filling, they seem dry. His saliva glands have stopped working.

By five-o'clock he is weak with nerves, actually trembling, and toys with the idea of riding the train home without collecting his test results, but he manages to drag himself back to the clinic, where he presents himself at reception, and then sits down. The level of fear in the room has doubled since this morning, now peopled by those awaiting their results. This time he does not have to wait, and is ushered at once into the same room as this morning. He assumes this speed heralds bad news. It's the next logical step in the downward spiral of his life.

"I won't keep you in suspense unnecessarily, sir." It's the same woman as this morning, only now she looks tired. "The result's negative. A negative test. Here, you can see for yourself."

She holds out the lab test sheet for him to see. He notices he's also been tested for syphilis and Hepatitis B. All negative. "Oh," he says, this limp remark full of huge relief. "So I'm okay?"

"Absolutely okay," she says, smiling. "And I'm very pleased. Now go on home. And whatever it is you were planning to do," she adds, knowing that they all make ridiculous promises to fulfil their dreams when death stares them in the eye, "just do it anyway."

"Alright," says Keith, still bewildered, still uncertain. "Perhaps I will." And by the time he arrives home to Bob and Derek, he has decided that she's absolutely right.

"Are you okay, Keithie?" Derek asks as Keith flops down in an armchair. He is alarmed by his friend's flushed cheeks and wild, glittering eyes.

"I'm fine," he says. "Just had a bit of a close shave, that's all." But he does not elaborate any further, and does not say where he has been.

After dinner, he falls deeply asleep on the sofa in the middle of his favourite tv programme, which The Bookends take as a good sign, and they gently help him up the stairs to bed with all the care of solicitous parents.

Next morning Keith wakes feeling refreshed, more purposeful than he has been in a very long time. Finally, he is going to take some action, and wrestle the reigns of his life out of fate's hands and into his own. He's going to find Martin. And with this in mind he decides, over a breakfast eaten alone in The Bookends' pristine kitchen, to drive into Portsmouth this morning, and find out Rebecca's address.

As he arrives at the Tricorn car park in the city centre, he remembers someone telling him that the building once won second prize in a contest to find the ugliest building in Britain. How much worse than actually winning, he thinks as his car slides neatly between two others – and how typical of this unwieldy city. Then he steps into the fresh air and winds his way down the grey concrete stairway to street level, feeling light with excitement about what he is doing. He heads for the central library beneath a low sky, confident of his plan, and on arrival at the building moves directly to the area in which the telephone directories are housed.

Picking out the directory covering the Guildford area, he turns to the R's with eager fingers, then remembers that this is the initial of her first name. The name she will be listed under begins with a K. He tells himself to calm down and turns to the relevant page, which he scans several times, but there are no Kilbrides listed. Disappointed, Keith slams the book shut with a heavy thud, causing several studious heads to turn in his direction, affronted. He smiles 'sorry', but actually doesn't care.

Having no other business in Portsmouth, he drives back home straight away, where he broods for several hours in a defeated mood. But as he stares at the afternoon soap operas, tea in hand, he suddenly hits on another idea, gleaned from a tv detective story. He doesn't think it will work, but it's worth trying, so he pulls out Rebecca's old letter to him, phones directory enquiries, and pretends he has a problem.

"Hello, I'm trying to get a number in Guildford, but I'm having trouble getting through," he says.

"Which number do you require?" asks the plastic voice at the other end.

"A Rebecca Kilbride, Guildford 176554." He knows this is not the correct number, he has deliberately transposed the two central digits.

"Could you repeat the number?" asks the voice, inflecting the sentence in an odd way, in the manner of all telephonists.

"Guildford 176554."

There is the sound of keys being depressed on a keyboard at the other end of the line. Then: "There's no such number listed, I'm afraid, sir. That number has not been recognised."

"For Rebecca Kilbride?"

"I'll just check that for you, sir," says the sing-song voice, tapping more keys on the computer. Then: "R. Kilbride is listed as ex-directory, sir. Can you repeat the number you've been trying?" Keith repeats the bogus number. "That's not the number we have here, sir," the voice informs him.

Keith clicks his tongue in mock agitation. "But that's the number she gave me. Damn! Are you sure?"

"Would that be R. Kilbride of Montgomery Road, Guildford?" enquires the helpful voice.

"Yes, that's right," says Keith, jotting down the address. "Montgomery Road."

"Then the number you require is 01483 175654. The two middle digits have been muddled."

"Thank you."

"Thank you for calling."

As he puts the phone down Keith punches the air, elated at the success of his B movie detective work. That night he does not sleep. Instead, he writes a triumphant account of his efforts in his journal.

The following day, he fills his car with petrol and drives to Guildford, where he parks in the British Rail car park. On the shiny station concourse, so much cleaner than others he has seen, he buys a street map of the city then sits down on a low red bar, which runs all around the concourse, to study it. Montgomery Road is not far away, about a mile from the station on the other side of the city centre, and Keith makes for it at once, tucking the blue cardboard-bound map into his coat pocket. He guesses it will take him no longer to walk than it would to drive.

The wind is chilly, and Keith pulls up the collar of his coat to protect himself from it as he walks. When he has been climbing uphill for some time, away from the city centre, during which time he has seen the houses change from modest to large, then to downright enormous, he checks the map again to see if he's still walking in the right direction. Rebecca can't possibly live in an area like this, he thinks, unless her designing is on an altogether different level from what he imagined. But he's right. Montgomery Road should be the next turning on the left.

It is only when he reaches the turning and looks down the road, in which the houses have suddenly shrunk back to normal size, that he realises he doesn't know the number of Rebecca's house. Keith walks into the middle of the road and stops, looking down this street, his destination, like a man who has just woken from a dream. He realises, at this moment, that he doesn't know why he's here, or what he expects to do next.

The road is long, falling away from him in a gentle slope, and Keith walks down it slowly. All the houses have gardens and most of these have mature trees in them, which Keith finds oppressive. The low November sky is heavy, raked by the leafless fingers of these trees, adding to his sense of weight. As he walks, Keith finds that few of the houses show any signs of life. Most stand like dark sentinels, waiting for their owners to return. He ignores these dark houses, interested only in those with lights on, with people inside, and makes a mental note of each one he finds. By the time he has reached the end of the road, he has counted sixteen.

After loitering around for half an hour, Keith begins to feel the insidious cold penetrate his clothing. He stands with his back to the increasing wind, to protect his face, and thrusts his hands deep into his pockets. He has not brought gloves. He stamps his way back up the road, checking in every lighted window as he passes, then journeys back down, but this hardly warms him. By lunch time he is thoroughly chilled, but ignores the rumbling of his stomach and the yearning in his limbs for the comfort of a café. He maintains his vigil, growing colder, more wooden-feeling by the minute. He will not give up.

Keith stays in Montgomery Road all afternoon, pacing up and down until the first street lamps begin to glow, still with no plan in his head and no idea what he's doing. Finally, frozen and dejected, he makes his way back to the station car park in the gathering dusk, the wind whipping his long hair into his face as he walks. When he removes his keys from his pocket, to unlock the car door, he finds that his fingers won't work properly. They are too numb. Throughout the homeward journey he keeps the heater on full, driving with his head pressed to the side window. He feels every bump and tremor through the glass, and thinks constantly of Martin. When he arrives home, he notices a small greasy smudge on the window, where his head has been.

Two days later he returns to Montgomery Road, wrapped up in scarf, thick gloves, and a hat borrowed from Derek – his Russian hat. He waits all day for a glimpse of his child, but sees no one at all. Once again he returns home dejected, and once again he sits up in his room far into the night, writing to his son, telling him how close he has come; that it won't be long now. When two further visits to Guildford prove equally unsuccessful, Keith knows there is only one course of action left to take.

"I've decided to move out," he tells The Bookends on the evening of his fourth excursion, over dinner. "I think it's time."

Bob is secretly relieved. Having Keith staying with them has proved an enormous strain. He knows Derek has found it hard to cope with. He has, too. But despite the fact that Keith's leaving would mean a return to their old privacy, Bob worries about this sudden announcement; he doesn't like it at all. He looks across the table at his friend now, sees his wild hair, which has remained uncut – and largely unwashed – since his release from prison, and reflects how much this is a physical sign of the sea-change which Keith has clearly undergone. "But why? And where would you go?" he asks.

"I've been here long enough," Keith replies, fiddling with his fork. "I mean, you said I could stay here until I found my feet. Well, now I have." He takes a mouthful of potato and swallows it. "It's not a sudden decision," he adds, answering Derek's questioning eyebrows, "I've been thinking about it for a while."

"But how will you manage?" Derek asks, taking a swig

of water from his tumbler.

"I can use my savings to rent a place, until I get a job," Keith says. "It's no problem."

Bob frowns. "If you're sure," he says, then pauses to swallow some more food. "Where were you thinking of moving to?"

"Guildford," says Keith.

"Guildford!" cry The Bookends simultaneously. "Why would anyone want to go there?"

"It's got much better job prospects than anywhere round here," Keith replies. "I've been researching it. I've even been up there a couple of times."

This finally satisfies Bob, who has fretted about Keith's lack of motivation during the two months he has been staying with them, understandable as it may be. It is the first time Keith has mentioned work, and Bob hopes it signals his return to his former self, or at least the beginning of that process. And he can understand why Keith might want to move away from here, go somewhere new, start a new life. "That's good to hear, Keith," he smiles. "It sounds like a good plan." Then, over the rim of his glass: "I suppose you'll be needing some help with moving?"

"It's a bit early for all that," Keith replies, "I'll have to find somewhere to live first."

CHAPTER TWENTY-THREE

Monica usually hates the run up to Christmas, with it's fake jollity, phoney family spirit, and those hideous Christmas lights (which no one on earth could possibly find thrilling) strung across the High Street. The whole thing sticks in her throat. 'Away in a Manger', that 'Jesus' shit, everything. None of it would be so bad, perhaps, if there was proper winter weather to go with it, but there never is. All it ever does is drizzle and the chance of snow is practically zero.

She decided several years ago to stop celebrating Christmas at all. Of course she pays her respects to the pagan solstice on the 21st, but the 25th passes her unnoticed. She always opens her presents early on purpose. But this year is different. She feels a rush of energy, a drawing together, a calling, and she's certain it's because of the man at Montgomery Road.

She's been studying him for three weeks now, through the porthole window in her eyrie, and finds him fascinating. It's not just his appearance – a strange mixture of student, crustie, and zec – which has captured her interest, but also his manner. His face, which she has scrutinized closely through her father's binos, is younger than she first thought, a little younger than Lenny's, but he has the demeanour of a much older person. And he seems shifty. All this makes him very interesting, and Monica has given him the nick-name of Dick, because she thinks he might be a private eye. She can think of no other reason why he should have suddenly appeared out of nowhere, to loiter in Montgomery Road all day. She is impressed by the professional way in which he remains ever-present in the street without actually drawing attention to himself. A difficult mixture, the gift of a true private Dick. She wouldn't be surprised if she's the only one who's even noticed him.

She has observed two other things in her studies of Dick. First, he seems to be casing a particular house, (number twenty six, although from her own private investigations she can see nothing special about it,) and second, he always pretends to be doing something else whenever she walks by – tying a shoelace, perhaps, or studying a map. This is conclusive proof that he is more than just a casual weirdo, and Monica has decided she likes him.

Strangest of all is that, if he beaded his hair, they would not look dissimilar. He has that same thinness about the face, the same eyes, the same hands. He could be her brother. It is this similarity, more than anything, which leads her to believe that this is the man who will be her vessel, her saviour; this man who will lead her to her destiny. The twin she never had. She ignores the fact that his skin is dark and swarthy; that he is twenty years older than her.

Later, Monica studies an auspicious Tarot spread, including nine cards from the Major Arcana, which is laid out before her on the kitchen table. She smiles a knowing smile. The King of Swords makes it clear that a dark man (Dick?) will come into her life within six days, and initiate a sequence of events which will lead, eventually, to her nirvana, to the Radical Separation she craves.

Now she knows it will be safe to meet him at last. It will even be safe to tell him her name. She doesn't usually do this. Once you tell people your name, they begin to own you, possess you. It's like the Aborigines and photographs – to tell a stranger your name is to give them your soul. But this man, Dick, is different. The way he stands, his slow movements, and his obvious missionary zeal, mark him as a kindred spirit. He's the One, the Phantom Twin Brother.

CHAPTER TWENTY-FOUR

Michael Whiting is also waiting to be delivered by fate, but he is fast losing his patience. For some time now he has been expecting Lenny to crack, to come crawling into his office on hands and knees, begging to be spared, but to his considerable irritation neither of these things have happened. If anything, Lenny's mood has improved. This has upset him.

The real problem, Michael reflects as he sits in his office chair, shuffling pieces of paper about his desk in an agitated manner, is that he is bored to death. He's bored of his life of one-night-stands; bored of the transient, synthetic happiness of drugs. And at the core of it all, he is bored of being a dentist. He doesn't need to do it any more, financially, he tells himself. He could retire and buy a little cottage in the lake district, go walking in the hills, buy a labrador. But that doesn't interest him either. There is no room in his heart for that, because it has been possessed by a lust for vengeance. Vengeance against Lenny. He's forgotten the reason.

To begin with, Michael had been sure he could predict what Lenny would do in the course of this little game, but now he is not so confident. As he sticks paper clips to the large cylindrical magnet which stands on his desk, and arranges them in soothing patterns, he realises that he is not in complete control. Lenny has not behaved in the way Michael thought he would, and this has thrown him.

Still swirling the paper clips about the face of his giant magnet, it occurs to Michael that Lenny might be even stupider, less perceptive, than he had given him credit for. It suddenly strikes him that Lenny might not realise that he, Michael, is responsible for the terrorizing notes. But no. Not since the episode with the creepy daughter. Who else would he blame?

Michael stands up and moves to the window, staring out at the leafless trees bending in the gale outside, and mulls it all over. It is possible that the daughter didn't read

Lance's letter at all, just dropped it in a bin on her way home, which would be a pity. Or she could have read it but not confronted Lenny with it, which would still be of no use to him.

This was not the plan. The girl was supposed to run screaming into the surgery (giving Michael cause to sack her father), then show the letter to her beautiful mother, thus ruining his private life. Finally she was to have hysterics in the High Street, publicly disowning her queer dad; Lenny was supposed to be reduced to a pleading nobody over whom Michael would have absolute power – the power to crush or the power to save – and if he tried to leave, the secret would be out in seconds.

But somewhere, Michael has made a miscalculation, and this makes him uneasy. If he wants the game to continue from here, he will have to force the issue, which will make him less powerful. With a sigh, he thrusts his hands deep into his pockets, his right hand finding some change which his nervous fingers jangle against his thigh. Then, his mind suddenly made up, he strides downstairs, through reception – nodding good morning to Wendy as he passes – and into Lenny's surgery. He doesn't knock, patients won't start arriving for another ten minutes.

When Michael enters, Lenny is lying in his chair staring at the ceiling, a mug of coffee in his hand, and he jumps with surprise at the sudden disturbance. Some coffee slops out of his mug and on to his robe, the stain spreading and lightening for few moments before resolving into a tiny map of India.

"Might I have a word with you, Lenny?" Michael asks, his hand still resting on the door handle. He pulls the door to behind him, but doesn't close it completely. He wants this conversation to be overheard, apparently accidentally. "It won't take long," he adds in his most unctuous voice.

"Of course," says Lenny.

"I'll come straight to the point," says Michael, drawing in a tight breath. "I don't think I'll be needing you any more."

Lenny's face registers shock, precisely the effect Michael intended. "Might I ask why?" Lenny asks in his usual formal manner.

"It's about Monica," Michael replies, giving the words peculiar weight, enjoying the power trip.

"Monica! What about her?" Lenny says, his voice high-pitched.

"Oh come on, don't give me that," says Michael, bluffing. He doesn't know what Monica did with the letter, maybe nothing, but decides to take a gamble anyway. "Surely she gave you the letter? I did ask her to." There is a long silence, and they both look at one another. "Look, we don't want your sort working here, Lenny," Michael says at last, "or rather, *I* don't. I don't enjoy having them as patients, and I certainly don't enjoy having them as colleagues. Have I made myself clear?" His voice has risen. He is not in control.

"You've no grounds whatsoever," Lenny cries in return, clearly not intimidated.

"You're ridiculous," says Michael. "Don't think I didn't take a copy of that letter. And I'm sure the Dental Council would be very interested. Didn't you know, they've begun to compile a list of mary dentists?"

"Go ahead and tell them," says Lenny in a chilling voice, absolutely calm. "It's not illegal to be gay."

Michael is temporarily thrown. Once again, the script has been re-written behind his back. He takes another tack. "So how *did* Monica greet the news that her daddy's a poof?" he croons in a voice like sour cream.

"If you want to know, she was wonderful. Sorry to disappoint you," Lenny says.

"And what about Zoe?" says Michael, losing his swagger by the second. "I hope you've been practising safe sex. For her sake, not yours."

Lenny stares back at Michael with a new expression, one that Michael hasn't seen before. "You really are pathetic," he says, right in Michael's face. Then, after a contemptuous pause: "Let me tell you, I've spent years of my life hiding from people like you. I've spent years thinking I was disgusting. But I had it completely wrong. It's you, people like you, who are disgusting. I rcfuse to associate with you for another minute." Lenny tears off his robe and marches out of the surgery with Michael trailing behind him. He scatters Wendy and Diane as he pushes past. Michael looks on as Lenny unhooks his coat from the coat rack, puts it on in a deliberate, mannered display of defiance, and turns to the assembled trio. "I hope you enjoyed the side show," Lenny says to the two women, who are staring at him with cow eyes. And then he leaves.

Michael, feeling winded, stands in the doorway for some moments, looking down at his polished shoes, which reflect two small images of his frowning face back up at him. This is the vengeance he craved, the victory he wanted. Lenny has been pushed out. Why, then, does he feel so small, so defeated? "You'd better phone for a locum," he tells Wendy in a wooden voice, then returns slowly to his own surgery.

CHAPTER TWENTY-FIVE

As Keith walks past the drama school this morning on his way up Lancaster Place, the usual route from his grotty digs to Montgomery Road, he is struck by the lack of noise from within. Until last week, when term ended, he was regaled every day by the strains of old pop songs with a heavy beat, over which a strident voice would be shouting time: "One! Two! Three! Four! and Five and Six and Seven and back". He looks at his watch now, nine-ten, and thinks they must all be barking mad to do physical jerks at this hour of the morning. He can't imagine ever being that motivated about anything. That part of his soul has been cauterized by three years in prison. He does not call his daily trips to Montgomery Road, looking for Martin, motivation – it's something far stronger than that. It's compulsion. A familiar driving feeling which he remembers of old, that fits him like a squeezing second skin. He loves it, he hates it, it's inexorable and must be answered.

As he trudges uphill, away from the city centre, he recalls the moment he first caught sight of his son – laughing as he ran to his mother on the doorstep. For an instant his vision had blurred, and a searing pain had lanced through his head before resolving at last into stony acknowledgement of Rebecca's cruel lie. Martin was there in front of him – happy, healthy, somewhat big for his age. In that moment, Keith had been assailed by a love so intense it threatened to overwhelm him. Now, he smiles at the memory and stops, looking down the road which now seems almost like a second home, and makes his way to his customary vantage point.

As he stations himself behind the post box, which stands five houses down from Rebecca's house, on the far side, Keith wonders if he will see his son today. He hopes he will with a passion so bright it almost hurts, but he knows it is by no means certain. On days when the weather is bad, and sometimes on fine days too, Martin remains indoors all day. When this happens, Keith returns to his meagre room on the other side of the city cold and depressed, and remains restless for the rest of the evening. He finds it impossible to sleep after a day on which he has caught no glimpse of the boy he loves. He thinks the chances of seeing Martin today are good, however; the sky is high with a pale sun swimming in it.

As he waits, he runs the tips of his gloved fingers over the uneven red paint of the post box, and wonders if the girl/woman will wander past again this morning. He's seen her quite frequently of late, always peering at him in an odd way, not afraid to linger and let him know she's looking at him. He assumes she lives close by, and tries to guess how old she is. She has one of those faces which is impossible to put an age to. If he tried, he might find he was ten years out either way. The first time he saw her he was convinced she was verging on middle age, sweeping down the road with her eyes cast down, fixed to the pavement, apparently looking for something. But last time, two days ago, he looked at her face directly as she approached and thought she might be a schoolgirl. Thinking of that white staring face now makes him shiver. He's sure she's dying of some terrible disease. She has that quality about her, as if she is not properly attached to the world.

He is torn from these thoughts by the sight of his quarry, Rebecca, who has appeared on the front steps of her house bundled up against the weather. She is wearing a large white anorak which resembles a duvet. "Come along, John-o," she calls, turning to her son. Keith is transfixed. It's the first time he's heard her call his son's name, and he's shocked to find that it's not Martin after all. It's *John*. Inexplicably disturbed, he focuses on the domestic scene in front of him.

"No, that's not what we do with those," Rebecca is saying to her son as she helps him over the lip of the front door, prising a tiny yellow wellington boot from his little gloved hand as she does so. She puts the wellington on the floor, just inside the front door, then shuts and locks it. John says something Keith can't hear, and Rebecca answers him. "Yes, it is. Look, you can see your breath." She blows a puff of misting air from her mouth, and John does the same, laughing.

Keith leans against the post box, watching in rapt attention. He lives for these moments, these glimpses of his son, each time freshly struck by the miracle of creation, of cell division, of birth. How could that small amount of colourless fluid, excreted from his body and so casually handed over in a Marmite jar, have created this wonderful, living child? He watches as John, so much bigger, blonder than he expected, stomps after his mother, dressed in a red quilted coat with the hood drawn up around his face. He is wearing tiny blue jeans, and green woolly gloves. As the pair draw level with him, on the other side of the road, Keith pulls up the collar of his coat and begins to walk off in the opposite direction. He doesn't want to be recognised by Rebecca, though he doubts she would anyway. He simply isn't the person she met.

Making off up the road he hears his son's baby voice: "Is it Hrissmas yet, mummy?"

"No, that's tomorrow," Rebecca replies. Her voice is full of smiles. "Come on, let's see if Amy's at the park, shall we?"

Christmas. He'd completely forgotten about it. He's sent no cards, and has no money for presents. It's too late now, anyway. He feels a pang of guilt, realising he'd promised to visit The Bookends, and his parents, over the holidays. That was weeks ago, and he hasn't spoken to any of them since. In fact, he has spoken to no one since he moved to Guildford just over a month ago. Feeling suddenly alone, Keith turns to watch his son walk down the road at his mother's side, then drifts back down to the post box which he then leans against. He can feel the steely cold of the metal against his right shoulder, even through his coat. Then another thought hits him like a brick, out of nowhere: it's exactly four years ago, to the day, that he first met Nick on Brighton sea front.

The memory of that name, not even formed on his lips, sends him into a towering rage. Without knowing what he is doing, his hands curl into fists and begin to strike the post box like a punch bag, slowly at first, but soon with gathering speed and violence. He doesn't realise it, but he is grunting wildly as he throws his punches, cracking his knuckles against the metal drum time and again, the padded gloves offering little protection to his bruising flesh.

"Hey!" says a voice at his side.

The fit leaves Keith as abruptly as it took hold of him and he stops in mid swing, feeling like a fool, and stares down at his hands. Then he looks across to the one who spoke. It's the girl/woman, who is also staring down at his clenched fists.

"What are you doing?" she asks.

Keith shrugs, relaxes his hands and lets his arms fall to his sides. "Uh . . . I was, uh . . . " He can think of nothing that doesn't sound ridiculous. Then: "I was pretending it was someone I used to know."

"Are you a private detective?" the white girl asks him, her face tipped up towards his.

"No, I'm not," Keith says, laughing at the bizarre question. He looks at the girl carefully for the first time, and decides that she *is* a schoolgirl after all, probably no more than fifteen. How had he thought she could be his age?

"I think you are. But of course, you couldn't possibly say so," she replies, swiping at her errant, beaded fringe, which has escaped from beneath the rim of her red beret. The beaded locks remind Keith of an ethnic necklace. "That's okay," the girl continues as she lifts the beret and stuffs the wayward coils back in, "I can live with that. Anyway, I'm *not* a private detective. But I am interested in people. Like you, for instance. You've been here for ages. What are you doing? What's so interesting about number twenty-six?"

Keith is startled by this. "What do you mean?" he stammers.

"I mean, it's number twenty-six you're interested it, isn't it? I know. I've been watching you."

"Have you?" Keith is growing wary. The voice of this girl, dreamy yet forceful at the same time, makes him nervous. For some absurd reason he imagines, just for a moment, that she's a witch.

"You see that house over there?" she says, pointing to a large property adjacent to the end of Montgomery Road. "That's where I live. And that little round window in the roof, there, is where I've been watching you from. It's my bedroom. You've been here every day for three weeks, and a few times before that. I've written down the dates." She looks him up and down. "You're always wearing the same glads, though," she adds. Then she beams an unearthly smile at him, perfect teeth in a wizened schoolgirl face. "See! *I* should be the detective. Can I call you Dick?"

"What?"

"Dick. As in 'Private Dick'."

Keith warms to this idea. In so many ways he is not the man who was Keith Lewis, the Principal, and a new name seems appropriate. He smiles at the girl. "Dick's fine," he says. "Yes, call me Dick."

"Thanks."

"And what do they call you?"

Monica stands on the pavement, looking up at Keith. "Names bind you, you realise," she says. "But if you want to know, it's Monica."

"Monica," says Keith, trying out the name. He's never known of anyone with this name before, except the tennis player who was stabbed.

"Right," says Monica, standing on one foot, resting the other on top of it. "So, what *are* you doing here?"

Keith has been living with his plan, his pipe-dream, for so long that he has convinced himself his argument is rational. He feels safe with it, safe enough to articulate it to this strange girl. "I want to abduct the boy who lives here," he says simply. He doesn't complicate the issue by telling her the child is his own son.

"That's amazing," cries Monica, her face lighting up with interest. Keith can detect no shock, not even surprise, in her voice, and this truly surprises him. She has not even asked him why he wants to do it. He feels a cold, amorphous fear pouring over his heart, but just for a second. "Are you a criminal?" Monica asks him after a moment.

"No, not really," he answers. "Although I have been to prison."

"Really?" Monica squeals, as if he has just told her he's David Bowie. "How long were you there, or have you been lots of times?"

"No, just once. For three years." His voice is dead, and he wonders why Monica is so excited. Suddenly it feels as if she's sucking the life out of him.

"When are you going to do it? The abduction," Monica asks in a wobbly voice, higher than the voice she has spoken in up to now. Keith thinks he can hear traces of a northern accent in it, which he hadn't noticed at first.

"I don't know. Soon, perhaps." Saying it out loud makes it seem real and ineluctable. He's beginning to believe that he might really do it.

"Can I help you?" Monica asks.

Keith stares at her.

"Well? Can I?" she asks again. Then, receiving no answer: "Of course, I could always go to the police."

Keith is dumbfounded. This is the most unexpected turn of all. He doubts that the police would take much heed of a fanciful teenager reporting a planned abduction in Guildford, but he has learnt to trust no one and will take no chances. "This isn't a game," he says, his voice blade sharp.

"Absolutely not," says Monica.

There is something dissembling and hard about the way she says this, like steel wrapped in cotton wool, which chills Keith. Suddenly, the girl seems much older, more in control. He doesn't like it, but finds himself saying: "I'll think about it. Yes. Perhaps. It would be easier with two."

"Boxing day is a good day," Monica tells him.

"Why?" Keith asks.

"Just is," says Monica. And without warning she turns, and begins to walk up the road towards her house.

Keith supposes she might be right. People are relaxed, more off guard, over the holidays. "Merry Christmas, Monica," he calls after her.

She turns back to him, a stream of white breath rushing from her mouth and away behind her as she says: "I don't believe in Christmas. It's a myth. Will you be here tomorrow?"

Keith shrugs. "I don't know," he says, too quietly for Monica to hear.

"See you on Boxing Day, then," Monica replies, raising a pale arm in farewell before walking away with purposeful steps. Keith notices that the nails of her ungloved hands are varnished black.

Keith stands on the cold pavement for some minutes, staring at nothing. He feels prodded into a corner now, hurried, goaded into action by this strange girl – a status much more unpleasant than the fantasy world he has been inhabiting until now. It has all happened so fast that his mind is like putty. He can't think straight. He breathes deeply, the cold air vibrant in his lungs, and reminds himself that his plan of kidnap is not outrageous but rational, even reasonable. The world has been unjust. He has had three years of his life stolen from him and because of this he has no job, no home, and no prospect of either; he has also been gang-raped, further robbing him of any vestigial self-esteem that might have survived Mortonlake. The only thing he has left is his child, and he doesn't see why he should be deprived of him, too. Besides, he will be very gentle, and no harm whatsoever will come to John. He only intends to borrow him for an hour or two. He won't even realise that he has been abducted. Keith will take care of him, spoil him, love him. It isn't really kidnap, when it's his own son.

Lost in these dark ruminations, Keith nearly misses Rebecca and John as they return from the park. John's little cheeks are pink from the bracing cold, and Keith longs to run over and touch him; to do something as simple as run the back of his index finger over John's wonderful face; to feel that warmth and softness; to say 'I love you' out loud. He watches as mother and child proceed to their front door, John's little hand held with the gentlest of pressures by his mother. As Rebecca fumbles in her bag for the key with clumsy gloved fingers, John turns, looks directly at Keith, smiles and waves. Keith is turned to stone, feeling love and grief in equal measure.

"The man won't wave," says John to his mother.

"Because he doesn't know you, John-o," says Rebecca without looking round. She has found the key, is now turning it in the lock. "Come on, in we go," she says.

Keith stares at the closed front door, tears in his eyes. He loves John, he really does.

He spends that evening in a state of anxiety surpassing all others, sleeping little. He feels weak and exhausted, his body heavy. A constant headache hovers behind his eyes. The following day, Christmas day, is the most miserable he has ever experienced – including those in Mortonlake – spent lying on his lumpy bed worrying about John, hearing occasional traffic idle by, eating nothing. He lies awake all that night, vacillating between poles of rational and irrational thought.

At four a.m. on the morning of Boxing Day, he decides that he can't possibly go through with his planned abduction. He sees it as ridiculous. But at six he remembers Monica, and has visions of her making an attempt of her own. He wishes he hadn't told her about it now. She's too weird. With sinking heart he realises that there is no other way forward. He has to go through with it, he has to protect his child. Once again he feels trapped, feels that fate is playing his hand for him.

At eight-thirty he finds himself sitting in his car outside Rebecca's house, staring out of the window. He hopes that Monica won't arrive. The back seat is strewn with little bars of chocolate, packets of crisps and peanuts, cartons of Ribena and orange juice, and sweets, which Keith bought at the service station this morning when he filled the car with petrol. They are for John, to keep him happy. There is also a small colouring book with a yellow cover, featuring a teddy bear, but as he glances back at it Keith realises he didn't buy any crayons. Quickly, he rummages in the glove compartment and the door trays, and manages to find an old green biro and a pencil, which he tosses on to the back seat next to the book. Then he grips the steering wheel with both hands, takes in a breath and sighs. He moves the car twenty yards further down the street, away from the house.

As he comes to a stop he catches sight of Monica in his rear-view mirror, and is amazed. She has dressed formally, as if for a debutante ball, in a long black dress adorned with lace and tassels, pulled in tight at the waist then flowing down to mid-calf. A crimson shawl, also tasselled, is draped over her otherwise bare shoulders, and is decorated by hundreds of silver and gold sequins. Her beaded hair is loose and hangs shoulder length all round, framing a face which wears full make-up. A large silver Star of David hangs from her left ear. She looks twenty-five and sassy, and he wonders why she has gone to all this trouble.

"Hello Dick," she says through the window as she draws level, and Keith opens the door to let her in. She smells of cinnamon and sandalwood. It's not unpleasant, but very strong. "You came, then," she smiles as she settles into her seat and arranges her dress about her. "I half thought you wouldn't."

"Me too," says Keith.

"So what's the plan?" Monica asks. "What happens next?"

Keith has not worked it out very well. His plan is vague to say the least. "I thought I'd wait near the park, and grab John as he goes past with his mother," he explains.

Monica's eyes are wide and glittering. "John? How do you know his name is John?" she demands, her tone urgent.

"Why? What's wrong with that?" says Keith, flustered.

"Nothing at all. It's perfect!" Monica laughs, her mood suddenly sunny. "Thank you, Em!"

"What?" says Keith.

"Oh, nothing," says Monica. "I was thinking out loud." There is a short silence, during which Monica examines her make-up in a vanity mirror which she pulls from a canvas bag strung about her neck. Keith finds the bag somehow disturbing, so at odds with her otherwise immaculate attire. "You can't do it on your own, you realise," Monica says as she smooths down an eyebrow with the little finger of her right hand. "You need two people. Someone has to distract the mother's attention, otherwise she'll see you take the child. And what if they don't come to the park, or if there's more than one adult with him?"

Keith shrugs, his sleep-deprived brain sluggish. "We'll have to try again another time, I suppose," he says.

They wait in the car for over an hour, the radio tuned to a jazz station. As time goes on, Keith becomes increasingly nervous, doubting his ability to carry out his plan. At nine-forty he decides, with a measure of relief, that Rebecca and John are not going to appear this morning, and prepares to leave. But at that moment, he sights his quarry coming towards them down the pavement. He adjusts the rear-view mirror to a more advantageous angle, to gain a better perspective on how close they are, and as he does so Monica steps out of the car and on to the pavement. She stands there waiting, looking debonair, almost beautiful, as Rebecca approaches.

"Excuse me, but can you tell me the way to Ripley Court?" Monica asks. The woman gives her a questioning look. "I've been invited to a champagne breakfast party," Monica adds with a conspiratorial smile. "I'm supposed to be there at ten, but I think I'm going to be late. It's somewhere near here, isn't it?"

Rebecca stands with one hand on her hip, the other holding the hand of her son as she thinks. "Yes," she laughs. "It's just up the hill."

"That sounds right. Near a hospital? I was told to look out for a hospital," says Monica.

"Oh, there's several up that way. Do you know which one?" asks Rebecca.

"St Bart's. I think it's psychiatric," Monica replies, not missing a beat.

As the conversation continues, growing more complicated, John wriggles his captive hand out of its tiny yellow glove, and smiles at his joke. His mother is still holding the empty glove in her left hand as he begins to walk away. She points up the hill, giving directions, whilst Monica smiles and nods, asking more questions. She does not notice that her son is now walking towards Keith, who is squatting down by the open back door of his car, and smiling.

"Hello, John," says Keith.

"How do you know my name?" says John. His face is a frown.

"I'm . . . a friend of mummy's," Keith says.

"No," says John, sure of this point, shaking his head. Then he sees the sweets ranged on the back seat of the car and his face becomes animated.

"Would you like some?" Keith asks the child, indicating the confectionary. "You can climb in and get it, if you want."

"I should wait for mummy," John says slowly.

"That's what we're going to do!" says Keith, making it sound exciting. "We'll wait for her in the car, and then when she's finished talking to that lady, we'll give her a big surprise. She won't expect us to jump out of the car at her, will she?"

John smiles. This is a good idea. He likes mummy's friend, even if he does look as if he needs a bath. "All right," he agrees, climbing into the car.

Keith, his innards feeling like water, quietly shuts the door, then gets in himself and moves off slowly, taking the first turning on the left.

"Where are we going?" John shouts worriedly.

"Only round the corner, John-o. We're going to wait for mummy here."

"I want to get out," John says in a wobbly voice, scared and upset. "I don't like it here."

Keith is torn apart by the fear in his son's eyes. "It's okay, John-o, there's nothing to worry about," he says in a soothing voice, as much to himself as his son. "It's daddy. I'm your daddy. Do you recognise me?" Keith pulls his lank hair into a pony tail with his hands, and turns round to face John properly. "See? It's daddy," he says. But John cringes away from him, frightened now, and begins to cry. Keith bites the back of his knuckles in horror, as unhappy as the child, and lets his hair fall back over his face.

Suddenly Monica flings the door open and jumps in, wild-eyed and out of breath. "Drive!" she commands.

"What happened?" asks Keith, glancing across to Monica.

"I left her on the street," Monica replies between gasps for air. "I lost her. She didn't see where I went."

Behind the steering wheel Keith's eyes are glazed, not seeing the road. He drives automatically, with no idea at all where he is going, or what he should do next. Originally he had imagined doing this alone. He had planned to take John back to his flat, where they would play games, get to know each other, have fun. But now he is with Monica and everything has changed. He can't think of a way to get rid of her. At the same time, he doesn't want to take her back to the flat with John, it might draw too much attention. And besides, it just doesn't feel right. "What shall we do now?" he asks Monica in a quiet voice, not wanting John to know there is no plan. "Where shall we go?"

"Manchester," says Monica. She says it emphatically, as if she's been thinking about it; as if it makes sense.

Keith is nonplussed, but in the absence of any suggestion of his own, acquiesces with a nod. He glances up at the small digital clock above the rear-view mirror, where garish green figures announce the time: nine-fifty-two.

As they proceed northwards through Woking, eventually picking up the M25, John begins to cry again and asks where they are going. Keith tries to placate him with the colouring book but John ignores it, his sobs growing more noisy and uncontrolled. Soon he is screaming for his mother, terrified, his little fists pounding against the back of Keith's seat, his hot face stained with tears and snot.

"Can't you do something with him?" Keith says to Monica. He feels monstrous.

Monica gives Keith a sideways look, then rummages in her canvas bag for something. "Do you like peppermints?" she asks the child over her shoulder. He nods, shoulders heaving, disconsolate. "Here then," Monica says, handing him an Opal Mint. "They're chewy."

John munches the sweet without enthusiasm, still crying. "I want to go home," he wails. But before long his sobs subside and he falls into an uneasy, stubborn silence.

"That's done it," says Monica with a satisfied smile. "He'll be quiet now."

"What?" says Keith, distracted.

"I spiked the mints," she replies, her voice flat. "Not with anything heavy," she adds quickly. "Just a little something to make him spacey. He'll probably fall asleep."

Keith is suddenly gripped by fear. He feels thoroughly out of his depth, and soon develops a severe headache which lodges itself behind his right eye, impairing his vision. Part of him knows that he should stop the car and bring this whole hideous affair to an end, yet another part knows he can't. He is too deeply involved already. As the car speeds on, leaving the M1 to join the M6, the sky begins to darken and the ceiling of cloud lowers, disgorging torrential rain and reducing everything to miserable grey.

Keith is forced to slow down in the appalling conditions. With pounding head, he notices that Monica is growing visibly more agitated – turning the heater up and down, picking at her nails, and fiddling with the beads on her hair as she mumbles things through her lips. Things with lots of M's, a weird kind of chant. After half an hour of it Keith loses his patience and asks her to stop, worried that it might frighten his son, who is sitting like a docile puppet on the back seat. But she doesn't stop, just lowers her voice to an even more irritating whisper, her hair beads clattering between her busy fingers like a rosary as her lips move.

Finally, the pain in his head gets so bad that he has to shut his right eye to be able to see straight. The tail lights of the cars in front have become long red streaks, and he has no idea how near or far they are. "I'm going to have go stop at the next services," he says as they approach Stoke. "I need some pain killers, I can hardly see."

At this Monica stops her mumbling and leans forward, clutching at the dashboard with thin white hands. "You can't stop. You can't!" she screams. "We've got to get there before dark!" Her voice has risen to a high-pitched wail.

Keith stares at Monica, who has a steely gleam in her eye like religious glory. "For god's sake calm down!" he snaps. "Can't you see you're frightening him?" He jerks his head towards John, whose eyes stare wildly from a cataplectic body.

"But we can't stop," says Monica, her tone urgent. "That's not what they did. That's not how they did it. Don't you see, we have to be the same!"

Keith's headache is worsening by the minute, a new sharp pain meshing into the general ache as if someone were sticking a knitting needle through his right eyeball. "Look, we *are* stopping and that's all there is to it," he barks, making his sore head throb at the temples. "It'll only be for five minutes. There are some services in seven miles, we'll stop there. And for god's sake stop that moaning," he adds as Monica takes up her monotonous mumbling chant once more, staring vacuously before her like one in fugue.

The rain has stopped, the horizon brightening like a second dawn, by the time Keith pulls into the services car park. The livid green figures of the car clock, which seemed to glow with such unnatural brightness in the motorway gloom, grow dimmer as the light outside increases. Insistently they flash the time: One-eleven.

He is about to get out of the car when Monica suddenly lunges across him, her hands wildly scrabbling for the door lock. Two of her nails bend backwards as her fingers slide down the side of the door, trying to push the button. Her head is buried in Keith's lap, he can feel her hot breath through his clothes. "What the fuck are you doing?" he shouts as he wriggles from underneath her and pushes the door open with his shoulder, at last breaking her surprisingly strong grasp of the handle. Now he stands by the open door, but he's unable to shut it because Monica has slid across the two front seats, body outstretched, her arms flailing. In a mad attempt to stop him leaving, she bats at the legs of his trousers with her hands, trying to gain a purchase on the material, but as she does so her identity bracelet catches against the seat belt and flies off, falling to the ground at Keith's feet. And for an instant, Monica is still. Keith, taking advantage of the momentary pause in Monica's silent, furious attack, closes the door hard with his knee. "I'll be back in a minute," he yells through the steamed-up side window.

Shaken and disturbed, Keith takes two deep breaths,

and stares down at the roof of his car. He can hear John crying inside, whilst Monica lies motionless across the two front seats, head buried between her outstretched arms. Not wanting to leave John alone with Monica for any longer than necessary, he hurries across the car park and into the shop, where he snatches up a pack of soluble aspirin. He wants to be quick. But the man in the front of him pays for his goods by cheque, apparently filling in the details in slow motion. Meanwhile, Keith waits to be served with growing agitation and toys with running from the shop without paying. He almost throws his money at the cashier when his turn finally comes. As he runs back to the car park, he tears the packet of pain killers open and chews on the gritty, bitter pills, trying to swallow them. They dissolve into a mush which sticks in the back of his throat and will not go away however hard he swallows. Then he remembers the cartons of orange juice he bought for John, which have lain untouched on the back seat of the car since this morning, and hurries on.

But the car has gone.

At first he thinks he must have made a mistake, but as he looks around, checking his co-ordinates against surrounding landmarks, he realises he has not. And as he looks down at the space where his car should be, swallowing and swallowing, he notices the silver identity bracelet which a few minutes before had been clasped around Monica's wrist. He squats down, picks it up, and tosses it from one palm to the other in agitation, pouring it backwards and forwards. The metal is cool against his skin, and wet from the rain-washed tarmac. Dumbfounded, he stares around him like an idiot. He doesn't know what to do.

CHAPTER TWENTY-SIX

Monica has her foot pressed hard on the accelerator as she scorches up the motorway in the fast lane. Her eyes are keen, her reflexes fast, and when she comes up behind other cars, she pulls into the middle lane and overtakes them on the inside. The radio is on, playing something classical she doesn't recognise, and she is relaxed. She wishes she'd brought some incense with her, but chants the Mantra of Completion instead. The boy is curled up on the back seat, scrunched into a corner, sucking his thumb. He doesn't seem scared, just stoned. "Your name's John, right?" Monica asks him as she overtakes a grungey Volkswagen.

"Yes," says the boy, his voice thick.

"What's your other name?" she says.

"John Kilbride, twenty-six Montgomery Road, Guildford," says John, reciting the words his mother has taught him in a flat voice.

"John *what?*" In high excitement, Monica glances over her shoulder at the boy, and swerves out of the fast lane in front of a juggernaut hauling pine logs. "Did you say John Kilbride?" John nods, and Monica lets out an elated whoop. An excellent coincidence! She has always believed in divine synchronicity, and knows how powerful it can be. Why shouldn't he be called John Kilbride, why shouldn't it all link together? Holding her left hand up to her forehead and steering with her right, she begins to laugh.

"Are you happy?" asks John.

"Yes I am," says Monica, shaking her head, praising the Strong Goddess. "Christ, that's just fucking excellent."

"Only grown-ups swear," says John, frowning. "How old are you?"

"Twenty-two," Monica replies. "How old are you?"

"Four and three quarters," says John. Then, proudly: "I'm adopted."

"Lucky you," says Monica, smiling a slow smile as she guns the engine to its limit. "Real parents are a drag." She turns the radio up full blast.

"Where's my new daddy?" John asks, raising his voice over the music.

Monica is confused. "What are you talking about?" she says.

"We left daddy," John continues.

"He's not your daddy," Monica tells him, "he's just a man."

"He *is* my daddy. He knows my name." John says.

"Of course he isn't."

"When will we get daddy?" John demands again, undeterred.

"We're not going to get him. And he's not your daddy, so be quiet," Monica shouts, her temper flaring out of nowhere.

"But he is!" Then, in a loud wail: "I want to go home!"

Monica thumps the steering wheel with her hands. "Just shut up, shut up, shut up!" she screams.

CHAPTER TWENTY-SEVEN

Keith holds his hands to his aching head, and tries to think what to do. He is worried about John, and what will happen to him, but he's in check-mate. He can't possibly go to the police or he will end up in prison again, and yet he knows it's the most pragmatic course of action. It's the only way to ensure the safety of his son. These two thoughts seesaw in his mind as a light breeze plays on his bowed head.

Where on earth would the girl go? he wonders as he resumes tossing the broken identity bracelet from hand to hand. If he could just work that out he could go after her, somehow. Steal a car. Hire a taxi. Something. Casually, he glances down at the silver bracelet, turns it over and reads the inscription: M _ _ A. He arches an eyebrow in surprise. MONICA has six letters, but M _ _ A is only four.

He straightens up and paces the car park, trying to massage the pain away from his eyes. M _ _ A . . . what does it mean? If only the insistent throbbing in his head would recede, he'd be able to think properly, but now he feels as if he's squinting through a gauze, the flitting shapes of indistinct ideas whirling about in a meaningless kaleidoscopic blur. And then, slowly, as bile rises in his throat, it begins to fall into place: All Monica's mutterings in the car, Em this, and Em that; her delight at the name of John; her emphatic choice of Manchester as a destination. All these things coagulate in his mind to make a hideous whole. Then, with a start, he remembers his son's full name, and he is no longer in doubt. There was another John Kilbride, back in the sixties! And of course it is Boxing Day, significant for another victim of that murderous pair . . .

In a wash of absolute panic, Keith vomits up a foamy spume of pain killers, wipes his lips with the sleeve of his coat, then stands and runs into the service station. Now he knows exactly where Monica will be heading.

CHAPTER TWENTY-EIGHT

Monica leaves the M6 and skirts round the southeastern quarter of outer Manchester, making for Huddersfield. She doesn't need a map, she memorized the complex sequence of A and B roads she needs last night. Once through Mossley and Greenfield she finds a road she recognises from pictures in the Book Of Truth and the Testing Trial, and smiles. The road climbs steeply. Taking this road, she sees the surrounding countryside turn yellower, bleaker, leaving Manchester behind, sprawling below her in a black mass. It's too early for lights to be turned on, but only just. Tea time.

She brings the car to a halt at the side of the road after seven miles and climbs out, locking the child in. His dismayed, bewildered face stares out at her like a febrile ghost. "I'll be back soon," she calls through the window, then she glances quickly up and down the road, checking for cars. Satisfied that there is nobody in sight, she jumps the irrigation ditch which lines the roadside, climbs through the rusty barbed-wire fence dotted with windswept sheeps' wool, and marches off into the springy, peaty moorland.

After a few minutes' walk, she pulls a piece of paper from her pouch and begins to study it. It's a photocopy of a picture she found in the library, which shows the Living Goddess standing near a small sign Monica can't read (it's a gas pipe marker, the kind that look like miniature tombstones). In the picture, there is a rock in the background. Monica wanders about for some time, trying to match the real skyline of Hollin Brow to the photograph. She studies the picture intently, then looks up to check her surroundings as she moves about, looking for the rock. As the light begins to fade her task becomes more difficult, but she won't give up. She knows this detail is important. This is the part that has to be right. Once she has found the Knoll, then the magic can begin . . .

CHAPTER TWENTY-NINE

As Keith approaches yet another table at the cafeteria, all four occupants get up to leave, glancing in his direction and muttering as they do so. Keith slams his fist down on the orange formica top in frustration, causing the rattling of cups and a fluttering of napkins. He is feeling very ill now, his stomach burning, his legs aching, his headache almost unbearable. Miserable, he watches a small, half-empty pot of marmalade roll to the edge of the table with impossible slowness, then drop to the floor, where it spins under a chair.

Now he is completely at a loss. He has begged every person he can find for a lift northwards, both in the shop and here in the cafeteria, but has met with flat refusal, abuse, or silence on each occasion. Half his mind can see why no one is willing to give this wild man a lift, as he lurches from table to table with unruly hair and manic eyes, long coat flapping behind him. Who has ever heard of begging lifts in this way? But desperate situations call for extreme measures. Monica has taken his son, and any behaviour is reasonable in the light of that.

He moves on to the next table with his stomach burning and his temples full of engine throb, then sits down at an empty seat and rests his head on his folded arms. When he shuts his eyes he sees John.

"You looking for a lift, mate?" says a voice.

Keith jerks his head up and sees a man sitting opposite him, whom he had not noticed when he sat down. He's in his late thirties, with a large black moustache, short hair, and a work shirt. He's just finishing a meal. "Yes, I am," Keith tells the man, his voice wobbling. "Someone's just stolen my car, and I need to get to Manchester."

"I hope you've reported it?" the man asks.

"Uh . . . yeah," says Keith, off guard. "But I've got to get to Manchester as soon as possible. It's really important. I can't stay here."

"Then you're in luck, mate. I'm going that way myself,"

says the man with a smile, taking a last mouthful of sausage. "I'd be glad of the company."

Keith is overwhelmed with relief and gratitude. "Thanks," he says, "that's marvellous."

"You're welcome," says the man. "I'm Russ, by the way," he adds, extending a hand towards Keith.

"Keith," says Keith, shaking the proffered hand.

Russ wipes his moustache on a shiny white paper napkin, crunches it up in his fist, and drops it on to his plate. "All right, Keith. Waggons roll," he says.

As they make their way out of the cafeteria, Keith is surprised to find that they are not heading for the juggernauts – he had supposed Russ was a lorry driver. Instead, Russ leads him to a sleek black sports car, a Ferrari Testarossa, which squeals as he disarms the alarm. "It's my baby," says Russ, reading Keith's astonished face. "Penis substitute, or what?"

Keith gives the man a tense, humourless smile, and climbs in.

"I hope you like to go fast," Russ says, as he pulls out on to the motorway and accelerates away.

"Yes," says Keith in an absent voice, and lets himself sink into the plush leather seat, lost in thought.

As the car speeds along Keith grows anxious, worried that he has made the wrong decision once again. He feels guilty that he has not phoned the police about John. There's nothing he can do now, here in this car, and if something happens to John it will be his fault. As usual he has no plan.

Keith knows that he is supposed to talk, to keep Russ company – it's the standard payment for accepting a lift – but his mind is blank, white-washed by anxiety. He is only aware of thrumming lorries, and the fizzing tyres of the Ferrari as Russ scorches up the fast lane, overtaking everything. He almost welcomes the idea of hurtling headlong into an on-coming coach, or compressing into a bridge stanchion at ninety miles an hour. Anything would be better than this agony of vain hope, of wondering if he will be able to find John before it's too late . . .

After twenty minutes of unbroken silence, Keith, in

despair and now verging on hysterical tears, turns to Russ, who is humming softly to himself, and says: "I know it's an odd question, but have you ever heard of Myra Hindley?"

CHAPTER THIRTY

Lenny is sitting alone in the house, doing nothing. There is no radio playing, no soaring music, and no burbling television; neither is he reading, or engaged in any other activity. He is simply sitting in his study with the lights turned off, absorbing the silence. He feels soothed by it. Somehow, it's a different kind of silence from the one he is used to. This silence, the silence of an empty house, is benign, whereas the silence of things left unsaid, of things withheld, is brooding and oppressive.

Lenny and Zoe have lived in an angry silence such as this for the last twenty-two years, but now, at last, the spell has been broken. Zoe has left. On Christmas Eve she simply packed her bags and went, sellotaping a short note to the kitchen table, written in her meticulous, small hand, informing him that she was returning to her parents' house. Lenny knows it's because he resigned from his job. She couldn't understand why he did it. How could she know how it had felt to stand face to face with Michael and utter the word 'gay' for the first time in his life? Previously, he might have said 'invert' or 'homosexual' – if he had mentioned the subject at all – but he had known it was important to use that new, lighter word for Michael. He had not, however, expected it to make him feel so powerful, and he smiles to himself at the memory. As he stares out of the window, regarding a heavy winter sky pregnant with rain, he wonders what Zoe has told her parents. He feels sure it won't be the truth. She is too proud for that.

After a time, Lenny grows cold in the unheated study, and moves into the kitchen, where he settles down with a cup of coffee and the newspaper, which he spreads out on the table top. He sits where Monica usually sits, but she won't come in and disturb him this morning – she has gone off to a breakfast party dressed all in black, with impressive nails and jewellery. Dimly, he wonders who has invited her. As far as is aware, she has no friends in Guildford.

He scans the newspaper for interesting articles as he sips at his coffee, but the news is trivial, as it always is over the Christmas period – largely concerned with missions of mercy, stories about children, and palatable home affairs. Before long, he gives up on it, folding it shut and neatly putting it to one side.

Instead, he turns his attention to Monica's diary, which lies open on the table, by the wall. As usual, the text is written in strange Greek-looking characters, but on this page there is a sentence written in English capitals, which leaps out at him from the mass of unrecognisable shapes and squiggles: THE HANGED MAN (M.A. XII) DO WHAT YOU KNOW TO BE RIGHT WHEN ALL AROUND YOU THINK OTHERWISE. He doesn't know what the M.A. means, but he thinks the Hanged Man is a Tarot card, and guesses the rest must be it's meaning.

He is still pondering this when the door bell rings, and with something approaching happy lethargy, he walks down the hallway and opens the door to a curtain of dull rain. But his mood turns to instant alarm at the sight of the two police officers who now stand in front of him, shoulders hunched against the deluge. As he stares at their dark uniforms, he feels a sudden irrational surge of non-specific guilt.

"Good afternoon sir," says the shorter, older officer, who is wearing a hat more senior than that of a regular constable. "We're sorry to bother you, but we're conducting an enquiry in connection with a missing child. He went missing from Montgomery Road about three hours ago. We understand that a very thin woman with beaded hair was seen in the vicinity at the time, and your daughter apparently fits the description, according to the neighbours." The policeman gives Lenny an encouraging smile. "Is she in at all, your daughter? Just so we can clear it up. She might have some important information."

As the policeman speaks, the blood drains from Lenny's face, his stomach clenches, and his legs, literally, begin to shake. He leans on the door-jamb, feeling decidedly unwell, and has to fight a desire to shriek. "I think you'd better come in," he mumbles. The two policemen glance at one another, then step over the threshold.

Lenny takes them into the kitchen. "She's not here," he says, "she went to a party this morning . . ." He trails off, hearing for himself how implausible it sounds.

"Do you have a photograph of your daughter, sir?" asks the senior officer. "That would be sufficient for now. If she's not the girl we're after, then we won't trouble you further." He smiles at Lenny.

"I'll fetch one," says Lenny, and scoots into his study. He returns holding a framed picture of Monica, taken two months ago at her graduation ceremony, and shows it to the two policemen. In the picture she is staring out at the camera with a smile which belies her narrow face and dull eyes, with her beaded hair falling around her face. "Is this her?" Lenny asks, afraid of the answer. He already knows what it will be.

The policemen look at the picture with grave concentration, then the senior officer, the Inspector, speaks into his walkie-talkie. "Charlie Romeo twenty, we might have a positive ID here. Can you send a constable round? Over." There is a response from the other end. "That's eleven, Dower Row. Just round the corner. Over." He snaps his walkie-talkie back into it's holder, then turns to Lenny. "The mother lives in the next street, sir. If you don't mind, we'll get a PC to show her the picture now."

Lenny nods his head, too stunned to speak. Three minutes later, a PC arrives at the house and takes away the picture.

"One other thing, sir. Some of your neighbours have reported seeing a long-haired man in the area over the last few weeks," says the junior officer. "Do you know anything about that?"

"Nothing, I'm afraid. I'm not here during the day," Lenny says, and falls silent.

Suddenly, the walkie-talkie at the Inspector's side crackles into life, surprising all three men. "It's a positive ID, Charlie Romeo twenty," says a tinny voice. "She's the one."

The policemen ask Lenny to come to the police station

with them, to which he agrees, feeling detached from the world, as if in a bubble. Once there, sitting in a clean sparse interview room, he tells them everything he knows (which he now realises is very little) about his daughter and her habits. There is a tape machine on the desk, recording his words as he speaks them. He mentions Monica's interest in Tarot cards, her coded diaries, and her intellect, but tells them he has no real idea how she spends her time.

"And there is no precedent for this behaviour?" asks the Inspector when Lenny has run out of things to say. "You've not noticed anything strange?" Lenny shakes his head. "Please think," the policeman continues. "Trivial information, even though it may seem irrelevant, can often help us build up a picture. We need to establish where she might have gone, and what her motives are. Anything at all could prove useful."

Lenny is just about to re-iterate that he has no more to say when he remembers Monica's bedroom, and her strange altar. A cold panic rises in his throat as he brings it to mind – even thinking about it makes him feel bad. "There is something," he says in a voice as dry as leaves. "She has a secret altar, with candles and mirrors and newspaper clippings." At this the Inspector grows more alert, and Lenny falters. "And there's a dead bird . . . and a book . . . " Lenny adds, finding it all hard to say, "and a picture of Myra Hindley. It's hidden in her wardrobe. I found it by accident."

"Myra Hindley?" asks the Inspector, surprised. "Are you sure?"

"Quite sure," says Lenny.

"And what about the news clippings? What are they?"

"I don't know, I didn't read them," says Lenny.

"Okay, you stay here," the Inspector tells his junior. "I'm going to get mobile." Then he rises from his chair and orders a thorough search of Monica's bedroom, and the wardrobe in particular. Twenty minutes later, after a seasoned officer has reported back to him, describing the contents of the wardrobe in shocked tones, he places a call to the Greater Manchester Police headquarters, telling them there may be a copycat murderer on the loose.

CHAPTER THIRTY-ONE

The light is failing fast as the Ferrari rockets up the hill to Saddleworth Moor, and Keith looks out of the window in dismay, at the bleak, alien landscape which stretches for miles in all directions. He'd imagined, somehow, that once he got to the moor Monica would be easy to find. He was wrong. Slowly, he bangs his head against the window. "She could be anywhere," he keens, his arms cradling his torso as he rocks back and forth in his seat.

"Not today, she couldn't," says Russ, his face set. Like many Mancunians who were children in the Sixties, Russ is familiar with all the dates and locations of those grisly murders. "She'll be at Hollin Brow. Boxing day, nineteen sixty-four, they killed Lesley Ann Downey. That's where they buried her." The countryside is cast in tones of brown, the moorland grasses appearing almost luminous in the half-light, as the car slices through the December dusk. "They dug it up again, not long back, looking for more bodies," he adds. "Just up here."

As Russ stops speaking, they reach the top of the incline and the view ahead opens out. "That's my car," Keith cries, pointing down the road. "Stop here!"

Russ pulls the Ferrari to a halt, and Keith lurches out of the door, runs up to his car, and cups his hands against the windows to peer in. "He's not here! Oh my god, he's not here!" Keith shouts, his voice tearing the air with terror. And he runs off into the half-dark moor, stumbling over unseen tussocks of grass. He falls twice, but each time gets to his feet and runs again, with no idea of where he is going.

After five minutes he pauses in the twilight, breathless, and vomits up a mouthful of bile. And as he stands, wiping his lips with the back of his hand, he notices a figure on its knees in the distance, off to his right. On the throbbing wind he can just make out the sound of a voice chanting, and with that he knows it's Monica. Monica, on her knees, scrabbling at the peaty earth with her fingers, a blanket lying beside her. With desperate energy, he runs towards her with his head down, and as he runs the pain inside him expands, filling his head with a massive roaring sound, like the sound of distant engines. But he stops short of her, backing off as she stares up at him with astonished eyes.

"We're going to be famous, aren't we?" she croons. "You and me. We did it, just like them. You and me!" And then she laughs, a broken donkey bray which belches from her white, mud-streaked face. Above them, the air is alive with throbbing.

Keith avoids her eyes and looks down at the bundle of blankets at his feet. With a start, he recognises them as the ones from the boot of his car, and falls to his knees beside them in horror. "No! Please, no!" he whispers, and cradles the blankets, holding them tight to his chest, feeling the little body within. Then he stands, and stumbles away from Monica, who remains kneeling beside her half-dug grave. The roaring in his head increases as he pulls back the blankets and sees the face of his son, white and motionless, revealed beneath them. There is a large purple bruise over John's left eye, and a nasty contusion on his right temple, clotted with dried blood. Keith shuts his eyes, imagining the swift, crunching blow of a rock held by a black-nailed hand, and the cry of surprise, fear and pain that John must have uttered as his skull was broken. All around him now, and inside his head, there is nothing but the roaring engine sound, then the sky streaks with intense whirling lights, and sharp electronic voices rain down on him like a judgement from god. Broken, he drops to his knees, still holding his son to his chest, then falls backwards, unconscious, in a pool of hard yellow light.

CHAPTER THIRTY-TWO

Lenny sits on Monica's bed, staring down at his hands. The police have been through her room so many times now that it is almost unrecognisable – reduced to a jumble of clothes, records, and long-discarded soft toys strewn randomly across the floor. He has no stomach for the mess, yet has no will to touch it. It reflects too accurately the chaotic nature of his own circumstances. He would not know where to begin.

Lenny lifts his clouded eyes to survey the room, as he has done so many times in the past week, and notices how the stripped, bare walls counterpoint the hectic litter on the floor. The wardrobe doors have been removed, and Monica's altar has been carefully divested of all its icons; her photo montage has been sealed into a plastic bag and taken away, along with her books and Tarot cards. They are to be exhibits at the trial. All that remains of Monica's strange world is a plaster rectangle decorated with mirror shards, and some spent candles. Lenny looks at it now, and wonders how something essentially so anodyne could have been invested with such hideous purpose. It reminds him of nothing so much as a miniature fire place. Closing his eyes against a wash of pain and incomprehension, he wonders what will become of her.

❋ ❋ ❋ ❋ ❋

Lenny does not feel ready to visit Monica yet. She has murdered a child, taken a life. This is the litany which plays through his head as he walks towards the secure room to face his daughter.

Lenny shuffles in, diffident and nervous, his eyes fixed on the floor. He has to force himself look at Monica, and when he does, the breath leaves his lungs. She seems so calm, serene and unrepentant as she sits there, flanked by uniformed warders, that it sends a shiver through his body. It is the most humiliating moment of his life.

They do not speak.

Lenny moves over to the chair prepared for him and studies his daughter, who stares down at the tabletop before her, fingers fiddling with the clacking beads laced through her crazy hair. In this moment he knows that he will not come to visit her again.

He asks how she is, but receives no reply. Embarrassed, he eyes the electric clock on the wall behind her, watching the thin red hand sweeping smoothly round and round, measuring out the seconds of his visit. The silence between them grows thick and impenetrable with things unsaid.

They sit in this terrible silence for fifteen minutes, until Lenny gets up to leave. As his chair scrapes across the linoleum flooring, overly loud in the too-quiet room, Monica looks up and beams a perfect smile at him from her thin, corpse-pale face.

It is only later, as he sits at home in his quiet kitchen, that he realises what it was about her that unnerved him so. She had looked genuinely happy.

✻✻✻✻✻

For Lenny, the last week has been a whirl of painful duty, of answering questions and making statements. The house has been full of detectives, with police photographers taking polaroids of every inch of Monica's eyrie, as if this methodical act will, of itself, make sense of what has happened. Lenny himself has been piecing together the story of his monstrous child in recent days, but the sum of all the disparate parts of her secret life do not combine to make Monica, the child he has loved for so many years. If anything, she has receded still further, fragmenting into tiny pieces as she careens towards her nemesis.

He is still numbed by the news – his own daughter capable of such a crime – and he will never come to understand it. How could she have hidden her potential for such acts? Why have there been no signs? Or perhaps there have, and he simply didn't see them. He can see none now, as he looks about her pillaged room, and yet coming in here has been like slicing open a succulent fruit to find it rotten within.

People are so closed, he reflects. No one can ever really

know another person, it is too easy to keep secrets from one another. And from oneself. His own life has been built around subterfuge, half-truths, and lies, and perhaps so are the lives of everyone else. And this is the result: damage and destruction; disorder and chaos. He wants no more of such lives, no more of lies. He wants to go back to the beginning.

Lenny lies back on the bed and stares up at the ceiling, letting the stillness of the house enfold him like a comforting blanket. He has always considered himself as being alone, but as he lies here, a solitary man at last with no daughter and no wife for company, he realises that the being alone is only just beginning. He wants to let himself slip into it, a drowning man easing himself into a fast-flowing river, to be enclosed beneath the silent water. And he is not afraid.

Also Available

Packing It In
David Rees

This collection of essays, written and arranged to form a year long diary, opens with an all too brief visit to Australia, continues with a tour of New Zealand and a final visit to a much loved San Francisco, before returning to familiar Europe (Barcelona, Belgium Rome) and new perspectives on the recently liberated Eastern Bloc countries (highly individual observations of Moscow, St Petersburg, Odessa and Kiev). Written from the distinctive and idiosyncratic point of view of a singular gay man, this is a book filled with acute and sometimes acerbic views, written with a style that is at once easily conversational and utterly compelling.

'Rees achieves what should be the first aim of any travel writer, to make you regret you haven't seen what he has seen . . .'
Gay Times

ISBN 1-873741-07-3
£6.99

A Cat in the Tulips
David Evans

Both in the later flush of life, Ned Cresswell and Norman Rhodes, room-mates of pensionable age, set off on their annual weekend visit to enjoy a traditional spring break in a quiet Sussex village. Where angels would fear to tread, in rushes the feisty Ned – whilst the conciliatory Norman becomes more reluctantly involved. The village begins to hum, including various brushes with the law, an exciting cliff rescue, a hard-fought game of Scrabble, Agatha Christie in Eastbourne and a dreaded Sunday sherry party, the weekend lurches socially from near disaster to neocataclysm. Further complications ensue, despite Ned's forceful objections, when the currently catless Norman falls in love with an irresistible pussy looking for a new home. Comedy and thrills combine in this delightful and most British of novels.

'It's like Ovaltine with gin in it.'
                    Tony Warren, creator or Coronation Street

ISBN 1-873741-10-3
£7.50

Heroes Are Hard to Find
Sebastian Beaumont

A compelling, sometimes comic, sometimes almost unbearably moving novel about sexual infatuation, infidelity and deceit. It is also about disability, death and the joy of living.

'Highly recommended...' *Brighton Evening Argus*

'I cheered, felt proud and cried aloud (yes, real tears not stifled sobs) as the plot and the people became real to me...'
All Points North

ISBN 1-873741-08-1
£7.50

The Learning of Paul O'Neill
Graeme Woolaston

The Learning of Paul O'Neill follows the eponymous hero over nearly thirty years – from adolescence in Scotland in the mid-sixties to life in a South Coast seaside resort in the seventies and eighties and a return to a vibrant Glasgow in the early nineties. As the novel begins, fifteen-year-old Paul is learning fast about sexuality as his Scottish village childhood disintegrates around him. After many years in England, he returns to Scotland trying to come to terms with the sudden death of his lover. His return brings him face-to-face with the continuing effects of adolescent experiences he thought he had put behind him. And his involvement with an ambiguous, handsome married but bisexual man raises new questions about the shape of Paul's life as he arrives at the threshold of middle-age. This is an adult novel about gay experience and aspects of sexuality which some may find shocking but which are written about with an honesty that is as refreshing as it is frank.

ISBN 1-873741-12-X
£7.50

On the Edge
Sebastian Beaumont

An auspicious debut novel which combines elements of a thriller and passionate ambisextrous romance and provides an immensely readable narrative about late adolescence, sexuality and creativity.

'Mr Beaumont writes with assurance and perception...'   Tom Wakefield, Gay Times

ISBN 1-873741-00-6
£6.99

Ravens Brood
E F Benson

The latest in our highly successful series of reprints of novels by E F Benson dates from 1934 and was almost the last novel he wrote. After *Ravens Brood*, he published only two more novels, *Lucia's Progress* (1935) and *Trouble for Lucia* (1939). By 1940, this most quintessential of Edwardian writers was dead, leaving a legacy of at least one hundred books – destined for seeming oblivion. The 'rediscovery' in the 1960s of the 'Mapp and Lucia' novels was the slow beginning of a revival of interest in Benson's work – which has subsequently produced biographies and family studies and two societies dedicated to his memory.

But *Ravens Brood* is quite unique in the Benson canon, a novel utterly unlike anything he had written before or would ever write again. 'It bristles with sexuality from the moment we meet John Pentreath, farmer and religious bigot, at his Cornish farm near Penzance,' Geoffrey Palmer and Noel Lloyd wrote in their invaluable *E F Benson: As He Was*. 'In the first thirty pages there are references to fertility rituals phallic symbols, lustful boilings in the blood, trollops, shrews, whores and harlots, a cockney strumpet, witchcraft, lascivious leers, a menopausal false pregnancy, and all seasoned with a touch of blasphemy.' The book includes, too, the character of Willie Polhaven (the name is ripe with innuendo) – perhaps the most overtly homosexual of Benson's gallery of ambiguous young men. *Ravens Brood* is atmospheric and outrageous: a rollicking good read.

ISBN 1-873741-09-X
£7.50

Summer Set
David Evans

When pop singer Ludo Morgan's elderly bulldog pursues animal portraitist Victor Burke – wearing womens' underwear beneath his leathers – to late night Hampstead Heath a whole sequence of events is set in train. Rescued by the scantily clad and utterly delicious Nick Longingly, only son of his closest friend Kitty Llewellyn, Victor finds himself caught up in a web of emotional and physical intrigue which can only be resolved when the entire cast of this immensely diverting novel abandon London and head off for a weekend in Somerset.

'Quite simply the most delightful and appealing English gay work of fiction I've read all year. . .'   Scene Out
'A richly comic debut. . .'   Capital Gay
'Immensely entertaining. . .'   Patrick Gale, Gay Times

ISBN 1-873741-02-2
£7.50

Unreal City
Neil Powell

One week in a hot August, towards the end of the twentieth century, the lives of four men overlap and entangle, leaving three of them permanently uprooted and changed. *Unreal City* is their story, told at different times and from their various points of view. Set partly in a London nourished by its cultural past but oppressed by its political present, and partly in coastal East Anglia, it is also the story of two older men – an elderly, long silent novelist and his retired publisher – whose past friendship and subsequent bitterness cast unexpected shadows over the four main characters. *Unreal City* is about love and loyalty, paranoia and violence, the tension of urban gay life in the century's last decade but it is about much else too: the death of cities; the pubs of Suffolk; the streets of London, and the Underground – in more than one sense; Shakespeare's *Troilus and Cressida*; the consolation of music; the colour of tomatoes, and the North Sea. It is a richly allusive, intricately patterned, and at times very funny novel.

'*Unreal City* is brilliant, understated, but powerful and should have a wide-appeal' *Time Out*
'Excellent. I suggest you buy it immediately.' *Gay Times*
'An excellent, extremely satisfying novel.' *The Pink Paper*

ISBN 1-873741-04-9
£6.99

Vale of Tears: A problem shared
Peter Burton & Richard Smith

Culled from ten years of *Gay Times's* popular Vale of Tears problem page, this book, arranged problem-by-problem in an alphabetical sequence, is written in question and answer format and covers a wide range of subjects.

Problems with a lover? Who does the dishes? Interested in infantilism? Why is his sex drive lower than yours? Aids fears? Meeting the family? How to survive Christmas? Suffering from body odours? Piles? Crabs? Penis too small? Foreskin too tight? Trying to get rid of a lover?

Vale of Tears has some of the answers – and many more. Although highly entertaining and sometimes downright humorous, this compilation is very much a practical handbook which should find a place on the shelves of all gay men.

'*An indispensable guide to life's problems big or small . . .*'
Capital Gay

ISBN 1-873741-05-7
£6.99

Millivres Books can be ordered from any bookshop in the UK and from specialist bookshops overseas. If you prefer to order by mail, please send the full retail price and 80p (UK) or £2 (overseas) per title for postage and packing to:

Dept MBKS
Millivres Floor
Ground Floor
Worldwide House
116-134 Bayham Street
London NW1 0BA

A comprehensive catalogue is available on request.